The Ingredients of Us

The Ingredients of Us

A NOVEL

JENNIFER GOLD

LAKE UNION
PUBLISHING

Text copyright © 2019 by Nicole Jennifer Persun
All rights reserved.

Published by Lake Union Publishing, Seattle

www.apub.com

Amazon, the Amazon logo, and Lake Union Publishing are trademarks of Amazon.com, Inc., or its affiliates.

ISBN-13: 9781542042666 (hardcover)
ISBN-10: 1542042666 (hardcover)
ISBN-13: 9781542042673 (paperback)
ISBN-10: 1542042674 (paperback)

Cover design by Shasti O'Leary Soudant

Printed in the United States of America

First Edition

For NILA

August 13, 2015

One day after Elle found out

Imagine your husband cheated on you; what do you bake? Pies are too cheerful, cookies too festive, chocolate mousse too sensual—you probably decide on jam. Something to pulverize. Blackberry jam, to be specific, made straight from the gnarled bush that has overtaken your potting shed in the back—the bush, heavy with berries, that your lying husband promised to prune but never did.

Blackberry jam: 4 cups of berries, 1 cup of sugar, 1 teaspoon of cornstarch, spices; grind the black globules, boil the mixture until thick, and store in the fridge with a dash of lemon juice mixed in.

Blackberry jam: tart, dense, and passive aggressive, something you might spread on toast like gelatinous fury early in the morning while tears pour down your face as you imagine all the seedy things he's done.

~

Standing in the doorway between the hallway and the bedroom she shares with her husband, Elle knows Tom has been sleeping with another woman. He's untucking his dress shirt, hanging his tie from the bedpost, oblivious. Home late. Thursday. Elle clears her throat, a faint sound, barely a breath's worth of air rasping at the back of her mouth. It's all she can manage. Her face feels as though she's standing before an oven.

"Tom," she says, and in that moment she realizes she's wearing his old T-shirt out of habit. *Shit.*

Now, he's folding his trousers; his eyes flicker up toward her. "Oh, hi, honey."

She tucks her hair behind her ears, then holds her own elbows in a kind of self-embrace. Her mother always told her, "Life is easier if you stay on everyone's good side."

Elle says, "Can we talk?"

His tight mouth wavers on the edge of a frown, and it seems to Elle that he knows she knows. But whether he loves the other woman, Elle is not so sure.

August 18, 2015

Six days after Elle found out

Elle sits on the couch in their living room because she can't stand to look at the man upstairs any longer. It's two in the morning, and there's rain on the roof. She's too defeated to make tea, so she sits there in the dark, bare legs curled beneath her, shoulders wrapped in an old throw. Eyes burning, mouth sour from the yelling, she stares out the window at the showers, all lit up and shimmering under the streetlight on the corner. The gutters gurgle with overflow, plunking water onto the rhododendron that crowds the house. Its waxy leaves bob in the darkness. All the neighbors' house lights are off.

Tom is upstairs in their bed, though she should have made *him* sleep on the couch. Grinding her teeth, she thinks, *Fuck him.*

As time passes, the rain gradually subsides into a Seattle haze, obscuring the street outside. Elle glances at the clock on the DVD player: a quarter to three. She has been on the couch since one, and her legs ache for movement. Unfolding them like a fawn, she walks gently, as if for the first time, into the kitchen. She considers baking something—it is her one true refuge from anything and everything. The backs of her knees are tingling; out of habit, she twists the wedding ring on her finger. It's her day off, but maybe she'll go to the bakery anyway.

She yearns to sink her fingers into dough, and it would be good to get out of the house.

Lingering a moment longer, she eases the ring off and places it by the sink. It hardly sparkles anymore, so clouded from soap residue and flour. Then she tiptoes upstairs.

Tom is snoring loudly. Their cat, Velcro, kneads the bedspread beside him while Elle grabs a pair of pants and a bra. She can see the lines of Tom's good physique even in the dim lighting, the contours of his arms stretched up by his head. His hair is still dark—only just recently has it started to turn gray on the sides—and while she can't see his face clearly now, she knows it has few wrinkles. Laugh lines, mainly.

She used to love to look at him, felt proud to hang on his arm and sit across from him at the pricey oyster house on the waterfront downtown. That was before the city built the Ferris wheel. Now in his image all she sees are the missed calls, late nights wondering where he was, less—and then practically no—conversation or sex. Worst of all, she sees the foreign influence of another woman: new aftershave, more frequent haircuts, songs stuck in his head that she's never heard before.

She should have known. How could she have been so blind?

Downstairs, she finds her car keys and purse and heads out the door. In the car, she uses an old tube of mascara from the cupholder to bring life to her eyes. It's three thirty when she arrives at the bakery. Elle's employee turned best friend turned co-owner, Bonnie, has already parked her car in the small lot behind the building; the fluorescent lights of the back room are on. Elle debates heading back home, but when Tom enters her mind, she feels a sharp twinge in her stomach. So she gets out of her car and goes inside.

August 4, 2015

Eight days before Elle found out

The new space is for her second bakery, on the Eastside, in Bellevue. It has high ceilings, wide counters, and a spacious back room. Elle follows the Realtor, Gina, over the hardwood floors, their footsteps echoing through the empty front room. It's larger than her current bakery, more modern and upscale. Already, she can imagine furnishing it with tables, pastry cases, and mixers. She can picture stocking the back shelves with napkins, cups, pastry bags, flour and sugar containers, rows of tart molds, pie plates, baking sheets. A rollaway cooling rack overflowing with gingersnap cookies and cinnamon twists.

While Gina leads her through the space, Elle takes photos to show Tom later. With her purse strap around her shoulder, elbow resting on its opening, she hugs the supple leather, swaying on her feet. "I love it," she says. "It's perfect."

Gina smiles a wide, gum-showing smile. "You and Bonnie have good taste. Do you want to sign off on it now?"

"Not yet; I need to check the budget again. This is a little outside our price range."

Running her hand along the counter, Gina nods.

"Are there any others interested?"

"This is a prime location. You should reevaluate your numbers quickly," Gina says. "Shall we?"

Elle follows Gina out the door and watches her lock up. "I'll be prompt."

They shake hands, and then Gina is on her way. Elle looks around, admiring the street. A cyclist darts by while a woman with two children window-shops across the street. Somewhere overhead, a bird chirps.

Pulling out her phone, Elle texts Bonnie: *You were right. It's exactly what we wanted.* Next, she calls Tom—he's at work, but she can't wait to tell him about the space, even if it's just his voice mail. "Sweetheart, it's perfect," she says into the phone. "We'll have to talk about the price—it's higher than we wanted—but it's perfect. I think I've found our second bakery. Can you believe it? Me, with a chain of bakeries. I'm shaking. Let's talk more later."

Hanging up, Elle peers in the window once more, her heart racing. The next phase in her career is right there before her, just waiting for her to sign the papers.

August 18, 2015

Six days after Elle found out

Despite the early hour, when Elle walks inside, the bakery is already warm from the ovens. Bonnie looks up from a spread of dough as Elle closes the door, her brow wrinkled, and before Elle can put on her apron, she says, "It's Tuesday."

"I know." Elle considers saying more but shakes her head. Bonnie already knows about Tom's affair, and the bakery is Elle's escape.

Without asking questions, Bonnie walks over and wraps her arms around Elle. "I'll call Mindy and tell her not to come in."

"No, pretend I'm not here."

Grasping Elle's shoulders, Bonnie says, "I think you need to move out, Elle. Or make him move out. It's not healthy for you to keep living with him."

"But moving just makes it seem so *real*, you know?" Bonnie gives her a look, so Elle continues, "I just don't know if I'm ready for that."

Bonnie takes up her rolling pin again. "You'll never be ready. You can't prepare yourself for finding out your husband cheated; you just find out. And then you do something about it."

Cheated. The word lingers in the air, a foul smell. "You say it like it's in the past."

Bonnie frowns. "It isn't?"

"I think he's still seeing her." Elle feels disgusted saying it out loud. "What if I drove him to her?"

"No, Elle, you didn't. He's an asshole—that's what happened. You didn't do a damn thing." Bonnie runs a pizza wheel through her slab of dough.

Before Elle can say more, Mindy walks in. "Elle, what are you doing here?" Her face is done up nicely, and around her is an aura of coconut body spray. She's the type of pretty, competent twentysomething that makes Elle feel old and plain.

"I thought I'd come in today and make a couple out-of-the-ordinary desserts," Elle says.

"Like what?"

She hasn't thought about that part yet. Pressing her tongue to the roof of her mouth, she considers what she's in the mood for. "How about lemon tarts?"

"Lemon tarts!" Mindy exclaims, hanging her purse on a hook. "Your lemon tarts are the reason I wanted to work here in the first place."

"Mindy, put these in the oven, would you?" Bonnie interrupts, handing the girl a sheet of pastries.

Mindy grasps the tray and yanks an oven door open. The scrape of the metal tray on the oven rack echoes throughout the entire shop, otherwise morning-silent. After Mindy disappears into the front, Elle leans against one of the smaller tables, facing Bonnie.

"Lemon tarts," Elle says with a sigh.

"It's been a while."

"It reminds me: I should call my mother."

"Speaking of calls . . . Gina. Have you decided about the new space?"

Elle's fingers curl on the edge of the table. "I'll call her back later."

Bonnie wipes the tabletop with a wet rag, clearing away the excess flour. "Are you going to do it, then?"

"I don't know yet," Elle says. "With Tom . . ." She spreads her hands. Tom was going to help pay for the new bakery from his business account. They haven't spoken about it since she confronted him about the affair last week.

"Don't let him stand in the way of your dreams."

"Well, if we can't work through it, it's not like he would—" She cuts herself short. She hasn't told Bonnie that Tom never wanted another bakery or that her money for it is tied up in his name.

"Work through it?"

"Some couples can work through this sort of thing."

"Do you *want* to work through it?" There's an edge of disapproval in Bonnie's voice.

Grasping the handle of the walk-in fridge, Elle says, "I need to think about it."

"I'll help Mindy open the front," Bonnie says, then over her shoulder, softer, "Love you."

"Love you," Elle says, stepping into the cold.

~

Her old recipes are kept on the top of a supply shelf, and it has been a while since she's brought them down. The five-inch binder barely holds together and is covered in a thick layer of dust and flour; it's so dingy that she can't even make out the Sweetheart Bakery logo under the front slipcover, and she doesn't bother to wipe it off. Inside, the scraps of paper are frayed and stained with vanilla extract and cocoa, crusty with sugar, stuck together with egg. Her blue handwriting has bled where pages got wet. It is a haphazard, glorious collection. All her old recipes are here, from when she still bothered to write them down. Many she knows by heart now, but she forgot the liveliness with which she wrote them. Pages upon pages of recipes doubling as memories of those early days, when the Sweetheart Bakery was young and so was her relationship with Tom.

She digs for the lemon-tarts sheet and finds it toward the back. It is especially damaged by egg, with little brown specks of old lemon peel clinging to the fibers of the page. After briefly running her finger down the center of the ingredients list, Elle gathers what she'll need, checking the walk-in once more to ensure she has piecrust already made, stored, and chilled—of course she does. Then, with her ingredients set out before her, she studies the smudged cursive on the page and gets to work.

Turn Something Sour into Something Sweet with Lemon Curd Tarts

Lemon tarts are something you make for tea parties with your mother, for brunch with your in-laws, or for when you want to take your mind off something sour. You'll need 5 lemons, 5 eggs, 1 cup of sugar, and a stick of chilled butter—no matter the occasion, lemon tarts are always well received. Simmer an inch of water in the bottom of a saucepan. Juice and zest your lemons until your wrist hurts and there's a haze of lemon in the air. Taste the tartness on your tongue; it might sting your eyes; you'll realize you have a paper cut on the side of your index finger. As if you yourself were a lemon, let your bitterness pour into this recipe—the more the better. In this case, life's lemons yield sweet lemon curd.

Combine the egg yolks with the sugar in a metal bowl until smooth; then add the lemon juice and zest. Whisk until your forearm and your shoulder ache. Reduce your simmering water to low heat and place your metal egg-lemon bowl on top of the saucepan. Now keep whisking—the mixture will gain body and become light yellow as it heats. The thickening process can take up to 10 minutes of hand whisking; it'll wear you out. Take your sour mood out on the curd. The more difficult it becomes, the closer you are; you'll know when it's ready.

Remove from the heat and stir in your butter a cube at a time. The curd should turn glassy and translucent at this point, but don't worry if this is not the case, since even a cloudy curd will taste lovely. Once the butter is incorporated, transfer your curd into a clean container and cover with plastic wrap, ensuring that the plastic is touching the surface of the curd, before storing in the fridge. Lemon curd goes well on everything: ice cream, toast, waffles. If you're making tarts after all, roll out some piecrust, blind-bake it at 350° in some greased tart pans until just underdone, add the curd, and then bake until the crust is golden. I like to decorate the tarts with berries and powdered sugar.

By now you should feel better about whatever was making you bitter. If not, eat the ugliest tart, serve the rest, and call it a day. After all, life's lemons never stay around for long.

Elle bustles to the front of the bakery and slides two trays of tarts into the pastry case. Early-morning sun streams through the front windows, muted and warm. Mindy is chatting with Sal and Henrietta, two regulars. The couple are both in their eighties and always arrive just after opening to grab two plain oven-warm croissants; Elle has always admired the way they sit in the front window, holding hands and speaking softly to each other. She had always hoped she and Tom would be like that someday.

Today, however, Sal and Henrietta are joined by a young woman. Mindy helps them drag a third chair to their spot, while the woman carries a plate with a cream cheese danish. Elle hesitates by the pastry case, watching. Bonnie did a nice job with the danish topping this morning: thinly sliced peaches are fanned like angels' wings atop the dollop of cream cheese frosting. The woman takes an eager bite of the danish before she's even settled.

Elle turns away, only partially warmed by the woman's pleasant expression, but then she hears her name and turns back. Henrietta is beckoning her over. Elle is too bedraggled to socialize, but she can't say no. While Mindy helps the next customers, Elle shuffles over to Sal and Henrietta's table.

"Good morning," Elle says.

"I thought you didn't work on Tuesdays?" Henrietta asks.

"Today I do," Elle says. "I see you have a visitor."

"Yes, dear, this is our granddaughter, Rebecca." Henrietta's knobby, unsteady hand pats Rebecca's arm lovingly. "Rebecca, Elle owns this fine bakery."

Rebecca, already halfway through her danish, says, "Nice to meet you."

"You, too," Elle says.

"Grandma says you might open a place on the Eastside?" Rebecca wipes the corner of her mouth with a napkin. "If so, I would come in all the time."

With a twinge in her heart, Elle says, "I believe Henrietta is a little ahead of me on that front."

"Nonsense," Sal says in his soft, gasping voice. "Simply a dream yet to manifest."

Elle presses her lips together. "Maybe."

"Don't let us keep you, busy bee," Henrietta says, waving her off. "I'm sure you have many things to make."

"Yes, always. Thanks for trekking all the way from the Eastside, Rebecca." Elle touches Sal's shoulder, adding, "Your grandparents are my biggest cheerleaders."

"Well, now you have a third," Rebecca says over her last bite of danish.

Elle smiles, nods, and returns to the back. As a means of useful distraction, she focuses on cleaning up her work space.

It's nearing seven o'clock when she finishes wiping down the back. She takes a final bite of the ugly, messed-up tart she saved, then swipes her finger through a glob of curd left on the plate. It tastes like spring rain, the summer before pastry school, mint-tea afternoons with her mother, and mulch from her father's peony gardens. Her eyes lift toward the supply shelf, where her binder of recipes was hibernating. A few fake peonies that her father gave her on opening day lie along the top of the shelf, grimy and faded. She misses him a little extra during hard times and wishes that she could talk to him about Tom—he always knew what to do, an optimist to her mother's pessimistic tendencies.

Tasting the last hints of lemon along her gums, Elle rests her elbows on the table, pushing her fingers into her temples. The sounds of the shop filter into the back, muffled and bustling.

~

At the end of the day, gritty and covered in flour, Elle checks her phone, only to find a missed call from Tom. Bonnie and Mindy have both left, and Elle, alone in the shop, is trying to decide where to go. She's not ready to go home, not ready to face Tom. But she should listen to his message. On the front counter, her phone sits beside her purse and a second deformed lemon tart she was saving for herself. She decides that once she listens to the message from Tom, she will have the tart. It'll make her feel better after hearing his voice. Counting down from ten, when Elle reaches one, she hits the play button on her voice mail.

There's some static, and then his voice cuts in. "Listen, Elle, with all that's going on—what you said earlier, if that's how it's going to go—I don't think I can help you with the second bakery. I'm sorry. It's not personal; I just don't think it's a good idea. We can talk about it more later, if you want. I just thought I would call while it was on my mind." Click.

Heat rising inside her chest, she taps Tom's name on her screen. It rings a few times, and then his voice comes through. "Hello?"

"I can't believe you," Elle says. She can feel her vocal cords tightening, filling with water. Her wrist quivers, causing the phone to wobble against her ear.

"Elle, we both know it doesn't make sense to start a new business venture with our current . . . situation."

"*Situation.*" Elle bites her bottom lip. "The only *situation* is that you *cheated* on me, Tom. Look what you've done to our lives."

"It just doesn't make sense right now, all right? You get that, right?"

"You never wanted a second bakery," she says.

"Correct. I didn't." A pause. "I wanted to start a family, and you were selfish and dragged us into more work."

"But we agreed—"

"I'm not moving forward with the new bakery," Tom says, his voice steady.

"You can't just back out of our lives like this."

"Why not? You did a long time ago."

His words pierce her deeply. She shakes her head, her other hand coming up to cover her mouth. It feels as though she can't breathe, as though a thousand pie weights have been placed on top of her rib cage. Time slows down. She ends the call and sinks to the floor. She rubs her eyes, and her mascara comes off on her fingers. There's no way she can afford to pay for the new bakery on her own, for a new lease and renovation. And of course Tom is right—it makes no sense to tangle their finances together even more, but the reality of it is harsh, like a plunge into ice water. All that she has worked for seems lost. Is her single hole-in-the-wall bakery as far as her career will go?

Staring at her flour-covered shoes, Elle remembers the ugly lemon tart. She reaches for it, and it falls onto the floor not far from where she sits. For a moment she just looks at it, the stiff dough cup tilted on the honeycomb floor mat, the curd crawling onto the black rubber. Elle leans forward and scoops it up. Half the lemon curd spilled out, but what remains is clean. She removes a few black particles from the textured dough, then takes a bite. No matter the flecks of dirt, the crust is perfect—flaky and subtle—and the lemon curd is tart and sweet. At least something is as it should be.

August 28, 2015

Sixteen days after Elle found out

She's been thinking about it all day in anticipation. Only three more hours until Elle will meet Bonnie and some of her friends for a night out of drinking, dancing, forgetting. For the occasion, she bought new heels and a sheer blouse. She won't need to shower and put them on for another two hours, and time is crawling. She leans against her kitchen countertop in sweats, trying to focus on something else but finding it impossible.

Afternoon light pours through the curtains, splashing on Elle's back, the counter, and her binder of recipes. She brought the book home from the bakery after Bonnie kicked her out, insisting she rest. Now, she thinks maybe she should bake something to pass the time, something to take to the bar tonight. She hasn't been out like this for years—is it still customary to bring something along when meeting friends? Not to a bar, right? But her mother always said that thoughtfulness takes one far in life, and that policy has never led her astray.

She's too thoughtful—that's her problem. Never a slip, never a mistake.

Which leads her back to tonight. The very thought of going out makes Elle's palms sweat. She might call it innocent fun, but deep down something inside her wants more. She craves a man's affection, an encounter to make her feel wanted, as if she has not just been cast aside. Revenge. Thumbing through her binder, she lands on the perfect recipe.

Triple-Layer Espresso Seduction Brownies

You need a night out, but you're a little nervous. Or maybe you're a little vengeful. You bought something that fits a little tight or that's a little see through; you're going to wear it tonight. If ever you needed a recipe with energy, richness, seduction—these brownies are it. 1 ½ cups of butter, 4 ½ cups of sugar, 1 ½ tablespoons of vanilla. 6 eggs, 2 ¼ cups of flour, 1 ½ cups of cocoa. A pinch of salt and inhibition. Beat your wet ingredients, then sift the dry and fold them together. Simple. These brownies are effortless seduction.

Pour the batter into a greased pan; don't allow them over an inch in thickness. Bake at 350° for about a half hour. They'll come out hard and dense, and that is just how you want them. They are only one layer of the total package.

For frosting, you'll need 4 shots of espresso, a pound of butter, a splash of milk, a teaspoon of vanilla, and plenty of confectioners' sugar. Beat the butter by itself before you pour in the liquids. Add the sugar in single-cup stages until the frosting reaches your desired consistency (it should be thick, but we all have our preferences). For good measure, bring along a sense of humor and energy too. Mix on high until fluffy; have a taste, then another. You might need to adjust by adding more sugar or milk. Trace your finger along the inside of your mixing bowl; savor the way the frosting melts into nothing on your tongue, leaving behind only the memory of its presence, like a beautiful woman leaving a room.

Spread the frosting over the brownies evenly, a trail of a gown. Refrigerate.

For the final touch, a wink, heat 8 ounces of high-quality dark chocolate and a half cup of heavy whipping cream in a double boiler. Or use a microwave on low power—no one will know the difference. Hand mix until smooth, and then pour this liquid mischief over your brownie bottoms and espresso frosting; it will try to seduce you, but you must resist. Refrigerate for at least 2 hours so the frostings have time to cool and settle. Lick the ganache spoon if you must to stave off your temptation until it's time for the main attraction.

～

Elle stands in their house before the mirror in the bedroom they've occupied together for seven years, and she considers an outfit she'll wear to a bar where she intends to meet and possibly seduce a man who is *not* her husband. She probably won't go through with it; the thought itself gives her a sense of shame. She isn't that woman, not really.

The idea nonetheless excites her.

In her diaphanous blouse, black bra, dark jeans, and new heels, Elle turns away from the mirror and tries not to think about it. Any of it.

～

It takes forever to find the place and even longer to find parking. Enérvé is nestled in the heart of Pioneer Square, a secret location delivered only by word of mouth. According to Bonnie, it's a new speakeasy-style bar and dance hall—it doesn't even have a website, just a convoluted Facebook page with a few blurry, dark images. Now doubting her clothing is appropriate, Elle stumbles over the uneven cobbles in her heels, past interchangeable groups of homeless people and millennials. The long, low moan of a foghorn bellows through the maze of brick buildings; sea mist is moving in, enveloping the streets in a gray embrace. With thoughts of what the night might bring, her palms become clammy again.

She wonders what Tom is doing tonight. If it were five years ago and he were here with her, he would have his arm around her. He would make her feel safe on the open street, guiding her over the steaming sewage grates, steering her around the puddles. But she hasn't seen him in days, and those sentiments are over. In fact, he is probably with the other woman right now.

She pictures Tom's arm draped across thin, bony shoulders. The other woman is probably petite but with a round ass from squatting at the gym. The other woman probably still wears thongs, little red ones that are so delicate they have to air-dry in her apartment bathroom. Have they gone out to a bar somewhere far from Elle's normal radius? Or did he take her to Enérvé, a rom-com scene poised to play out as soon as Elle arrives? (In the scene, Elle would throw a drink in Tom's face, and the other woman would squeal and call her a bitch.) More likely, Tom is probably at the woman's place, naked. He could be inside her right now. It's all Elle's speculation. Equally likely, Tom could be at home. Since confronting him, Elle hasn't asked for details. She doesn't really want to know.

Clutching her purse full of brownies, Elle hurries down an alley toward what she hopes is Enérvé's entrance; it's halfway down the narrow street, bricks giving way to a passion-red door with bass thumping just on the other side, as if the building itself has a pulse. After she pays the cover and whispers the code word—*evergreen*—the bouncer lets her through without checking her ID. As she slips past, his attention refocuses on a gaggle of hipsters rounding the bend.

Inside, it smells like mahogany and aged upholstery, old-fashioneds and body heat. To the left is the bar, an impressive wall of backlit shelving harboring an array of glistening liquors in all shapes—triangular bottles, skull-shaped bottles, stout bottles filled halfway with amber, tall ones that are clear. To the right is a dance floor, not quite packed yet but filling up. She expected the music to be swing, but it's a strange mix of horns and techno, so loud that the bass could give her heart palpitations.

With her feet planted just beyond the door, she watches as the hipsters pass her, bringing a gust of night air in with them. They hand a few tweed jackets to the coat girl, two men splitting off toward the bar while a white woman with dreadlocks and a man with a nose ring head toward the dance floor. They twist and shake under a dappling of colorful disco lights; they're probably already drunk. Elle looks down to text Bonnie—*Here, where are you?*—and when she looks up again, the couple is out of sight, lost in the crowd.

Skirting the edge of the room, Elle heads to the bar to wait for Bonnie's reply. She orders a glass of something with vodka, one of Enérvé's specialty cocktails, and tells the bartender to keep her tab open. With her heels hooked around the bottom rung of her barstool, Elle takes a sip and looks around. Despite the unmistakably *Seattle* vibe of the place, many of the other patrons are not hipsters. In fact, the floor is filled with short-skirted, half-drunk, cigarette-smoking UW students and their V-neck-wearing, tattooed, Corvette-driving boyfriends—or so Elle would guess. She was one of them once. Or rather, she was *among* them. She never would have been found in a bar like this; she spent most of her college and postcollege weekends in bookstores or going to sleep early so she could get up and go to the bakery where she worked, a strict place that expected her promptly at 3:00 a.m. for her shift. No, even back then she would have felt uncomfortable here, would have clung to the bar as she's doing right now, sipping on something that goes down easily, waiting for the friend who dragged her here to rescue her.

~

Elle is halfway through her fruity drink—already feeling the vodka—when Bonnie finally texts back. Elle gets up, adjusts her blouse, picks up her drink, and walks straight across the dance floor, skidding on the pinpoints of her heels, trying to get to her friend quickly through the crop tops and Goodwill jackets but failing in the confusion. By the time she spots Bonnie and the two other women with her, the rest of her drink is mostly spilled from all the bumps and *sorrys* and side steps. The women are seated in one of a handful of somewhat-isolated couch clusters on the other side of the club: a haven compared to the uncharted waters surrounding the bar. The music is more muffled in their alcove too. Elle is instantly relieved to see them and sits down.

As a way of greeting, Bonnie says, "Elle, you actually look *sexy!*"

"Gee, thanks." She turns to the other women. "I'm Elle."

"Kelli."

"Angela."

Elle automatically likes them, just for the fact that they appear to be in their thirties, too, and seem friendly. Kelli's hair is dark and straight; Angela wears a classy day-to-night blazer. Elle feels as though she fits in with the trio of women beside her.

After deeper introductions—Kelli is a teacher, Angela a lawyer—and more drink orders, Elle suddenly remembers the brownies in her purse and, slightly embarrassed, presents them to the group. Bonnie laughs, but Kelli and Angela are all over them.

"Damn good," Kelli says, her mouth full.

Angela nods in agreement. "But do they have any . . ." She trails off and tips her head.

Elle doesn't understand, but before she can raise a question, Bonnie cuts in. "Pot?" Her chuckle is more like a snort. "If Elle made them? No, not a chance."

"I could get you some," Angela says to Elle. "Good stuff. My coworker—"

"I'm good," Elle says. She feels the heat of embarrassment swelling her throat.

"They're delicious as is, Elle," Kelli says, running her fingers through a strand of her long black hair. "It's obvious you're a professional."

"I wasn't saying they weren't good," Angela says. Now she seems embarrassed too.

Elle spreads her hands, trying to be lighthearted, trying to move the subject along. "I'm just glad you like them."

"Oh, you made her uncomfortable, Angela," Bonnie says.

"Can I have the recipe?" Kelli asks.

"Elle's working on a recipe book, actually," Bonnie says.

Elle shakes her head. "I have a big collection that I've written myself. Everyone thinks I should try to publish it."

"My sister is a literary agent," Kelli says. "Lily Zhang—look her up."

"I'd buy it," Angela says.

Elle smiles and looks at her hands, wordless.

Bonnie says, "You're adorable."

They all break into laughter, and Elle tells herself it's no big deal. They like the brownies—marijuana or not—and Elle is glad she brought them, even if it *was* an unnecessary gesture. Kelli eats three before their new drinks are even delivered, and Elle decides her offering is a success.

~

"So," Angela says, touching Elle's arm, "Bonnie told us about your . . . situation."

She was just forgetting about Tom, just beginning to loosen up. The shift in conversation comes like clouds moving over the sun. "My situation?"

"Your . . ." Kelli pauses, obviously struggling for a better way to say something that simply can't be said with tenderness, no matter what words are chosen.

Divorce.

Elle doesn't want to say it, either, so instead she says, "Husband? It's okay; I'm not sure what I should call him anymore either."

"Well, we're really sorry," Angela says. "Have you chosen a lawyer?"

"I haven't thought about it, actually. I don't really know how to handle the whole thing."

"You handle it with little mercy, that's what you do," Bonnie says. "You strip him of all his worth—take the house, his money, anything you can." Kelli laughs, and Bonnie turns to her. "I'm not kidding."

"I don't want the house or his money," Elle says.

"Yes, you do!" Bonnie says. "Don't let him screw you, Elle."

"Not likely. He hasn't screwed me for months," Elle replies, taking a sip of her martini.

The women giggle, and Angela hands Elle her card. "Regardless of what you want, email me. There's a good divorce lawyer in our building."

Elle nods. "Thanks." She looks down at the card. The logo is familiar, but it takes her a moment to place it. "You work at Charlie's office?"

"Where else?" Angela asks.

The thought of Bonnie's husband makes Elle squirm in her seat a little.

"She's his *superior*," Bonnie says.

Angela swipes her hand through the air. "Not really—we work in different parts of the firm." She takes a sip from her drink, clearly suppressing a grin.

Elle just smiles. As the conversation takes a turn, her mind wanders to Charlie. She's always done her best to avoid talking to him or spending much time around him at all, despite him being her best friend's husband. Seven years, and they still haven't said a word about how they met. And now that Elle thinks about it, this is the first time she has been out, really *out*, having too much to drink and too much fun, since that awkward encounter.

September 12, 2008

About seven years before Elle found out

Elle and Bonnie are perched at the bar, knees touching, leaning toward each other in close conversation over the noise of the other patrons and the music and the bartender's clinks and shakes. They're at a place called the Woozy Gull, somewhere in Capitol Hill. Letting loose for the first time in who knows how long, what with the wedding plans and Tom's new online tutoring business and the search for another employee to hire for the bakery. Bonnie's telling Elle about her new beau, a man named Charlie who works as a mediation lawyer for business disputes, which sounds terribly boring to Elle, but Bonnie thinks it's sexy as hell.

"He wears a suit to work," Bonnie says, taking a sip of her cosmo. "I've never dated a man who wore a suit to work."

Elle thinks of Tom coming back to their apartment from the university with his over-the-shoulder bag, always a newspaper rolled up and sticking out of one of the pockets like it's 1955. The sound the bag makes when he plops it on the floor, a dull but chaotic clunk of books and notebooks shifting inside the canvas.

"I wish Tom had to wear suits," Elle says.

"Yeah, but he has the hot-professor look going on."

Elle laughs. "Maybe when his business takes off and he's a CEO, he'll have to wear suits."

"A girl can dream," Bonnie says.

Elle adjusts her skirt and picks up her drink.

Bonnie finishes hers and scoots off her stool. "Order me another, will you? I'm going to use the bathroom."

When Bonnie has disappeared into the crowd, Elle turns toward the bar. The bartender is shaking a drink, pouring it into a frosted martini glass. Elle waves at a waitress who has just slipped behind the bar and orders another cosmo for Bonnie—Elle's barely halfway through her own.

"We have a tab open," Elle says to the waitress.

"Put it on mine." A man sidles up next to Elle. "And I'll have a Johnnie Walker Black, neat."

"Thanks," Elle says, facing more toward the bar than toward the man next to her. She feels for her engagement ring on her finger and realizes she took it off while making cookie dough at the bakery. She must've forgotten it there.

The man settles on Bonnie's stool, and when Elle finally does regard him, she can't bring herself to tell him it's taken. He's dark and elegant, a black suit over black skin—a cat, and this is his pounce. Elle can't think of why he came over to her, but the attention is exciting. Her eyes fall to his engraved tie clip holding in place a silk tie, then rise back up to his face.

"J," he says, holding out his hand.

Elle takes it—warm and a little calloused—and they shake.

"Here alone?"

"My friend's in the bathroom."

"Then I'm guessing I stole her seat," he says, leaning a little closer. "I don't suppose I could steal her friend too?"

She wants to say with sarcasm, *Nice line*, until she glimpses her flushed cheeks in the bar mirror. Tom is at their new house painting before they move their furniture in this weekend. The thought is mundane compared to this moment, the excitement filling her limbs, making her feel awash with tingly heat. She can't remember the last time she was hit on—not that she goes out much—but it's flattering, reaffirming. Ever since the engagement, things haven't been as hot and heavy with Tom as they used to be.

She takes a sip of her drink and looks away from J, unable to respond. In the silence, he settles a little closer and begins to draw circles on her knee under the counter. She nearly chokes on her final sip, but before she can react any further, Bonnie emerges from the crowd. Elle swivels in her chair, J's fingers slipping from her leg.

"Charlie!" Bonnie says, a smile breaking across her face.

Seeming to snap out of a trance, J sits up straight as a pin, then stands and wraps his arms around Bonnie. "Sweetheart," he says, "what a nice surprise."

Elle's eyebrows crease. *This* is Charlie? Did he give her a fake name? She looks away, her chest growing hot. Bonnie's boyfriend. She's suddenly awash with a sour, cold guilt as she grasps what has happened. Does Bonnie not realize? Did she not see his hand traveling up her thigh? Elle smooths her skirt over her knees, uncrosses and recrosses her legs.

"Crashing girls' night?" Bonnie's asking.

Charlie points to Elle, his eyes widening. "Elle?" Then again, with more energy, "Elle! What a coincidence. I'm Charlie. Charlie Jones."

"And you stole my seat," Bonnie says, scooting onto the stool again.

"I had no idea," he says.

"If you're not crashing girls' night, what are you doing here?"

"Just happy hour with the guys—why did you come here?"

"You said it was good, so Elle and I decided to try it."

"Your cosmo," the bartender says, setting down Bonnie's second drink.

Before she can grasp it, Elle lifts it from the counter and takes a long gulp. She turns to the bartender and says, "I'm sorry; I meant *two* cosmos."

Bonnie smiles, but her brow is tight.

"Well, I'll let you get back to it," Charlie says, grabbing his scotch off the counter.

Bonnie lifts her chin, and they share a quick peck. "I'll see you later?"

"It's a date," he says, kissing her again. He lifts his hand, fingers spread, at Elle and says, "Nice to meet you," before heading back to a corner booth with three other men.

Next to Elle at the bar again, Bonnie looks over her shoulder. "Did he seem weird to you?"

Elle's eyes dart from Charlie to her drink; mortified, she can't bring herself to tell the truth, not right now. "I don't know; I haven't met him before. Why?"

"He seemed weird," Bonnie says. "Like, caught off guard."

Elle shrugs, sipping at her cosmo. "Could just be a surprise. He wasn't expecting to see you."

"I guess," Bonnie says, reaching for the stem of her freshly delivered cosmo. "See what I mean about the suit, though?"

Elle nods. "Yes, really nice."

"And he seems like a good guy. Always answers my calls, buys me flowers."

Elle nods again, thinking about Tom, probably all covered in paint. She imagines getting home, kissing him, insisting she help wash the paint off. Stepping into the shower together. She loves Tom, she thinks to herself. Supportive, funny, smart Tom who doesn't wear suits. All of a sudden, she can't wait to get home to him.

August 28, 2015

Sixteen days after Elle found out

More chatting, more laughing, more drinking at Enérvé. Elle thought maybe more men would come by, but no one has. Then, later in the night, a pushing and laughing trio arrives with a plate of french fries.

"Finally, something we *really* want!" Bonnie says, smothering a fry in ketchup.

Angela, who is now on her third martini, hair mussed, blazer slung to the side, leans forward. "Do you boys have names?" Her tank top is see through in the flashing lights.

Elle's head swims, the muted bass coming up through the floor and rattling all the way to her collarbones. The men look young but not as young as some of the college students on the dance floor. She guesses late twenties, feeling in over her head. What do they want with *her*, or any of them, nearly ten years older? The attention makes her feel even dizzier; she adjusts her blouse.

"I'm Sean," one says. He's tan, with perfect lips, and has that clean, tidy look that says he's close with his mother.

"Damon." Big muscles, dark eyes. Elle automatically dislikes him, the player vibe he lets off.

"Owen." His voice is sure as oak. It reminds Elle of her husband, and she becomes wary. It was Tom's voice, a dangerous voice, that attracted her in the first place.

Sean gestures toward one of the empty chairs in the women's little circle and asks if they can sit, but Damon and Owen are already settling in.

"Sit, but we're not sharing these," Angela says, lifting up a fry.

Damon settles next to Bonnie on the small fainting couch. "We'll order another plate."

Owen situates himself on an ottoman near Kelli's chair. "So now that you know our names, what are yours?"

"Kelli. And I'm married." She wiggles her ring finger as proof.

Owen lifts his hands. "Point taken."

Sean looks at Elle. "Your name?"

"Elle." She points to Bonnie, who has her mouth full. "Fry girl over there is Bonnie."

Angela lifts her near-empty glass. "Angela."

"Let's get you another one of those," Damon says.

"If you're trying to get me drunk—"

"You're too late," Bonnie finishes.

Damon turns to her and puts his arm along the back of the couch. "Do you need another, you know, to wash down those fries?"

Bonnie gives him a chin-down sarcastic look. She wiggles her ring finger at him, too, and he lowers his arm back to his side.

Sean chuckles and tosses a glance at Owen, who then asks Elle, "Do you need another one too?"

She doesn't. She's already had two and can feel the sting of sugar and vodka in the top of her chest.

She picks up a couple of fries and shrugs. "I think I'm good."

"Well, that's no fun," he says. "You might have more fun if you had another."

Before Elle can reply, Kelli jumps in. "She's not fun the way she is?"

"Seems a little uptight to me," Damon says. Sean glares at him—not so much a scolding look as a don't-blow-it look.

Uptight. Elle is beginning to loathe the whole situation; she lifts off her seat, smooths her jeans, and sits a little straighter . . . then realizes her action and slumps. Maybe Damon's assessment is true.

Angela, sobering into irritation, says, "Insulting women isn't a way to pick them up."

Owen retorts, "Who says we wanted to pick any of you up?" He's trying to keep things light, but the conversation has already curdled.

"So you just came over to give us fries, and that's it?" Kelli asks.

Damon shakes his head. "I wouldn't be picking her up, anyway," he says, nodding his head at Elle, "so you have nothing to worry about."

Trying to ignore her tipsiness, Elle says, "Excuse me?"

"No offense, but you're not my type," Damon says. "I don't want to say prudish, but . . ."

"How could you know? You just sat down." Her esophagus is closing with humiliation. Why defend herself against him—why care at all? In that moment her mind circles back to Tom, and perhaps she really *is* that undesirable after all.

"Funny how 'no offense' is always followed by something offensive," Bonnie says, sitting a little straighter. "Why don't you guys just go?"

Owen scoffs. "Oh, c'mon."

Bonnie hits him with a hard stare. "Take your fries with you." She lifts the platter and waves it at him. "Go on."

With a couple of irritated huffs, the trio gets up. Sean is the last to make himself scarce. "Sorry, girls. Damon's a dick when he's drunk." He catches up to his buddies, and they share in a few shoves, some wide-mouthed conversation inaudible with the music.

"Seems like a dick regardless," Bonnie says.

"You're obviously not a prude," Kelli says.

"Yeah," Angela agrees, sitting back, adjusting her tank top.

"No, maybe I am," Elle says. "Maybe I don't come off as very fun."

"You don't come off as easy," Bonnie replies. "Big difference."

~

Angela eventually rushes off to throw up in the bathroom, Bonnie running after to hold her hair. Kelli stays with their purses, watching the seats, while Elle goes to pay her tab. She's still buzzing and wants to stay longer, but the sugar in the drinks is catching up to her, and it's late, and her friends seem done. She wishes she could lift her tension, but drinking it down hasn't helped. This night has been a disaster.

Then Owen is beside her in the blue of the lights, his deep voice riding over the wail of a remixed clarinet solo thump, thump, thumping full blast by the bar. "Elle," he says, leaning in, "sorry about earlier."

Elle crosses her arms, heart pounding. "Are you?"

The music is too loud for her to catch his response, but his eyes appear genuine—at least she would like to think so. The next question is unmistakable: "Dance?"

The vodka in her chest flares, and her hands go to her hips. "Sure you want to dance with a prude?"

His brow creases, and he steps closer. "What?"

The song is reaching its climax, the bass increasing in speed. "You won't get anywhere," Elle says in his ear.

The music fades, and he says, "I don't want to sleep with you."

"No?"

"I just want to dance."

Elle is surprised and a little disappointed. She wants him to want her. She wants to turn *him* down.

"Um, okay," is all she can think to say. She tries to appear disinterested, but really, his voice is alluring. She finds him sexy. She wants to prove him wrong, prove Tom wrong. As she stands on her tiptoes in her new shoes, her ankles wobble.

Owen says, "So?"

She shrugs as a new song starts up, slipping her credit card into her pocket. "Well, since I know you're not going to try anything, why not?" Kelli can stay with the purses a few minutes longer—no harm in that.

He smiles and offers his hand, and she takes it.

~

Everything seems to slow down while her senses battle with the alcohol. The blue lights flash and shimmer like a lake, as if she were underwater, Owen distracting enough for her to forget that her marriage is drowning.

Among the couples grinding on each other, Elle swings to the music, not really knowing how to dance to the rapid beat but liking it anyway. Owen looks familiar with it, pumping his fist and shifting his weight from foot to foot. After a song or two, he leans in, his lips almost to her ear, and asks, "How about that drink?"

She nods, and he disappears toward the bar. While he's gone, she looks at the other dancers and tries to mimic their gyrations. She feels silly, especially without a partner, but she doesn't care as much as she might if she were sober. Feeling a buzz in her pocket—perhaps a necessary interruption to her poor dancing—she checks her phone. Bonnie texted: *You okay?*

Still moving her shoulders with the bass, Elle texts back: *Dancing with Owen.*

Bonnie's reply is instant: a winky face. Then: *Taking Angela home. Be safe.*

Phone back in her pocket, Elle starts to dance again, moving her hips like the other dancers.

Before long, Owen shows up with two beers. "Nice moves, prude," he says with a grin.

Elle laughs, grabs a beer from his hand, and takes a sip. Then she circles her hips very much unlike a prude until he chuckles and comes closer. Swaying against him, Elle can smell his cologne and a little sweat. It sends chills down to her thighs. She likes the scent. She has more beer. Moves closer. Soon, his hand is on her hip. It feels different—no man other than Tom has touched her like this in years—but somehow very *right*. Before she can react, he's dancing behind her, his hips guiding hers, his nonbeer hand around her front and holding fast at one of her belt loops.

His breath is hot on her neck, his hand steadying her as they move as one, and Elle begins to lose herself. Beers disappear, and more appear. Bass vibrates through her stomach, and gradually Owen's hands become more daring. The one familiarized with her belt loop glides under her blouse along her belly. The other brushes her hair off her neck so he can kiss behind her ear. It feels good. It feels erotic in a way Elle has forgotten about. She turns to face him, feels his hands moving on her back, then over her ass. She feels his cock hard against her leg, his tongue in her mouth.

She's gone now. Gone with Owen. Outside, down the street, into a cab. Gone.

~

The avenues rush past them in the form of traffic lights and taillights and streetlights and lit-up, late-night OPEN signs. Elle tries to hold on to that carnal feeling that flooded her body on the dance floor of the club, but sobriety is catching up to her. Owen sits a full foot away, and she can't tell if he's being shy or cold—or perhaps he's losing his steam too. Perhaps he's second-guessing going home with a woman older than him and tamer. Elle has never done this before, but Owen must have, with girls probably half Elle's age, two times as kinky. The sting in her throat grows more acidic as each city block passes.

What is she doing?

As time unfolds in the stillness of the cab, Owen finally moves closer, warming to her again, and Elle is mildly reassured of his desire for her. It's supposed to be meaningless, isn't it? Yet Elle yearns for him to feel as though this somehow matters, that somehow she's different, better than all the rest. But sex isn't like a recipe—there are no set steps to follow—so knowing what he really thinks of her and expecting to be more than just another fuck is useless. There is no way this stranger can validate her sexual appeal, especially not to her husband.

His hand slides high onto her thigh, his little finger an inch from her zipper, and he twists his torso toward her. Lips find skin beneath collarbone. The scent of him reaches her nose again and mingles with the cab smell. She feels the vodka rising up, and she has to open her eyes and stare at the road ahead.

Owen doesn't seem to notice, his face buried in the crease of her neck, breath warming her hair. Maybe he does really want her. Elle tries to enjoy it, but every time her eyes close and she thinks about what she's doing, she feels sick again and is forced to stare ahead at the open streets. She holds desperately to the looseness of her inebriation, not wanting to lose the heat Owen is generating between her legs, not wanting to sober up and allow Tom to enter her mind.

Instead, she cranks the window down a notch. Cool air filters in, fresh with salt from the bay. She returns her attention to Owen's lips, which are now traveling up toward her ear. He takes the diamond stud into his mouth and gives a light suck, and Elle feels her intoxication coming back. His hand slips under her blouse and pushes up over her bra with enough pressure to make her lungs seize. Their mouths meet, and then his hands are in her hair, tipping her head to allow for a kiss deep enough to reach all the way down.

His taste, despite the staleness of beer, is inviting, and paired with the way he moves—new in the nuance but the same as any man in the mechanics—it has her losing herself again. With each trying flood of thoughts of her husband, Elle blocks them with the image of Owen. She can feel the solidness of him behind his cotton T-shirt, muscles bunched in readiness. She is lost in the heat, in his hands, in a cab heading up the downtown hills.

Anytime during the Good Times with Tom

Years before Elle found out

It could be any date night. Perhaps Tom takes her to Ray's in Ballard. They share a bottle of Chateau Ste. Michelle Dry Riesling, even though Tom is more of a negroni man. The wine goes well with her market halibut and the view of the bay. He has the filet mignon, and judging by the bite he offers her, it's exquisite.

Or perhaps it's that Mexican place somewhere in Ravenna, operated out of an old house. The wall paint is chipping, but the air is sweet with the aroma of freshly cut tomatillos. They have margaritas and share chicken mole, with extra chips and fresh guacamole on the side.

No matter where they go, it has been a long day, a bad day for Elle. She probably dropped a pie, or an angry customer yelled at Bonnie, or old milk ruined a batch of cake batter. She probably almost said no to Tom's spontaneous idea for a dinner date. As usual, though, she's glad she didn't. The crème brûlée or fried ice cream is reason enough—let alone the way he makes the negativity melt away.

Finished, they walk out into the blustery air. The sun set some time ago. On the wooden planks that lead to the valet or the gravel walkway leading to their car or anywhere else outside the restaurants they frequent, Tom pulls Elle close. More often than not, her legs are chilly in the sudden outside temperature. How comfortable it was inside the restaurant, how welcoming; out here, they are bald to the wind off the water or through the trees or even to a drizzle of misty rain. She smiles up at him.

Tom drives the two of them back to his place, her place, or later, their place. He blasts the heat so she can warm up her bare legs. Her body feels light and airy, and the narrow streets and sleepy houses slip past them in a haze. She looks out the window, but she's not paying attention to anything outside. Tom's hand is on her thigh—the way it usually is. If it's a Saturday, he hums softly to *The Swing Years* on the radio. At a red light, the streets empty, he leans over and lifts her chin. The kiss is long, and she loses count of the seconds passing by. It's long enough for the hand on her leg to lift to her cheek, her neck, her hair. Their tongues brush lightly.

Who knows how long the light is green before someone drives up behind them, before the rearview mirror betrays the moment, a flash of headlights across their eyelids? They part; Tom eases on the gas. On any other day, Elle would feel bad about blocking the intersection, but on date night she doesn't.

No matter what, she says, "This was a good idea."

He's a smart-ass, but she likes it: "Told you."

A wistful or lively voice comes through the car speakers, listing musicians and song titles from the last set of swing or rock or sometimes pop. *That was . . .* But the names are unrecognizable to Elle, as again, Tom's hand comes to rest on her leg.

Back to the bedroom, they go through the familiar motions: she slips out of her heels, he unzips her dress, she slides his belt out of the belt loops, he guides her to the bed. They make love easily. Afterward, she gets up to go to the bathroom; Tom is asleep when she comes back. She nestles beside him, and he wakes long enough to kiss her again, to whisper that he loves her. He snores lightly, a lullaby.

This is the way life is meant to be, she always thinks, close to dozing. This night—and every date night with Tom—is what love looks like.

August 28, 2015

Sixteen days after Elle found out

As Owen unlocks the door to his apartment, with that deep voice of his that sounds so much like Tom's, he says, "I didn't mean what I said at the bar. I'm very attracted to you."

Grasping his fingers in hers, Elle steps past him into the darkness of his apartment.

~

In his bedroom, as he guides her blouse off her shoulders, he says, "Look at you."

~

As he rolls the condom on, he says, as if in a trance, "I'm so hard for you."

~

As he finishes, he says her name. God, for the life of her, she wishes he wouldn't say anything.

~

In the silence, his turning under the sheets is as loud as the foghorn outside the bar. He whispers something she chooses not to hear, blood rushing in her ears. Momentarily, she mistakes his presence for Tom's. His breathing beside her is deafening.

She decides to get out of bed in three . . . two . . .

~

The toilet is brown yellow, with little hairs all over the broken seat, and Elle hovers above it, naked, urging herself to pee. The whole bathroom smells like piss, but Elle appreciates the privacy. Staring at the sink, she wonders how many girls Owen has had over. She flushes and stands up straight. Two Durex wrappers are nestled among some old toilet paper tubes behind the toilet on the floor, with skeletal spiders in cobwebs and grime from who knows how long ago. It could be the alcohol, but she doesn't care: she's still tipsy and wobbly and sour in her chest, and she should probably shower, but the tub is so in need of a cleaning that she would feel dirtier just by getting into it.

Right now, sleep sounds best. She's never done this before; will Owen expect her to leave, or can she stay, just for a few hours?

Elle pads into the bedroom and finds him asleep, sprawled out on the mattress. His naked behind is pale against the dark sheets. In the doorway, she listens to his muffled snores, and her body slumps. A similar image from her honeymoon comes to mind, filled with a haze of laughter and pouncing into bed and Tom holding her and kissing her cheeks.

She turns back into the bathroom and closes the door, faces the smudged mirror. Her eyes become blurry. She seizes a breath, then another. She longs to place her hands on the countertop and weep but doesn't because of the crusted toothpaste on its surface. Elle refuses to break down, but a red strand of some other woman's hair confirms that she is one of the many—one of the many Owen has invited over, one of the many having one-night stands, one of the many getting divorced and crumbling.

In his apartment, somewhere in Seattle, surrounded by run-down, boy-ignored mildew and hardened toothpaste and condom wrappers, Elle stares into the mirror in silence. Naked, she sighs deep into her body and wills her throat to relax.

She doesn't hate herself as she thought she might for going home with a man who isn't Tom. She feels a sort of grounded lightness from the release of sex, a stained contentment. Maybe even a little pride, for going through with it, for taking a risk, for doing something for herself for once—even if it was to spite Tom. And for a moment she is able to forget, able to look into her own eyes in the mirror without wishing to close them.

August 29, 2015

Seventeen days after Elle found out

The air outside Owen's unventilated apartment is thin and clear, the sky pearly-peachy at seven a.m. Autumn's crispness grows stronger as the weeks pass, but the day looks like summer. It's too bright for Elle, but she breathes deep into her lungs anyway, trying to fill herself with freshness. Her mouth is more than sour, and her hands smell like condom. Her headache is a tree—a thick trunk starting at the base of her neck, working its way up, branching into her temples, behind her ears, and into the roof of her crown. The worn, gray sidewalk feels hard up into her knees but hurts the most in the balls of her feet. She wants to take off her four-inch heels, but she's not a woman who would walk barefoot in the city. Still, morning is when Seattle looks its most beautiful, the sea fog lifting and the tall buildings casting their shadows across the steep streets.

Elle is forced to take an Uber, since her car is in a parking garage near the club. Preoccupied with the radio the whole time, her driver drops her by the wide alley to the club entrance. Out on the corner, Elle realizes that her car keys are in her purse, and the last time she saw her purse, it was with Kelli. Her Uber's exhaust pipe is already puffing into the steady traffic a block away, so she slips into the alley and texts

Bonnie—thank goodness she at least held on to her phone. While she waits for the reply, she looks around at the littered entrance of Enérvé: cigarette butts, a flask, wet neon flyers, green shards of glass, tipped trash cans, vomit, a thong. Why on earth would she go to a club? Why would she go home with a stranger? Is it really what single women do? Divorced women? It seems like it's either that or online dating, and both are equally depressing, just for different reasons.

Growing impatient, Elle calls Bonnie, but she doesn't pick up. Elle realizes Bonnie must be at the bakery. A minute later Bonnie replies via text: *Took Angela home. Kelli has your purse.* Then Kelli's address. Elle's phone is almost dead, and she repeats the address to herself. *Coming in later?* Bonnie asks, to which Elle replies, *Yes*. Before she can reply to Bonnie's next question—*What happened last night with Owen?*—the Apple symbol pops up, and her phone goes black. Thank God. Elle isn't ready to face that question, anyway. It's too early, she's too hungover, and she hasn't yet washed the shame off her body. Stale sex clings to her, and all she wants to do is shower, but first she needs her purse and her keys. She hails a cab and heads to Kelli's neighborhood.

The drive is expensive, but Elle appreciates the solitude, admiring the golden leaves on cherry trees as she zooms past, the dying breath of summer not yet fully exhaled.

February 14, 2006

About nine and a half years before Elle found out

The first day at the Sweetheart Bakery is a blur of flour and oven timers and fingerprints collecting on the glass of the pastry cases. Elle has been up since two a.m. working to fill them, and now it's almost seven p.m., and the doors are closed, the cases empty. Tiny bulbs light up the vacant, crumb-covered trays and illuminate the finger smudges revealing which pastries were most coveted. The rest of the bakery's front lights are off, and Elle's employee, Bonnie, has gone out back to wash the floor mats. Alone among the butter-colored walls and the hum of refrigerators, Elle sighs. Still more to make. She welcomes the ache in her palms, forearms, and shoulders. It's the kind of fatigue that makes her feel accomplished.

Today is the day she opened her very own bakery. No more strict bosses or crying in back rooms; no more guilt over lumpy frostings or tensing muscles during taste tests; no more panicking in the parking lot when something goes wrong; no more grudges held for pies she dropped on the floor two years before. No more doubting her abilities—finally, baking is hers and hers alone to enjoy, to savor, to own.

Elle flips the case lights off and heads into the back room, where the fluorescents still buzz, casting the silver tables and mixers in metallic white. Before digging into her final recipe—cinnamon rolls, for the next morning—Elle searches inside her purse for her cell phone. She hits speed dial two, and it rings only once before she gets an answer: "So how did it go?"

"Hi, Dad," Elle says, leaning against the largest silver table in the back room. "It went great. Sold out of nearly everything."

"That's my girl!" he says. "I'm so proud of you, Elle-Belle. How many twenty-six-year-olds own their own business?"

"Lots of them do."

"All right, aside from all those young tech yahoos—I'm talking about a *real* business."

She smiles to herself, unable to help it. "I can't thank you enough for your help."

"Not another word. It's the best investment we ever made." She can hear the sleep in his voice, an end-of-the-day crackle that sounds like she called while he was settling down for the night. He goes on, "How does it feel to be in charge?"

"Liberating," she says. "How are you?"

"Oh, don't say it like that."

"Like what?"

"Like I have cancer."

"You *do* have cancer." He remains silent. "How are you, Dad?" Elle says, trying to lighten her voice.

"I'm doing well. I'm proud of my girl."

"You already said that."

"I would let you talk to your mother, but she's having her shower before bed."

"Just tell her I called," Elle says, not really minding. Her mother was never really on board with her father's financial input into her bakery. "And thank you for the flowers," she says, her eyes focusing on a large bouquet of fake peonies sitting by her small mixer.

"Of course. I'm sorry I couldn't send you some real ones from the garden; it's not the season."

"They're perfect. They'll stay in my back room forever this way."

There's some rustling around on his end. "Have you thought more about a recipe book?"

She clenches her teeth, a reaction she's had since she was a girl. It happens every time her father pushes her to work just an ounce harder when she's already spread thin. One more page of math homework. One more lap in track. Now a cookbook. "I don't understand why you want me to write one—you and Mom don't bake."

"Since you keep refusing to mail me scones, I would like a recipe book to chew on."

Elle lets out a breath of laughter.

"Seriously, though. You're good. I think you could write a bestseller. A successful bakery owner with a cookbook—it happens all the time."

"It's been one day, Dad."

"All I'm saying is to write down a recipe every once in a while. You can't always rely on memory."

"I have a lot on my plate—" Elle cuts herself short at the sound of coughing on the other end of the line. His coughing has become more watery by the week, and the sound of it makes Elle's skin prickle. She closes her eyes. "Are you all right?"

He rumbles his throat, and then there's some more rustling. "Fine, fine. I should let you go. You're probably tired from your first day."

Elle finds herself nodding; she shouldn't keep him up. "I'll call you in the next few days."

"Take your time, sweetheart," he says.

"I love you, Dad."

"I love you too."

The line clicks, and Elle lowers her phone from her face, her cheek warm. A recipe book. Her father's spunk is aggravatingly persuasive. All her recipes are better variations of old ones she's gathered from numerous books over the years. Torn pages with sections crossed out, notes in the margins, or sheets fully handwritten. Stacks of them in a box, spilling out of fat folders. She imagines her father's coughing and resolves to at least pick up a binder—something to organize the sheets of paper. Perhaps she should take up a pen right here and now, rewrite some of the oldest ones, but she remembers her next task: cinnamon rolls. The last thing on her list before she can go home.

Her first day off, she decides, she'll start writing them all down.

As she pulls out ingredients, her mind wanders to Tom, who is probably done teaching his evening class by now. He stopped by during a late-morning rush, before his first class of the day, and bought three pastries: two bear claws and a berry turnover. Elle only had time to hand him his three white pastry bags, give him a quick peck, and then rush off to her next task. It was nice of him to stop by at all—she knows it was out of his way. Elle grips the table. She's only known Tom just over a month, and yet she's crazy about him. He's the first man not to be scared away by her ambition or the demand of her career.

Her fantasizing is interrupted when Bonnie comes in the back door, dragging a mat. Straightening it into place along the edge of a fridge, Bonnie stands and brushes her hands on her jeans. "Mats are clean."

"Thank you," Elle says, probably smiling a little too big. She's never had an employee before—she even went so far as to dig out one of her old business-school textbooks to glean a little insight. Still, she feels almost guilty giving orders, already too pushy—she doesn't want to be like her old bosses, always critical. She wants to be a *friend* kind of boss.

"I'll Windex the cases next?"

"Sure," Elle says, then, "Thank you."

Bonnie disappears into the front, and soon Elle hears the squeak of the Windex nozzle, the tear of paper towels.

Cinnamon rolls.

Elle turns toward the flour bins. Before she even dips her two-cupper into the white powder, she hears voices up front. Bonnie introducing herself, and then a man's voice—Tom's voice, unmistakably deep, as smooth as a cinnamon roll's caramel topping. Before Elle can think to set down her measuring cup, Bonnie calls back to her, "Elle, Tom is here."

"Coming." Her voice comes out higher pitched than she expected, quivering at the *ing*. Relax, she tells herself. Re-lax. She smooths her apron, tucks a stray strand of hair behind her ears. He always makes her feel flustered.

"Elle?" Bonnie calls again.

"Yes, coming!" She hurries out into the front to see Tom up by the counter, flowers in one hand and a takeout bag in the other. Bonnie's chitchatting with him, Windex bottle dangling from her index finger.

When Elle gets closer, Tom's whole face lifts into a smile. "Look at you," he says. "Bonnie says it went great." Elle nods, feeling bashful over the gifts. "I brought you some orange chicken."

"And flowers," Bonnie says.

Elle grins. "I see that. You didn't have to . . ." She walks out from behind the counter, kisses him briefly "I didn't expect you to come down."

"Well, it *is* Valentine's Day," he says, gesturing to the pink construction paper hearts taped all over the walls and counter. "And we have to celebrate." He sets down the takeout, lifting the flowers. "Do you have a vase for these?"

"I'll grab one," Bonnie says. "Don't touch the glass; I just cleaned it," she adds, disappearing into the back.

"This is really sweet," Elle says, moving into his arms.

"Least I could do."

"I was going to call you once I was finished here."

"I'd never hear from you, Miss Business Owner."

Elle gives him a little shove. "It's our first Valentine's! I would have."

"Maybe at midnight, and then you'd be heading to bed so you could come back here at two a.m. and do it all over again."

"Nuh-uh!"

Tom gives her a quick peck. "It's okay. I'll give you a pass this time, since it's the grand opening."

"How *kind* of you," Elle says, then more seriously, "I'm almost done here."

Tom shakes his head as Bonnie comes back into the room with a vase, already filled with water. Tom hands over the flowers, and Bonnie takes them out of their plastic packaging before setting the vase near the cash register. "Beautiful," Bonnie says. "He's a keeper."

Elle glances at Tom, and he offers a tight half smile, almost bashful.

"Well, I know how to take a hint," Bonnie says. "Is there anything else you need me to do, or should I scram already and leave you two alone?"

"You can go," Elle says, then adds, "Thanks for all your help today, Bonnie."

"A great first day," she says, then heads into the back again. Elle hears the crinkling of a windbreaker before the back door slams shut.

Tom turns to her. "Alone in *your* bakery."

Elle's not sure what to say. Caught between embarrassment and the lingering excitement from the day, Elle hugs Tom again. Breathing in his scent—a mix of dusty English books and Old Spice and cigarette smoke—she can't believe how supportive he's been through all the chaos. He even helped with the final coat of paint.

Tom breaks the silence. "Should we dig into the food?"

"Yes," Elle says. "Thank you—this is so sweet."

They sit down at one of three tables in the front room, the one by the window. Elle can feel the damp chill coming off the glass. She glances out, the street vast and dark beyond the warmth of the bakery—*her* bakery.

"Oh—I almost forgot." Tom stands. "Stay right there."

Elle watches him hurry out the door, down the street, and out of view. She unpacks the food: two big containers, plus a small one that must be extra rice. Reading the tops of the containers, she places the Pad 2* in front of Tom's seat and the Or 1* in front of herself, the rice in the middle. She's rifling through stray napkins in the bag, looking for utensils, when Tom comes back in with a bottle.

"Champagne?" Elle says.

He lifts the bottle as if to show it off. "We're celebrating, aren't we?"

"I guess so," Elle says as he circles behind the counter for two cups. "And thanks for making mine less spicy this time."

Sitting back down, he says, "Please, after all the coughing last time? Never again."

The mention of coughing reminds Elle of her father, giving her just a touch of sorrow. "I have a sensitive palate."

"I know." Tom opens his pad thai container to a burst of steam and sticks his fork into the heap of noodles.

Elle opens her own container and takes a tentative bite of the orange chicken—not too spicy. Just the taste makes her realize how hungry she is, and she scoops up a bite twice the size of the last.

"So it went well?"

Elle bobs her head. "It was great. Better than I expected."

"You look so cute in your apron," Tom says.

Elle realizes she's still wearing it, the front caked with fruit fillings and flour. "Oh, gross. I should take this off."

"I just said you look cute," Tom says. "Eat."

Elle straightens her apron, as if that'll help the mess, and takes another bite.

"Did you know that the word *apron* actually used to be *napron*? *A napron*. Over time, the *n* migrated over to the *a* to get *an apron*."

"Huh," Elle says. "I'm glad the *n* migrated. *Napron*? Sounds silly."

"Well, nowadays it does."

Elle laughs. "When are you going to open that bottle of champagne?"

"You want it now?"

"Well, yeah," she says, spooning more rice into her chicken container. "Then I have to get back to work."

"Seriously?"

"One more recipe."

"Just one?"

"I promise," Elle says.

"All right, then," he says. He tears the foil off the champagne bottle, unscrews the wire cap, and eases the cork out. The loud pop makes Elle jump, and Tom laughs. With vapor still stirring around the top of the bottle, he pours the champagne into the two plastic cups. Watching him, she thinks to herself how he is the first man she has ever felt this way about, who has ever seemed *lasting*.

"Cheers," he says, lifting his cup.

They tap rims with a cheap-sounding clack, then drink. The bubbles sting Elle's tongue a little, but they flutter warmly in her chest. She promptly takes another sip.

"Good?" Tom asks.

"Very," Elle says. "Thank you."

"Sorry it's not chilled."

"I didn't even think of it."

He chuckles. "Good."

They finish their meals and cups of bubbly in relative silence, glancing up at each other every now and again. By the time she's done with her orange chicken, she can feel the gentle spin of the champagne making her pleasantly tipsy.

Tom takes her hand and squeezes it, but before he can speak, Elle says, "Cinnamon rolls."

"You *have* to?" he protests.

"I *have* to," she says. "But you can stay here with me while I make them, if you want."

"Will you let me lick the spoon?"

"Only if you're good," Elle says, standing. Again, she feels that gentle spin, and she pauses a moment before leading Tom into the back room. In her head, she envisions how she would write down the recipe.

Sultry Cinnamon Rolls

Cinnamon rolls are best for impressing customers or guests— or, better yet, your sweetheart. Spray two quarter-sheet cake pans with plenty of flour-based cooking spray and set aside. No need to preheat your oven—the rolls will need to rest overnight before you bake them fresh in the morning.

Making cinnamon rolls is a courtship; they take all evening. Start slow. The dough is first. Briefly whisk 6 ½ cups of flour, 2 teaspoons of salt, and ¾ cup of sugar in a large bowl. Next, warm 2 cups of milk, 1 cup of water, and ½ cup of butter to 120°, or even a little warmer, add 3 tablespoons of active dry yeast, and allow it a few minutes to proof. The liquid will be slick—add it, steaming, to the drys, and ease your fingers into the bowl, like easing into a hot bath. The liquid will be almost too hot to touch; embrace the tingling sensation, the silky way it envelops your skin. Breathe in the scent of yeast, activated by the milk, warmly pungent and welcoming. Loosely knead until the dough holds together before transferring it into a clean bowl greased with cooking spray. Cover with plastic wrap and place somewhere high, such as on top of your cupboards or fridge—the heat will help the dough rise.

Now the filling, but not before a kiss from your sweetheart. Microwave 1 ½ cups of butter until it is half-melted, half-firm; share more kisses as the seconds count down. Pour the butter into your mixing bowl along with 2 cups of brown sugar, and beat until combined. This is where the recipe gains energy; feel the thrum of the mixer with your palm. Add 4 tablespoons of cinnamon and 2 tablespoons of maple syrup. Add an extra teaspoon of cinnamon, if you like its sweet spice. Beat the ingredients until the butter stiffens; admire the mixer's enthusiasm, its unwavering rhythm. Go another minute before you let it rest.

The topping requires heat. In a saucepan, warm ½ cup of butter, 2 ½ cups of brown sugar, 1/3 cup of vegetable oil, 1/3 cup of corn syrup, ¼ cup of maple syrup, and ½ cup of honey until they mingle. Stir until it's as smooth as your lover's voice. Never simmer, never boil. Your heat is an intimate whisper, not a shout. Keep stirring for another few minutes, until the sugar has dissolved and the mixture appears almost glassy. Spread 4 cups of chopped pecans evenly over your greased quarter sheets, pour the topping into the pans until it fills every corner, and let it cool.

Retrieve your dough from its high place. The plastic wrap will be a dome over the bowl, and the dough will be twice its size already, resembling a honeycomb along the edges. Inhale as you release the wrap—there is nothing like the scent of a sweet yeast dough. Clear a large surface, cover with 2 cups of flour, and spray your hands with cooking spray—you'll need the slip. Grazing your hands along the inside edges of the bowl, gingerly cup the dough and transfer it to your surface. It'll feel silky and malleable in your palms, warm and taut. Knead it into an oblong oval; then take up your rolling pin. Rolling outward, stretch the dough into a large rectangle, about 2 centimeters thick.

This is when things come together.

Spread your filling over every inch of the dough, and then loosely roll it widthwise. Your sweetheart might pinch or tickle you at this point. Tell them you're almost done, and cut the roll into 12 equal sections. Place those in the quarter-sheet pans on top of the caramel sauce, and cover with plastic wrap, leaving the cinnamon rolls in the fridge overnight—you'll bake them in the morning.

Note: While making cinnamon rolls is a courtship, never let them interfere with your lover's courting. Some nights, it's better to let them go unmade.

Before Elle is able to even spread flour across her table, Tom is kissing her neck, running his hands over her waist, biting her ear. Trying to focus on her ingredients, she says, "Tom," but he's unrelenting, and finally she gives in to his lips. "All right," she whispers against his mouth. "But if a customer complains about no cinnamon rolls tomorrow, I'm giving them your number."

"Worth it," Tom says, gathering her closer into his arms.

~

It's eleven at night, and Elle has to go to work in four hours, but for now baking is far from her thoughts. Tom exhales beside her, his bare chest sinking in her peripheral. On her back, her body feels slightly chilled in the open air of his bedroom. The sheets are crumpled somewhere at the base of his bed. Together, they're enwrapped in the gauzy glow of his bedside lamp. Her mind is unfocused, suspended between coherent thought and an abyss of gradually diminishing pleasure. Coming off the high of their lovemaking, she feels heavy, as if she might never get up, as if she might lie here forever, content.

Tom sighs again, kisses her forehead, rolls out of bed. He disappears, and the hall is illuminated with the light from the bathroom. Elle hears the sink running. She remains on her back for a few moments more, then gets up herself. Rather than retrieving her clothes from off the floor, she finds Tom's T-shirt and slips it on. The cotton is smooth against her skin, and it smells overwhelmingly like Tom.

Just as he's coming back into the room, Elle's climbing back into bed.

"That's almost as cute as your apron," Tom says. Still naked, he flops onto the bed and slips under the covers, settling beside her.

"Don't you mean *napron*?"

A quick breath of laughter. "Right," he says. He wraps his arm around her. "That was great."

Elle snuggles closer, her head on his left bicep. She links her left fingers with his, his palm enveloping the back of her hand. "I never realized how big your hands are."

"My hands, huh?" He squeezes her close, and she chuckles.

Inspecting his fingers in the soft light, she hesitates to speak. She's said too much too soon in the past, and it has only been a month. But after the long day and the champagne and *tonight*, Elle feels her filters slipping. Still staring at his fingers, she says, "I'm glad I met you."

Instantly, he responds, "Me too."

Elle feels her cheeks pull into a smile. Staring at the little dark hairs on his knuckles, hairs she never really noticed before, she says, "You're just too good to be true—" She stops short. There, faint, on his left ring finger, is the trace of a tan line. Her chest constricts, and her throat suddenly feels flooded and tight.

Tom's saying, "I feel the same way. I've been having so much fun with you. And your baking doesn't hurt either . . ."

She can't stop staring at his finger in the lamp glow. Maybe a trick of the light? She shifts his hand, but no, the tan line is still there. How did she not see it before? Of course, the answer is obvious: they haven't been this *close* before. Suddenly claustrophobically hot, her skin bristles at each point of contact with the man beside her. He's still talking, but she can't hear him anymore. Is he really married? Is she his mistress? Elle thinks about the wife, who is probably oblivious, who would certainly hate Elle for what she's done. Overwhelmed with a blistering sense of guilt, she sits up.

Tom hushes, sitting up as well to place his hand on Elle's back. "What is it? What's wrong?"

She wants to yell, to slap him, to leave, but she remains anchored where she sits, one leg curled under her, the other hanging off the edge of the bed.

"Elle?" Tom asks.

Deep in her belly, her muscles tighten. In his T-shirt, without underwear, she feels dirty.

His voice becomes low, serious. "Elle, what's wrong?"

Chin to collarbone, she looks over her shoulder at him. "There's a tan line on your ring finger."

His face scrunches, and he tugs the blanket toward his belly button. "That's not what you think."

"No?" Elle tries to muster more attitude but buckles under the tension. She turns away again, not wanting to see his face.

"I'm getting divorced," Tom says.

Trying to wrap her head around the situation, Elle doesn't respond.

"We've been separated for two months now. You think I share this apartment with a woman?"

Elle lifts her gaze to the bare room. He's right—it doesn't look like a woman lives here.

"I was going to tell you, of course. But, you know, things were going so well . . . I was putting it off."

Elle isn't sure whether she should be relieved or angry. She looks at the clock: 11:24. "I should go."

"Please don't."

"I should go," she repeats, standing. She picks her clothes up off the floor.

"Elle, your car is at the bakery."

Shit. "I'll walk."

"You can't *walk.*" He stands up, blocking the doorway.

Clothes bundled in her arms, she says, "Let me leave, please."

"I want to talk about this," Tom says. "You said yourself, 'too good to be true.'"

"Yeah, that's right. Too good to be *true.*"

"I mean . . ." He runs a hand over his face. "I mean, let's talk about this."

She wants to leave. She wants to hit him. But she just stands there, in his T-shirt, looking at his naked body in the doorway. Suddenly, she has the urge to laugh. He's naked. How can she fight with him while he's completely naked? How did the night go from perfect to absolutely awful? And now it's almost absurd.

"You're naked," Elle says.

"Okay," Tom says, still harried.

Elle drops her clothes on the floor and sits on the edge of the bed. She's been up for almost twenty-four hours. "I'm tired."

His arms, which were on either side of the doorframe, drop to his sides. "I know." He sits down next to her but leaves plenty of space between them. "I'm sorry, Elle. I should have said something. I shouldn't have let it go this far without telling you."

"I really should go," Elle says, looking at him.

His expression is drawn, the lamp casting shadows across the angles of his face. With his hair a bit tousled, he looks worn. "Don't go."

Elle drops her chin to her chest, then leans her head against his shoulder. For a moment she thinks she can feel the warmth of his hand hover over her back, but it never lands.

"It's completely over with her, my . . . wife. It has been since before I met you," he says.

"Why did you break up?"

"She became . . . cold." He hesitates. "We didn't share the same views on having a family; it became clear that neither of us would bend."

"Her name?"

"Miranda."

She repeats the name softly, lifting her head to look him in the eye. "I want to see your divorce papers."

"You can watch me sign them," he says. "Just please don't go."

Overwhelmed by fatigue, by emotional strain, Elle says, "All right."

He helps her slip under the covers again, lifting and then laying the blanket over her body, hands not once grazing her.

"I'll sleep on the couch," Tom says.

A little relieved, she says, "Yes, all right." Let him feel bad about it.

"I'll wake you at two?"

"Three," Elle says.

"Three," Tom repeats, turning off the light.

~

Elle takes another long sip of coffee, finishing the cup, then sets it down and picks up her rolling pin. It's been an hour and a half already and three cups of coffee, and still she feels like the lights are too bright. She can't stop thinking about bed. And Tom. He woke her gently, helped her find her clothes, and drove her to the bakery. No complaints, no words at all, just, "I'd like to see you later," before she got out of the car. She said, "All right." Now she's not so sure. She can't shake the acidic feeling in her stomach she gets just thinking about it. A married man. She slept with a married man. On a technicality, sure, but she still feels cheated. He lied to her.

Elle runs a pizza cutter through her dough, cutting half of it into triangles, the other half into rectangles. She folds the croissants first, bending them into crescents. Then she makes the chocolate turnovers, sprinkling dark chocolate in lines across the little rectangles, folding them once, twice, a pinch to the ends and three slits along the tops. She pops a few spare chocolate chips into her mouth. A little floury, but sweet and bitter and good.

"I saw that," Bonnie says. She's readying the folded pastries for the oven just the way Elle trained her: adjusting them on the sheet, brushing them with egg wash, sprinkling almonds on the bear claws.

"Want some?" Elle says.

She nods, coming over to Elle's table to grab a small handful of chips. "They're a little—gritty. Have any sans flour?"

Elle shakes her head. "I already put the bag away. These are the stragglers."

Bonnie picks a few more off the table, blows on them, and pops them in her mouth. "Better than no chocolate, I suppose."

Elle gets back to rolling more dough.

Bonnie slides the bear claw tray into the oven and turns her attention on the croissants Elle just shaped. "Judging by the three cups of joe this morning, I'm guessing last night went well?"

Elle's taken a little off guard by the question. Swiping the pizza cutter through more dough, she says, "Um, yeah."

Bonnie rests a hand on her hip. "Okay, what happened?"

"Nothing."

Elle opens the walk-in to get some berry turnover filling. Even over the whir of the fans, she can hear Bonnie say, "I'm not convinced."

Pushing the heavy refrigerator door shut with her behind, Elle places the container of filling on the table and starts spooning small globs onto her dough squares. "Why not?"

"Because if it had gone well, you'd be smiling ear to ear. Something happened. Do you want to talk about it?"

"It's complicated."

"Point taken." Refocused on her work, Bonnie adds, "If you change your mind, I'm happy to listen."

Elle folds a square into a triangle, then flutes the edges—it's one of her favorite pastries to make. Two fingers on the dough's seam, one to scrunch the dough between them, a perfect ripple. She realizes now that Tom never told her whether he liked her pastries from yesterday. Why didn't he say anything?

Elle hesitates, then says, "Tom's married."

"*What?*" Bonnie sets down her brush. "Are you kidding?"

Elle shakes her head, fluting another turnover. This one has too much filling, and the purple berry juice oozes out the sides. "We were in bed last night, and I noticed the tan line on his finger."

"Oh, sweetie," Bonnie says. "How awful."

"He's getting divorced. Been separated for a few months now, just finalizing it."

"Oh . . . well, that's not so bad."

"I guess. Still, he didn't tell me."

"How long have you two been dating?"

"A little over a month."

Bonnie sucks air into her cheeks, making a hissing sound. "He should've told you."

"That's what I'm thinking."

Sliding another sheet into the oven, Bonnie comes to Elle's table and starts lifting the finished turnovers onto the last baking sheet. "So what happened when you confronted him?"

"He just . . . explained. We talked pretty late. Then I fell asleep."

"You stayed at his place?"

"My car was still here," Elle says. "He slept on the couch."

"*Aw,*" Bonnie says, egg washing the last of the turnovers. "That's kind of sweet."

"I guess," Elle says. "I didn't want to stay, but he insisted."

"Well, I'm surprised you haven't had a fourth cup of coffee."

"Ha. I was thinking about it."

Bonnie smiles, her blonde bangs falling across her face. They work in silence for a few minutes, cleaning up the mess of flour and egg on the tables. Bonnie then slides the first baked tray of pastries out of the oven, some corner folds that are to be topped with a dollop of thick cream cheese frosting and fresh fruit.

"So what are you going to do?" Bonnie asks, swiping some frosting off a spoon and onto a pastry.

Elle sighs. "I don't know yet. Is it overreacting to be mad at him?"

"I would be mad."

Elle slides the next ready tray out of the oven, the bear claws all puffy and golden. "But part of me feels like it's not a big deal. He's single; he didn't break any rules." She opens a container full of almond glaze and stirs it up with a fork.

"But he did lie to you," Bonnie says.

"Exactly," Elle says. "I mean, it's not like I ever asked if he was married and he said no, but he didn't go out of his way to tell me either."

"He should've told you."

"He said he was going to—he just didn't want to ruin what was going so well."

"I can understand that," Bonnie says, dusting her tray of pastries with powdered sugar. "But still."

Elle starts drizzling the bear claws with the almond glaze, realizing how much better she feels. It's nice to have a girlfriend to talk to. With the bakery opening and all her friends from college getting married and having babies, Elle hasn't had much time for girl talk.

Elle says, "I just feel jealous now, you know? Wondering what his wife is like, how I compare." And what would Elle's mother think?

"Oh, don't be like that," Bonnie says. "He's with *you*."

Elle sighs. "Yeah, for now."

"You're not going to break up with him, are you?"

"Do you think I should?"

Bonnie shakes her head. "I think he's just too handsome; that's the problem."

Switching over to chocolate drizzle for the chocolate turnovers, Elle adjusts her apron. Her *napron*. She smiles to herself. "I think I'm falling in love with him—*that's* the problem."

"*Oooooh*," Bonnie teases. "Just don't let him off the hook too easy."

"Oh, I'm still upset," Elle says. "I asked to see his divorce papers."

"Good."

Glancing at the clock—4:55 a.m.—Elle speeds up her task. Bonnie takes notice and speeds up, too, traying the pastries that are ready.

With the cases finally full—all but for the turnovers, which are still baking—Elle unlocks the front door and flips the CLOSED sign to OPEN.

Another half hour goes by before anyone comes in—the bell on the door ringing just as Bonnie is sliding the turnovers into the case—but it's the start of another busy day, that's for sure. While Bonnie helps an older man buy one of the still-warm turnovers, Elle pours herself a fourth cup of coffee and heads into the back room. Time to make those cinnamon rolls.

August 29, 2015

Seventeen days after Elle found out

The house is white and perfect. It looks like it was built yesterday. The lawn is neat as a golf course, and despite the season, the garden is full. Elle doesn't want to interrupt Kelli and her husband, who are probably asleep or eating breakfast. But she needs her purse. She needs to get back to the cabbie waiting for her with the meter running, needs to get her car, needs to go home. She walks up the path to the front door, checking out her reflection in the large shuttered windows. She looks like shit. She looks like she just had a one-night stand. Maybe she should come back later.

She knocks. No answer, no sound. She knocks again; nothing. They're asleep. She probably woke them. She rings the doorbell. A weight in her stomach pushes all the air out of her. What is she doing? What has her life come to?

Kelli opens the door.

"Elle!" she says. "You're looking for your purse." She's wearing a matching shirt-and-pants pajama set, blue, with little sea stars and urchins.

"Did I wake you? I'm sorry." Elle drags her palm across her face.

"No! Brett and I were just having our coffee." Kelli smiles warmly. "You look like you had *quite* the night."

Elle shakes her head.

"Well, come in. I'll get you some coffee." Kelli turns and walks farther inside.

"That's really kind of you, but the meter is running, and I'd like to get home," Elle says. She doesn't want to intrude, doesn't want to prolong her no-underwear, dirty-jeans, hungover-in-public embarrassment. She has also already seen enough of Kelli's perfect life.

"Right, yes. I understand completely," Kelli says. "I'll get your purse."

She disappears around the corner, and Elle is left on the stoop. Before Kelli comes back, her husband shuffles down the stairs into the foyer, slippers scuffing against the carpet. "Oh," he says. "Kelli's friend? Is she getting your purse?"

Elle nods.

He's tall, clean cut, save for a little morning stubble. He lifts his coffee cup. "Going for a refill. Want some?"

"No, thanks," she says. "Eager to get home."

"Yes, I remember those nights," he says as Kelli slides up beside him. He rests his arm across her shoulders in a half hug.

"Not anymore." Her lips pull tight, and a few almost-wrinkles crease at her eyes. "I convinced him to settle."

"I wouldn't call it settling, Mrs. Whitman." He drops a kiss on top of her head, and the weight in Elle's stomach presses toward her spine.

"I should go," she says, reaching for her purse in Kelli's hand.

"Oh, no more cab fare for you," Kelli says, holding tight. "It must've cost a fortune to get here."

Elle wants to scream. To race across the perfect lawn away from the perfect couple and hole herself up in her ruined life alone.

"It's fine, really."

Kelli turns back inside, then reappears with a set of keys. "I'll drive you. Brett, do you have cash?" She points at the cab.

"You don't have to—"

"Sure, sweets," he says, slippers scuffing out of sight.

Kelli hands Elle her purse and, throwing a coat over her pajamas, leads her to the silver Lexus parked in the driveway. There aren't even weeds growing in the lines between the concrete slabs, no oil stains or leaves or anything.

Inside the car, Kelli starts the ignition, and a monotone voice blares out of the speakers, saying something about the Roman Empire. Kelli startles and hits the power button on the console. "Sorry. Brett likes to listen to books on tape. Why so loud . . ." She spreads her hands. "It always makes me jolt when I start his car."

Elle can see him outside, paying the cabbie. He waves before heading back through their front door.

"You didn't have to pay for my cab," Elle says. "That was way too nice."

Kelli shrugs. "Schoolteacher mentality. I like taking care of people."

"Still," Elle says, "I met you yesterday."

Kelli gives her a brief glance and then a smile. "Any friend of Bonnie's is a friend of mine. Plus, you're going through enough trouble."

Suddenly Elle feels like a bitch. Kelli did nothing but be responsible, and Elle automatically envied her—and maybe even disliked her?—for having a good husband and home. Softening, she says, "Well, thank you. You've made my morning better."

Kelli nods, not saying any more. All but for the gentle rumble of the engine, the inside of the car falls quiet. Elle stares out the window as Kelli turns down this street and that, stopping and going at every deserted stop sign. It's still early, and it's Saturday, so the passing houses are hushed. She feels dirty and worn down. They're twenty minutes from her car in the city, and Elle's home—or her husband's home—is another half hour after that, and she doesn't think she can stand to wait even another second to wash Owen off her body and down the drain.

"Do you want some music?" Kelli asks, breaking the silence. She hits a button, and the radio comes on—some sort of soft popular-music station. Then her bubbly tone diminishes. "You're probably just impatient to get home, huh?"

"I feel like shit," Elle responds. What was she thinking, going to a club, sleeping with a younger guy? Crawling down a suburban road in Kelli's car makes it seem all the more ridiculous. Loud techno swing she can't understand, drinks that aren't wine, high heels, men ten years her junior—and Elle, trying to grind.

She breaks into a giggle, and Kelli does too. "What was I thinking, inviting you inside? You're probably aching for a shower."

Elle nods. "It's okay. Some coffee probably would help the hangover—I just feel *gross*."

Kelli becomes subdued again. "So you went home with him?"

"Yes." The topic hangs there for a second, filling the stuffy air of the car.

"How was it?"

"It was . . ." Elle sits there for a moment, ashamed but also feeling a sense of resolve. "It was necessary."

~

After getting her car from the garage and stopping at a drive-through Starbucks, Elle parks her car on the street in front of her lawn and walks up the stones and porch steps to her front door. She fumbles with her keys, but the door opens before she can slide the key into the lock. Tom.

Standing in front of him in the small space of the threshold, Elle can smell his new aftershave—which means he can probably smell last night all over her. She steps back to allow him room to walk by.

"You went out," he says tightly, lifting his golf caddie out the door.

Elle's head pounds, and she stumbles over her words. "Going golfing?"

"Yes, with a few buddies from work." He clicks his key fob, and the Accord in the driveway *bip-bip*s; the trunk pops. His lean arms effortlessly slide the clubs into the car. "Your mom called. She left a message."

"Okay," Elle says. She can't move; the joints in her knees refuse to bend.

Before Tom gets in his car, he says, "Nice blouse." His tone is level and unrevealing of his meaning. Then he's gone down the street.

She looks down and sees she buttoned her blouse up wrong, but the fabric is sheer enough in the late-morning light to reveal the outline of her bra. The faint sound of an engine fills the still neighborhood.

February 19, 2006

About nine and a half years before Elle found out

The bakery's first week went well, but Elle is glad it's over. Following Bonnie out the back door, she locks up before walking alongside her employee across the gravel to their cars.

"A successful week," Bonnie says, fiddling with her key fob.

In the tiny back parking lot, the only light is that of a streetlight near the front of the shop. Elle can barely make out the dumpsters a few yards away. The night air is frosty, foggy, and still.

Elle takes a long, deep breath, the cold waking her up. "I think so."

"Give yourself credit," Bonnie says. "It went great, and you know it."

A small smile pinches Elle's cheeks. "I'm exhausted."

Bonnie chuckles. "Me too."

"Any plans for your day off?" Elle has known Bonnie for barely two weeks, but after the late nights and the early mornings and her support with regard to Tom's divorce, she feels like she's known Bonnie for much longer.

"Not sure yet," Bonnie says. "Trying not to freeze my ass off, I guess. It's supposed to slip back down into the twenties."

"God, I'm ready for spring."

"Tell me about it." Bonnie shifts on her feet. "What about you? Any plans?"

"I'm seeing Tom tonight again," Elle says.

"Oooh. And how is that going?"

"We've talked a couple times since opening night," Elle says. "He's been really open about the divorce. Answers every question I ask."

"Do you feel better about the whole thing?"

"I do," Elle admits.

Bonnie folds her arms. "What really matters is—do you trust him?"

Elle looks out into the freezing darkness. Her pinkie toes are numb, and she scrunches her feet in her shoes. "I don't know if I trust him yet. I want to. I mean, what would you do?"

Bonnie grins. "Oh, I'd probably stick with him. Aside from this, he seems like a sweetheart."

"It's hard to stay mad at him."

"Especially since he came in every day this week to buy pastries."

A steamy breath of laughter swirls around Elle's face. "Right?" Her phone buzzes in her pocket. "Speak of the devil."

Bonnie unlocks her car. "Good *ni-ight*."

"I'll update you on Tuesday."

"You better!" Slamming her door, Bonnie turns on her car, headlights bursting against the back wall of the building.

Elle slips into her own car, setting her purse on the passenger seat. She twists the key in the ignition, and the engine rumbles to life. A blast of chilly air comes out of the vents, and Elle wiggles her toes again, willing the temperature to rise. Teeth chattering, she waves at Bonnie as she drives out of the parking lot, turning right. Elle turns left as she heads for Tom's.

~

Tom opens the door a few moments after Elle's knock.

"You're still up," Elle comments, stepping past him into the apartment.

"Reading," he says. "Anticipating, too, maybe." He kisses her cheek.

Elle drops her purse by the door, wanders over to the couch. There's a box of pizza on the coffee table, three slices missing.

"I can heat that up if you're hungry," Tom says.

Elle shakes her head. She should be hungry, but she isn't. Between the tiring week and the thought of more talk about their relationship, her appetite is slight. Things are still a little tense between them, still lumps in the batter that they need to whisk out.

Tom retrieves something from the kitchen, then sits down beside her on the couch. He holds out a plain, unsealed envelope. "I'm not trying to buy your affection," he says.

Taking the envelope, Elle flips it over and slides out its contents. There's a card with a sunflower on the front, which she reads first:

Elle, I'm going to get fat from all the pastries, but it's worth it. Congratulations on your first week. You inspire me.

— Tom

Elle smirks. "You don't *have* to eat the pastries."

"But they're so good," Tom says, resting his hand on her back. "And I want to be supportive."

"You can be supportive in other ways."

Tom glances at the gift in her hand, a white slip of card stock. She flips it over to find that it's a gift card to her favorite kitchen shop, with *$50* scrawled in the corner. Halfway through the week, she mentioned offhand that she needed more supplies: small things, like one more bench scraper, extra rubber spatulas, and a better whisk. Elle is surprised he listened.

For a moment, she stares at the gift card. The warmth is coming back into her toes, and her fingers are tingly against the textured paper. She beams up at him. "You're sweet."

"You said you still needed some things."

"I did."

"We can talk more, if you want." His expression is a strange mix of hopeful and hesitant—the same way she feels.

"We've been *talking* so much lately," Elle says. "Aren't you sick of it?"

Tom shrugs. "I really care about you."

"Well, I'm sick of talking," Elle admits, kissing him on the mouth. His kindness and openness and care overwhelm her. Tom is irresistible, and she doesn't want to resist him.

Tom pulls back slightly, his voice a murmur. "I want you to trust me."

Elle looks into his eyes. The room is dim, and she realizes how close they are, his arms around her, their faces barely parted. She's only known this man for six weeks, and yet he helped with preopening setup and picked up supplies and bought more baked goods than he needed—and now this. He wouldn't have done all that if he weren't genuine.

"I trust you," she says.

"We haven't really defined this yet, but I want you to be my girl-friend. I want to be exclusive."

Her breath catches momentarily. "I would like that."

"And I don't want to start things on the wrong foot."

She leans toward him, and they kiss again. She lightly bites his lip as they pull away. "I think we're starting things just fine."

Tom laughs and leans in for another kiss.

"Thank you for the gift card," Elle whispers against his mouth.

"I'll go with you tomorrow if you want."

Her voice is barely audible, her mind already thinking about other things. "Looking forward to it."

September 4, 2015

Owen was supposed to be a onetime thing.

Now they're in his bed again. Side by side. On their backs. Talking. He says she's sexy, says, "I like your softness—some of the girls I've been with are so *toned* it makes me feel like a lump. It's not feminine. A little jiggle is a good thing." He glances at her out of the corner of his eye. "I'm not trying to insult you."

She rolls to her side and pushes up off the mattress.

"Now, see, I insulted you," Owen says.

Elle stands. "Just give me a minute." Feeling suddenly very body aware, she steps over the dirty carpet into the bathroom.

Tom used to talk about her body, compliment her shape, and now he's with another woman. It doesn't mean anything. She can't do anything about it. Her hips will always be full; her breasts will always be not big enough; her thighs will always be too sinewy. These are things that she has never been able to change, not with diet or gyms or yoga or distaste. She did used to be toned, however. Lean. She ran track all through school and after, and the running made her ass and abs tight. Tom liked that. The tightness of her ass. The stockings she wore under her dresses and how her behind looked when Tom lifted the back of her skirt as they stepped out his apartment door—one last peek.

Now she's soft. Owen has said so. She quit running when she opened her bakery.

Elle smooths her hair in the mirror, then returns to Owen.

He's sitting up, flaccid penis lying against his thigh. "I was trying to compliment you," he says. On his face appears to be actual concern.

Elle goes to the other side of the bed and lies down. "I know."

With a sigh, he lies back as well, turns to his side. "What happened to your husband?" He regards her hand resting on her belly. Touches her ring finger. "I'm assuming by the tan line you were married? Or still are?"

Elle lifts her head, horrified. Such a familiar moment, yet now she's the married one. Cringing, she chews on the inside of her cheek.

Owen offers a smile. "I can be sensitive."

"Sure you can."

His smile widens before it sobers. "Really, though."

"He's fucking someone else."

"Oh." Owen relaxes onto his back again. "When did you . . . ?"

"A few weeks ago." Elle presses her fingers into her brow, then lifts her hand above her head so she can see the tan line. "How old are you?" she asks Owen.

"Twenty-three. I turn twenty-four next month."

Elle laughs, almost to a surprising volume. "Shit."

"Well, how old are you?" His voice sounds groggy. "I mean, I know it's rude to ask a woman, but—"

"Thirty-five."

He sounds surprised. "You don't fuck like you're thirty-five."

"I probably fuck like I'm in my forties."

Owen shakes his head. "No. If anything denotes your age, it's that you have experience. Which is sexy."

"What about my softness?"

"It's not *old* soft. And I said the soft was sexy."

Now Elle turns, elbow propping up her head. "So full of compliments tonight."

He turns now, too, brushing his hand over a breast and down to the strip of neatly groomed hair on her pubic bone. "I'm just horny." He kisses her, and the hand between her thighs increases pressure.

She's not in the mood, though. She pushes him back a little. "I'm done for the night," she says.

"Oh, fine." He flops onto his back again. "You know, what would be hot is if you shaved everything off."

Elle doesn't understand—and then she does. Irritation floods her muscles.

He's unaware. "Or waxed. Maybe that sort of thing is after your time. All the women my age are hairless down there—"

His age.

If he meant it as a joke, it's not funny. Elle reaches for her clothes.

"Where are you going?"

"You seriously don't know why I'm offended right now?"

"Well, you don't *have* to be hairless. It was just a suggestion."

"I'm done for the night, Owen," Elle says, yanking on her jeans, grabbing her purse. It shouldn't have lasted this long, anyway. It shouldn't have happened at all. *His age.* As if eleven years is all that long, all that much older.

"All right, but you don't have to—"

She's too humiliated to explain his mistake. "Good night, Owen."

"I was just saying—"

"Good night."

Elle rushes from the bedroom, out of his apartment, into the hallway. The fluorescent lighting and dingy light-blue paint make her feel as though she's under examination, as though every flaw is multiplied. She's mortified. Can he seriously be that ignorant about a woman's feelings? If she didn't see it before, she sees it now—Owen was a fleeting thing, and tonight she got him out of her system.

Briefly, she wonders if her husband's girlfriend shaves it all off. She's probably one of those toned girls Owen was talking about, but Tom always liked that, didn't he? He probably strayed because Elle stopped running, stopped shaving her legs twice per week, stopped wearing tights. Or perhaps it's more ineffable than that, the emotional equivalent of stale bread. The new woman is probably exciting. The new woman definitely shaves it all off.

Outside Owen's building, a siren blares.

~

When she gets home, Tom is there, in the kitchen, slicing a cucumber over a plate of lettuce. She always hated how he cut vegetables, the paring knife sliding toward his thumb, slice after slice. One slip, and he'd take off the tip. Now, she imagines him cutting himself, even wishes for it, briefly, if only because she'd like the house to herself. She's not in the mood to see him.

"You're home," he says without looking up. "Should I make you a salad?"

Elle pauses by the stairs. He's moved on to a bell pepper, finger-long red strips falling onto baby greens. His question feels sickeningly normal, as if he has a right to make her dinner after screwing someone else. It amazes her how everyday tasks continue, even after she confronted Tom. They go to work, pump gas, do the dishes, make dinner. Bell peppers still get sliced; dinner still gets made; time trudges forward. And yet everything has changed.

"I'm not hungry," Elle lies. In fact, she's starving. It's past eight o'clock, and she skipped dinner to see Owen, and after the sex and her humiliated drive home, she could eat ten of Tom's recklessly made salads.

"You sure?" he asks. "It's no trouble."

And why is he eating so late? Is it for the same reason Elle is just getting home? She's stung by the likelihood of that fact.

Impulsively, she drops her purse by the stairs and walks into the kitchen. "A little late for dinner, isn't it?"

Tom sets the bell pepper down on the bare counter, a spot of red juice landing on the clean surface. He's still wearing a pressed blue shirt, but it's rumpled, and his white undershirt shows through the undone top buttons. "I worked late."

"Oh?"

"*Yeah.*"

She's unconvinced. Betrayal seeps into her skin, staining her like blackberry juice. She can feel its dark color spreading through her, a bruising pain that makes her feel sleepless and exhausted all at once. She can't stand to look at his face, to think of where he's been—it sure as hell wasn't the office. Imagining him with that other woman, she glances away. A part of her wanted him to stop seeing her, but clearly that was a naive wish.

"How *is* work, by the way?" she asks.

"Don't patronize me."

"Come on, I really want to know." Maybe Owen's comments tonight had some truth to them; maybe Tom got tired of her unshaven, soft body.

"It was fine," Tom says. "Busy."

"Busy like happy hour busy?"

A flash of anger colors his face. Tightly, he says, "A web-developer problem, actually."

Ever since Tom started his business, he's struggled with periodic website issues. If it's an excuse, it's a good one, but Elle senses his sincerity—not that she's been a good judge of that in the past. Nonetheless, she says, "I'm sorry about that." Then, "I'm going upstairs."

"I'm not going to ask where you've been."

She doesn't move. Involuntarily, her face flushes—she can feel the pinkness tingling through her cheeks. Does Tom know about Owen? Has he entertained the same thoughts she has about him, thoughts to make his blood course hot, thoughts of Elle naked with someone else? She expected she would revel in Tom being jealous, but now she feels something else entirely. Is it guilt? She shouldn't feel guilty, not considering what Tom's done, but the worrisome prospect of him knowing makes her feel dirty.

In a small voice, she says, "You don't deserve to know where I've been."

Tom says, "I still care."

"No, you don't."

"You're still my wife."

She glares at him. "Am I, though? Because you haven't been acting like I am."

Tom doesn't speak. His shirtsleeves are rolled up, and he rests his fists on his hips.

"If you still saw me as your wife, you wouldn't have done this."

"That's not true—"

"Isn't it?" Thinking of Owen's insensitive words again, Elle wants to know, "What is it that I don't have?"

"What?"

Bitterly, she says, "Am I not pretty enough for you? Sexy enough?"

"Elle, stop."

"No," Elle says. "Tell me why you did it, Tom. What makes her so special?"

His brow is creased, his jaw set.

"It must be something," she presses, the pain of his disloyalty welling in her throat. "Tell me what it is, Tom. Tell me why."

"Stop it."

"Did you seek her out?"

He shakes his head. "No, I didn't."

"So she came on to you? That's how it happened?"

"What do you want to hear, Elle? It just happened."

He makes it sound so casual, like it happened *to* him. Like he was walking along and tripped, and there she was, suddenly beneath him.

A little hysterical, Elle continues, "And you didn't refuse her?"

"It just happened," he repeats.

"So she approached you, and what? You just went with it?"

"Yeah." Then, sounding more defeated, "Yeah, that's how it happened."

They both stand there in silence as Elle digests this fact. In the time that they've been arguing, the pepper—still on the counter—has beaded with moisture. The leaves in Tom's salad have flattened under the weight of the cucumber slices. The paring knife has grown visibly sticky from dried vegetable juice. Is it somehow better that Tom wasn't *looking* for an affair? That the woman came on to him? *No*, Elle thinks, and for the millionth time, *Fuck him*. There is no "better" way to cheat on your spouse.

"Was it that she's younger than me?" Elle asks. "Is that why you did it?"

"Of course not."

"I know I could've tried harder."

"What are you talking about? It's not—" He sighs, resting his hands on the counter. "There's nothing wrong with you."

Women have always been attracted to Tom. Sexy, charming, funny Tom. If it's true that the other woman came on to him, what made her different from all the others? It has to be something. "Was it because she was willing to do things I won't do?"

"Jesus, Elle, no." He shifts uneasily on his feet.

"Do I know her?" Elle whispers.

"Why are you asking all this?"

"Just answer me," she says. "Is she someone I know?"

"No," Tom says. "She's not anyone you know."

Elle considers asking him who, exactly, the other woman is, but she's not sure she can handle his answer. What good will it do her now?

"After all we've been through," Elle says, eyes brimming. She sighs, trying to dam the emotional flood with a feeling more palatable than the ache of betrayal—like maybe resentment. She fans the spark of anger inside her. "After . . . everything. How could you do it?"

Tom shrugs, his temples pulsing outward with the clench of his jaw. The oven clock ticks to 8:47.

"I hope you feel like shit," Elle says to him, then turns away.

He doesn't call or come after her.

June 2, 2006

A little over nine years before Elle found out

Elle is in Tom's apartment, hands in a bowl of scone dough, when she gets a call. It's the second day of June. A fan runs on overdrive in the small kitchen; the slight breeze hits the back of her neck, where sweat has dampened her hair. Tom answers for her, his smile disintegrating with the chirps coming from the receiver. Elle's brow creases as Tom slips the phone between her shoulder and ear. She's kneading as she listens to the voice on the other end.

"This is your aunt Sarah, dear." Her father's sister. "Listen . . ." She trails off, a pause.

Elle's stomach drops, anticipating the words; she stops kneading and adjusts the phone against her ear.

"Your father passed away early this morning."

Numb, she asks, "Dad's dead?"

"I'm so sorry, honey."

"What happened?"

"He passed in his sleep, dear."

"Was there . . ." Elle gulps for breath. "Was he in pain?"

"No, dear. He'd spent his last day in the garden. Went to bed early. Didn't wake up."

"Oh," Elle says. "Where's Mom?"

She hears faint, weepy breathing on the other end. Then her aunt's voice returns, high pitched and overly casual. "Oh, you know, already making arrangements."

"Thanks for calling, Auntie Sarah," Elle says stiffly, and she hangs up.

She looks at Tom, then closes her eyes. It is the moment she was so ready for—ready since they heard of the cancer—but now she is blindsided. Tearless. A wave expected to come, but its magnitude overlooked. She sinks to the floor. She thought images of her father would flash before her, but instead she's shocked by the blankness, already forgetting his face, which makes her panic.

Her dough-covered hands rise to her face, hiding her eyes. She feels thin, ephemeral. Tom wraps his arms around her as she holds back the dry sobs that strain her sternum. On the floor, heat from the oven emanates out toward her.

~

Again, they are in Tom's kitchen, fan running, Elle's hands in dough. This time, she already knows that her dad is gone. The funeral was three days previous, and the two of them are back from California. She is determined to finish the scones—they were his favorite. Looking down at the dough, she reminds herself that no one will call to interrupt this time. Scones are, perhaps, the only way to connect with her father from now on.

Behind her, Tom preheats the oven; she hears the click of the knob, the ticking of an old oven coming to life.

She has stayed with Tom since her return from the funeral, and peonies litter his apartment, vases of them everywhere, bought by Tom to cheer her up, their petals fluttering in the draft from the fan, bobbing on their long stems. Her father loved growing peonies—pink or white, always sweet—and he'd bring them into her childhood house, bringing, too, the ants that hid near their yellow pistils. The fragrance of them reminds her of home, of simplicity. She thinks of him cutting the peony stems in the kitchen, ants falling to the counter. Plant fertilizer floating like powdered sugar, wafting into the air as he sprinkled it into a vase. Petals littering the base of the sink.

Tom breaks her trance. "Elle." He slides his hands around her waist, brings his lips to her ear, then her neck, then her shoulder. "I love you."

She twists in his arms to face him, hands covered in flour, arms twined around his neck and held out so she won't dust him. Her father never met Tom and will never meet Tom; it's too late. Her father would have liked him, too, would have approved. She wants to cry, but she merely looks into Tom's solid eyes and says, "I love you too." It's not the first time she has said it, but somehow she feels odd speaking the words amid her melancholy.

Elle breaks free from his hold and goes back to kneading.

"Is there something I can do?" Tom asks.

There's nothing he can do. Her father is gone. "Do you have a cookie sheet?"

He nods and pulls it out.

"Parchment?" She's shaping the poppy seed–speckled dough into a square now, right on the counter.

"I'm not sure I do," he says.

"Cooking spray?"

"Yes." He gets the spray and coats the sheet.

Elle cuts the dough into little triangles using a steak knife and arranges them a few inches apart. Then she brushes them with egg and slides them into the oven. Tom turns on the sink so she can wash her hands.

"It's ten forty-five," Elle says. "They'll be done a little past eleven."

Tom gathers her into his arms again. "Take all the time you need being sad."

Elle feels a weight settle in the bottom of her chest, heavy on her lungs and in her heart. "Let's talk about something else," she says.

"All right," Tom says. "I was thinking I could take you away some weekend next month, maybe after the Fourth of July."

Elle steps back slightly, looking at Tom straight on. "Our first trip?"

"Well, yeah. You deserve a break, what with the bakery and California. You've been through enough, and I was thinking—I just thought—I wanted to spoil you a little bit." He touches her shoulder, then her cheek. "I found a B&B over near Olympic National Park, on Lake Sutherland, that we could try."

Leaning her face into his palm, Elle says, "That sounds perfect." She's in need of a break—from work, from family, from reality. And the next step with Tom excites her. Closing her eyes, Elle listens to the rapid pulse of the fan. With the perfume of peonies filling her nostrils, Elle is touched by a sense of sorrow yet again—her father will never walk her down the aisle.

September 7, 2015

Nearly four weeks after Elle found out

The morning light leads Elle to believe it'll be a clear day. In their guest room, the sheets are still rumpled from her restless sleep, and she doesn't bother straightening them. She tugs on a pair of shorts and a tee. She reties her ponytail, listening by the door for movement. The house is quiet, but it's early enough that Tom could still be home. She checks her watch: she's supposed to meet Bonnie in twenty minutes.

Turning the doorknob one millimeter at a time, Elle listens for footsteps. Nothing. She slips into the hallway. To the left, the doorway to their bedroom is dark—he must not be there. She pads downstairs, her shoulders relaxing as she walks into the kitchen to find an energy bar. He must've left early. Thank God.

"Heading out?"

His voice, gravelly from sleep, startles her.

She turns to see him seated on the couch, book in hand. Their eyes meet briefly before she looks away, searching for her purse.

"I made coffee." He lifts his steaming mug as proof.

"I thought you'd be at work already," she replies, an edge to her voice. She's not in the mood to talk; it's torture enough living in the same house.

"I'm leaving soon," he says. "Just wanted to finish this section."

"Poetry?" *Shit, why ask?* Is their life together so engrained that conversation with Tom is simply reflex? She clenches her teeth.

"Yeah," he says, as if nothing is wrong, as if it's a normal morning.

"I have to meet Bonnie." She can't stand the way his voice can still reach into her depths and stir something there.

"You sure you don't want coffee?"

Elle looks at him, truly seeing him for the first time in weeks. His eyes seem watery, the wrinkles that frame them appearing deeper than she thought they were. His mouth turns up slightly—in hope? Invitation? His bid for conversation makes her squirm.

"I have to meet Bonnie," she says again, grabbing her keys. She swings the front door shut behind her, not looking back. Halfway down the walkway, she realizes she's still wearing her house shoes, but she doesn't dare go back inside to change them.

~

Bonnie is already sitting at a table when Elle walks into the Ballard coffee shop. Elle sits down with a gusty sigh and reaches for the untouched coffee cup on her side of the table. In the foam is the pattern of a sprig—she delights in the little coffee-colored leaves before taking a sip. The latte is milky smooth.

"Thanks," she says to Bonnie, wiping foam from her lip.

"Apparently you needed it." Bonnie's skin is dewy, and she smells like apple shampoo.

Not having showered, Elle feels ragged, her cheeks puffy from sleep. "Tom was sitting in the living room reading. It's like living with a stranger; I creep around my own goddamn house just to avoid him."

"I would make him move out," Bonnie says.

The comment catches Elle off guard, like bumping shoulders with someone in a crowd, shaking things into focus. "I can't just—" But she doesn't finish the sentence. Of course she wants to leave him, but what's more shameful is her urge to stay.

"Aren't you seeing that lawyer Angela recommended?"

She takes another sip. "Later today, actually. If I can convince myself to follow through."

"You should," Bonnie says gently. "At least have your bases covered."

Elle nods, staring at the misshapen leaf pattern in her coffee. She drinks again, and the decoration disappears completely, leaving only the plain liquid underneath. Resting the cup back on the table, she says, "So . . . financials?"

It's a regular meeting they have together. Last month's numbers, this month's numbers. Planning for the future of the bakery. For a while, they go through the file Bonnie brought, reviewing their inventory and what they'll need to place on the coming shipment. Elle finishes her latte; Bonnie finishes hers. They order a morning glory muffin and share it down to the last crumb.

When they're finally done, Bonnie clasps her hands on top of the folder on the table. "I know things are up in the air, but have you thought more about the Eastside space? Gina said another buyer is interested."

It's the question Elle has been waiting for all morning, a knot building in her stomach. Without Tom's financial input, Elle can't match Bonnie's half of the deal, simple as that. She's been avoiding the topic because, well, any topic lately is filled with heartache.

Nodding, Elle says, "Look, Bonnie—"

"You can't do it without Tom."

"Yeah," she says, staring at her fingernails, the dishes on their table, anything to avoid her friend's face.

Bonnie sighs a long, disappointed sigh. "It's not your fault."

"Maybe it is."

"It's not." Bonnie touches Elle's arm. "What he did . . . it's not your fault."

"Still, what do we do? The interest is too high for a loan."

"Charlie and I can't spare any more, not with all the memory-care costs."

It's the first time in months that Bonnie has brought up her mother. A rapid descent into Alzheimer's left Bonnie and Charlie with the bill. Not to mention the emotional burden. It reminds Elle of her father, but in a way, she guesses she had it easier. At least cancer didn't take away his mind, his personality, and his memory of Elle's name.

"I know, Bonnie. I wouldn't expect you guys to pick up my slack."

"I just meant that we're both strapped."

"How's it going, by the way?"

A flash of sadness sweeps over Bonnie's face, only for a moment, before the corners of her lips turn up in a tender, coping smile. "Some days are better than others."

"I'm sorry."

"But about the bakery," Bonnie says, back to the matter at hand. "It's not over yet, Elle. If you divorce—"

"I'm not going to try to take all his money."

"Why not?"

"Because," Elle says, faltering.

"Look, Elle. As the founder, the new bakery is ultimately your decision. But be smart about it, would you? You've worked hard to get where you are. Don't let Tom steal that away from you—from us."

"It sounds like you *want* me to divorce him."

Bonnie frowns. "Don't *you*?"

"I don't know what I want," Elle says, looking away.

"You want another bakery, don't you?"

"Of course."

"You're not going to stay with him, are you?"

"I don't know what I want," Elle repeats, slower this time, growing upset. She's afraid she'll start bawling right here in the middle of the coffee shop.

Bonnie lowers her voice, her eyebrows knitting together. "Do you think you'll give him a second chance?"

"What's wrong with a second chance?"

"Nothing," Bonnie says. "But there's nothing wrong with standing up for yourself either."

Elle nods, looking off toward the front counter, where the barista is squirting chocolate syrup into a to-go cup. The customer waits nearby, staring at her phone.

"I'm sorry. I'm just trying to look out for you," Bonnie says.

Elle nods again, swiping a hand over her face.

"It's not over yet, okay?" Bonnie repeats. "We don't need to cry over it just yet."

With her lips pressed together, Elle smiles. "I won't call Gina until we're certain."

"The space might be gone by then," Bonnie says.

With a pang in her chest, Elle says, "There will be more. Gina already mentioned other locations available." She looks down at her hands, which are folded in her lap. "She's a Realtor. I know things happen at a different pace in their world. Other buyers are out of our control."

Bonnie meets Elle's eyes. "Whatever happens, I'm here for you, all right?"

"Don't make me teary eyed again."

"All right, then tell me this: did you see Owen again?"

"Oh, God," Elle says, "do I have a story for you."

June 29, 2006

A little over nine years before Elle found out

"Mom."

"Is that how you answer the phone now?"

"I'm just surprised to hear from you, that's all," Elle says. It's after hours at the bakery, lights off, and she's almost out the door.

"I can't call my daughter to see how she's doing?"

"Of course you can, Mom."

"Well?"

Elle sighs, the scent of bleach faintly tickling her nose. "I'm fine."

"Do you miss your father?" Her voice is the same cool, level tone as always, never roused by anything. They could be talking about the weather.

"Of course I do." Elle is defensive; conversations with her mother are usually strained, and they've been worse since the funeral.

"Well, me too," she says matter-of-factly, as if Elle doubts her, which is true. Her mother played the part of a widow, black shawl billowing like a butterfly, her face covered in a veil so no one could see the redness that was—or was not—in her eyes. Elle did not see her weep all weekend, though Elle suspects her mother does miss his companionship.

Her mother goes on, "I know you two were close; you seemed a wreck at the funeral."

"Understandably, yes," Elle says, her tone biting. Just the thought of her father has her quivering.

"Please, dear, I'm just trying to check up on my daughter."

Elle doesn't speak; her hands are achy from all the dough she just made for tomorrow. Her shoulders feel tense, and she has frosting in her hair. She wants to go home but feels held captive by her mother's conversation, unable to get in the car for fear of criticism about talking while driving.

"How's Tom?" her mother asks. "Still around?"

"What? Yes."

"I was concerned the funeral would strain things, your relationship being so new."

"It didn't scare him off, if that's what you mean," Elle says. "In fact, we're going on a trip soon."

"A trip?"

"A weekend getaway."

"Where?"

"A few hours outside the city," Elle says.

"So you two *are* serious," her mother says.

While it's not really funny, Elle can't help but laugh. "I took him to my father's funeral, Mom. How is *that* not serious?"

"It's just surprising, Elle; you've always been so independent. Never kept a man around for long."

Elle is silent. Her mother is like a lemon-drop candy: at first sweet and pleasing, but when you get close to her, the sugar dissolves, leaving something sour underneath. Such a contrast to Elle's father, who was more like caramel: smooth and sweet from first meeting until the end. Elle suspects her father loved his wife *because* she was a challenge; he had a knack for softening edges. And she made him think. Having been a corporate success, her father was always up for a debate. Yet he had a gentle side; he loved his wife and his daughter more than anything—except maybe his garden. Despite their contrast, Elle always got the sense that her parents were, overall, happy. Elle has always felt as though she got in the way of their marriage. Like she and her mother were in competition for her father's affection.

Her mother continues, "I'm just sorry I couldn't entertain you more while you were here."

Elle shakes her head, though her mother can't see her. "You had a lot on your plate, Mom."

"I just don't want Tom's impression to be that our family is poor at having guests. It was a hectic time."

Elle sighs. "He's much more laid back. We didn't need entertaining."

"Am I keeping you, honey?"

"Long day at work."

"Oh. Right. How's the bakery?"

"Fine, Mom."

"All right, well, I can take a hint," she says. "It's not a crime to check up on my own daughter, you know."

"I didn't say it was, Mom," Elle says, grabbing her purse, heading for the door. "I appreciate your call. I'm doing fine. Sad, but fine."

"I'm sad too," she says. "We all deal with grief in different ways. Don't let it affect your relationship with Tom. He seems like a good man."

"He *is* a good man."

"I would hate for you to lose him over inattention in your grief."

The comment strikes Elle. Though her mother has always been hard on her, she's never steered Elle wrong. She's the one who suggested baking classes, who told Elle to take the leap and move to Seattle for college. Hell, she was married for over thirty years; Elle has never had a relationship longer than one.

What constitutes inattention? She would ask her mother to clarify, but she's too tired. "I won't," Elle replies.

She thinks of Tom, of how loving he's been through all this. How kind he was when he met her mother, all five seconds of their visit before she was off again, critiquing the funeral flowers.

"I love you, Elle," her mother says. "Be good."

"I'll be good," Elle says, and she hangs up before her mother can say more.

July 7, 2006

A little over nine years before Elle found out

It took almost four hours for them to find Lake Sutherland—an hour of which was driving the wrong way and then backtracking after they missed their turn. Pulling up in Tom's blue '96 Tercel, the back crammed with two suitcases, spare windbreakers, hiking boots, and snacks, Elle is itching to stand up. She has to use the restroom—they stopped at a gas station twenty minutes earlier, but she couldn't stomach entering the Sani-Can baking in the sun around back, so she decided to hold it. As the tires crunch over the gravel, she squirms in her seat. Her jeans are stuck to her thighs, and she can't wait to slip into a sundress—or, better, leap into the lake. Behind the gravel roundabout drive, the other cars, the flower beds, and the huge B&B, she glimpses the water glistening against the backdrop of emerald pines.

She's only been to a B&B one other time, when she was a little girl, and she doesn't remember it very well, just the awkward breakfasts with other families and how on the last day she managed to pet one of the tame resident deer after a dare from her father. She swallows the memory. This B&B will be very different: romantic dinners, swimming, sex. Lying on the dock, gazing at the stars to the sound of the water lapping against the wooden boards. The whole weekend to themselves, just the two of them. Her heart quickens—it's as if she's on a drop tower at an amusement park. She can almost feel the rush of the lift, the weightless pause, and then the plunge, where her heart leaps into her mouth and the air rushes by and the ground is fast approaching, and at the last second, the tower halts, and then she's on her way up again. It's her first truly serious relationship. A smile parts her lips, and she thinks to herself that she has never loved anyone so much.

"Here we are," Tom says, pulling up beside two other cars. He squeezes Elle's knee. "Excited?"

"Not even a little bit," she says, grinning.

He pecks her on the cheek, opens his door. "Me neither."

A woman with long, tan legs steps out of the house and shuffles down the big porch. "Hello," she calls. "You must be Tom and Elle. Welcome to the Thompson Point Inn."

Tom shakes the woman's hand while Elle peels herself out of the car. She stretches, fans her face—it's cooler in the shade of the trees, but not by much.

"Yes, we have a reservation for three nights," Tom replies.

"Fabulous! I have the Heron Room almost ready for you, which has a wonderful view of the lake." The woman turns to Elle. "Holly. We spoke on the phone."

Holly is perhaps in her early thirties—much younger than Elle expected, especially for an innkeeper. She isn't wearing a bra under her tank top. Elle straightens her T-shirt over her stomach; her jeans are digging into her bladder. Suddenly Elle's need to pee isn't the only thing making her uncomfortable. "Nice to meet you," Elle says.

Tom grabs their bags, and the three of them head up the wraparound porch. It smells of lavender and syrup inside the inn, and the AC is almost too chilly.

"How long was your drive up?" Holly asks.

"Four hours."

"We got lost," Elle adds.

"Not lost," Tom says. "Just took a wrong turn."

"Well," Holly says with a clap of her hands, "let's get you checked in. Your room will just be another five minutes or so."

Five. Elle is overwhelmed by the ache in her stomach. She doesn't want to seem impatient, but she can't wait another five minutes. "I'm sorry—do you have a restroom I can use?"

"Oh, of course! The lobby restroom is just around the corner there, to the right."

"Thank you," Elle says a bit breathlessly, then heads down the hall toward her relief.

Before she rounds the corner, she looks back. Holly's hand is on Tom's arm. She's saying, "Four hours—I can't even sit through a two-hour movie without having to use the bathroom." Tom laughs, not seeming to notice Holly's hand. With a twinge of distaste, Elle hesitates—maybe she *can* hold it another few minutes? Again, Holly's voice: "I know I'm young to own a B&B, but it was my grandmother's. She raised me . . ." *No,* Elle can't wait any longer—she steps into the small restroom and latches the little hook-loop lock.

She sits and waits for her bladder to ease, her mind circling around the image of Holly and Tom in the hallway. Frustrated by her own jealousy, Elle tells herself that nothing's going to happen, that Holly's just being friendly. Women, no matter what their age, are always friendly with Tom—without seeming to do anything at all, he attracts it. The one time Elle brought it up to him, he brushed it off: "There's a difference between friendly and flirting," he said and left it at that. Not wanting to come off as insecure, Elle never mentioned it again.

She takes a deep breath, stands, and sucks in her stomach to button her jeans again. Tom could be the real deal, and she wants to put her best foot forward. She will not allow herself to ruin their trip with unnecessary insecurities. Tom isn't her past boyfriends, who told her she's too talkative, too independent, too . . . *not* the girl from the gym. Always the dumpee, never the dumper. No, Tom is different. He likes talking with her, he likes her independence, and she's never caught him even *glancing* at another woman. She can't let her jealousy cloud their first weekend away together.

Before she leaves the restroom, she tries to calm her nerves by looking around the small space. On the back of the toilet, the Kleenex holder has a watercolor image of a buck in a meadow. The hand towel is embroidered with a doe and fawn and hangs beneath a high, small windowsill cluttered with ceramic deer figurines. She counts at least seven deer in the tiny bathroom. Are all B&Bs like this? It's been a long time, and she can't remember the details of the last one she visited. Hastily, Elle pulls the towel off its bar and refolds it so there are no creases—everything is placed so precisely, and she can't leave it all rumpled from her use.

Unlatching the door, Elle listens for Holly's and Tom's voices but doesn't hear anyone. When she rounds the corner to the main room, no one is there. Discomfort prods at her delicate mood. Did Tom go to their room? She peeks outside and sees the Tercel; he isn't out there. Is he still with Holly? Turning back inside, she wanders farther into the main room, which has couches and a big guest book on the coffee table. The ceiling-to-floor windows reveal the shimmering lake, sunlight glaring off the water and spilling up into the crossbars of the high ceiling. Off to Elle's left is a hallway, and she sees room numbers and names on the doors, but she's too shy to venture down the unlit hall.

Just when she's about to head back out to the car—perhaps Tom *is* out there, and she just didn't see him—she hears his voice. She steps to the mouth of the hallway and spots him poking his head out of the last room on the right. "Elle. This way."

Her whole body fills with energy, and she hurries into their room, the Heron Room, complete with a placard on the door with a heron painted on it.

"I wasn't sure where you went," Elle says, feeling embarrassed.

"I didn't go far." Tom kisses her.

In that moment, she feels ridiculous about her jealous thoughts toward Holly—Tom was only making sure he and Elle were settled. She feels her shoulders relax; he's not her ex-boyfriends. This weekend is about them. "Are we all checked in?"

He nods, then closes the door behind them and stands behind her, hands on her arms, as she takes in their space. It's magnificent, if a little antiquated, but everything is clean and neat and bright. The bed is king size, with light-green sheets and pillows and an afghan woven with all shades of blue draped across the bottom. Among the fluffy decorative pillows is one small one with a needlepoint cover depicting a heron. Lying across the top of the dresser is a blue-gray feather that Elle guesses is a heron's, and off in one corner is a waist-high gray-painted heron sculpture made of what looks like old scrap metal, very independent-artist-esque.

"What do you think?"

"It's—there are so many herons!"

"There are even herons on the bathroom towels," Tom says.

"I bet. There were at least seven deer in the lobby restroom."

"No."

"Oh, yes."

He laughs. "Can you imagine the Turtle Room next door?"

Elle shakes her head. "Is it okay with you?"

"The room? It's perfect," he says.

"You sure?"

"Absolutely."

Elle twists around and kisses him, softly, on the mouth. She savors the feeling of his stubble against her lip. Hands on her waist, he pulls her closer, just for a moment, for a deeper kiss, and then they part, and Elle turns to explore the rest of their room. Slipping off her shoes, she pads across the soft carpet and into the bathroom.

"There *are* herons on the towels!" she says, voice echoing off the gray tiles. One of the towels is askew—Tom must've used it—and she straightens it before checking out their large shower. "Did you see the showerhead?"

"Also a heron?" Tom asks from the other room.

"No, but it's fancy!"

"How so?"

"It has all kinds of settings," Elle calls. She slides the glass door open and observes it more closely. "Soaker, mist, spray, and pulse," she reads.

"Pulse, huh?"

Elle walks out. Tom's lying on the bed with his hands behind his head. His button-down is tight around his biceps, and she likes the look of him, the veins on his forearms bulging from the heat.

"Maybe we can try out the pulse setting a little later," he says.

She feels a tingle through her lower belly. "Maybe." She puts her hands on her hips. "You aren't going to just lie around all day, are you?"

He sits up and takes her hand, pulls her into bed. "No, *we* are."

He tickles her waist, and Elle shrieks. Immediately, she slaps a hand over her mouth, realizing how loud that was, how there are other people in the B&B. Her eyes widen, and Tom falls into an easy chuckle.

"Come on," he says, "we're *supposed* to be relaxing. Unless you have some big plans you haven't told me about."

Elle touches his face. "Not really—but don't you want to check out the hot tub?"

He perks up a little. "We have a hot tub?"

Elle rolls off the bed and strides over to the sliding door. Pushing back the curtains, she unlatches the door and drags it open. The sun is fierce outside, and the heat on their secluded patio is almost unbearable. It takes a moment for Elle's eyes to adjust, with the lake water glaring so brightly. There's marshy grass ahead, leading down to the water, but off to the left is a small pine needle path to their hot tub.

Tom leans past her out the door to take a look. "I didn't know we had a hot tub."

Elle looks up at him. "Did I not mention that when you asked me to pick out a room?"

He shakes his head, lips spreading into a smile. "So if we're not going to lie around all afternoon, what did you have in mind?"

"We could explore town a little? Then grab some dinner?"

"*Then* the hot tub?"

"*Then* whatever you like."

"Okay," Tom says. "I'm going to hold you to that, though."

"I hope you do." With her finger, she traces the trail of freckles on the side of his neck, hand stopping at his collar. Serious, she says, "I'm glad to be here with you."

"Me too." He kisses her nose and heads back into the room. "So, town?"

"I'm just going to put on a dress; then we can go." She slides the door closed again and fans out the curtains—it's hot enough that she'd like to keep the sun out—then lets her eyes adjust to the dimness of the room. She's about to ask where Tom set her suitcase, but then she spots it, on her side of the bed, by a wooden nightstand holding a vase of peonies.

Peonies.

Elle didn't notice them when she first came in, but now that she sees them, she can smell them, and it makes her think of her father. Stopping in her tracks, Elle puts her hands over her mouth, trying to suppress the riptide of emotion threatening to pull her under. She is still fragile over the thought of her father—it has only been a month since the funeral.

Tom is changing into a T-shirt, and she hopes he doesn't notice, but of course he does, and he comes over to her. "Sweetheart, what's the matter?"

Just his acknowledgment of her tears is enough to push her over the edge, and she starts weeping, right there in the middle of their romantic B&B room, with all the herons watching, and Tom, who is probably tired of all her tears. "It's—my dad." She sucks in a breath. "The—" She points at the vase.

"Oh, sweetheart." Tom pulls her to his chest tightly, and it makes her cry even harder.

She is overwhelmed by memory, the scent of peonies taking her back into her childhood, climbing trees in their backyard while her father pruned the bushes and mowed the lawn. His garden gloves with the rubber palms and fingertips, his red lopping shears that were big to Elle but fit perfectly in his hand. The growl of the old push mower. Mulch splinters in her fingers that her mother would have to extract with a sewing needle. The kneepads her father had worn that looked like the knobby leg joints on the ants that hid in the inner petals of the flowers. Elle feels like she could cry forever, thinking about her father. Seeing the peonies makes her feel like the funeral was yesterday.

Tom holds her for a long time, swaying her a little and stroking her hair, not saying anything.

Finally, quieting down, she says, "I'm sorry."

"For what?"

"We're supposed to be having a good time alone together, and I'm crying."

Tom gives her a squeeze, then sits her on the bed. "Don't be sorry. If it were my father—" He shakes his head. "You're allowed to be upset."

Elle runs her knuckles under her nose and sniffles, trying not to drip. She has never been one of those girls who could be cute when they cry, and she hates for Tom to see her this way. He's seen her this way a lot lately. "No, I'm sorry."

"Stop it." Tom gets up and disappears into the bathroom. He comes back out with some tissues. He hands them to her, and she starts dabbing her eyes.

"I don't think I'll ever be able to look at peonies without thinking of him."

"I understand," Tom says. "But I think it's kind of nice that they're here, so coincidentally."

"Yes, because my tears are so romantic." She inspects her tissue; there are small black flakes from where her makeup has run. She swipes the tissue under each eye, trying to clean up any shadows of mascara under her eyelashes.

"Well, it's just that—it's as if he's here with us. Like he's giving us his blessing."

Elle pinches her lips together to keep them from quivering.

"It's our first trip away together."

Elle hopes it is the first of many.

"I mean, I never met Richard," Tom says, grasping her hand. He runs his fingers over hers. His eyes remain on her hand when he says, "I like the idea that he might be looking down on us. I would have liked for him to have liked me."

Elle sniffles. "He would have liked you a lot."

"Or he would have threatened me. 'If you ever hurt my daughter—'"

"You wouldn't hurt me."

Tom kisses her forehead.

"And he wasn't that kind of dad." Elle looks into Tom's eyes. "He really would have liked you."

Tom kisses her forehead again, this time with more pressure, lingering longer. He isn't dissuaded by her tears, Elle realizes. Their relationship might be new, but it's strong. He's been there for her through perhaps the most difficult thing she'll ever have to endure, has stuck by her when another man might have gone. The thought fills her with love.

"Now, enough tears," Tom says. "Why don't we go get an early dinner? We can pick up some wine and bring it back to the room."

"That sounds nice," Elle says.

September 7, 2015

Nearly four weeks after Elle found out

After spending the morning with Bonnie, Elle runs back home before her appointment with the lawyer. She slices an apple and changes her shoes. The house is quiet. With Tom still at work, she's able to rush from room to room, unafraid of bumping into him. She uses the opportunity to switch a load of laundry and carries some dry towels to the guest room. Out of habit, she included his clothes in her wash, and then she couldn't bear to let them stay wet and mold, so now her shirts are tumbling with his in the dryer, and it seems so stupid that even the most mundane parts of their lives have remained intact. The only bonus is that perhaps, upon finding his clean boxers in the dryer, Tom will feel like shit.

As she hurries back downstairs, it occurs to her that she ought to bring something with her to the lawyer's office. She didn't think to ask what would be pertinent, and his assistant wasn't helpful, a young-sounding guy who was in a hurry to get off the phone. Tax returns? She retrieves them from their cluttered home office, along with a few other documents with both their names listed.

A wash of melancholy passes over her. This morning, sitting on the couch, reading his book, Tom seemed almost *normal* again. For a few heartbeats, nostalgia grips Elle, and she wonders if she needs a divorce lawyer after all.

But she can practically hear Bonnie's words in her head: *At least have your bases covered.* Turning off the light, she reminds herself that it won't hurt just to keep the appointment.

Purse on shoulder, papers under one arm, she's almost out the door again when she remembers her apple slices—still in the kitchen—which she meant to eat in the car on the way. But she doesn't make it past the living room: out of the corner of her eye, she spots a crumpled piece of paper on their bare couch, standing out against the gray-blue uphol-stery. Curious, she unfolds the ball and finds it to be a receipt. Her eyes scan the single item, the total.

Roses. And they were expensive.

Sucking air in through her cheeks, she scans the receipt again. Tom hasn't bought her roses in years—maybe ever, knowing she doesn't par-ticularly like them—and then she spots the date. He bought them three weeks ago.

Realization embitters her mouth like bad fruit. Tom must've bought them for *her*.

Tingling with anger, with the threat of choking up, she balls the paper again and shoves it in her back pocket. If Elle hasn't been certain about the lawyer before, she is now.

July 7, 2006

Over nine years before Elle found out

Elle is feeling better after their dinner, though a little bloated too. They found a nice little Italian restaurant—a flyer had been left on the B&B's coffee table—and spent a quiet evening on the back deck of the place. The restaurant patio was draped with white awnings overhead and strings of lights, and Elle understood why it was so busy, being such a gem of a place. They stared into each other's eyes all night, holding hands across the table, their candle threatening to go out each time the warm breeze lifted. Talking about their future, childhood memories, interesting articles they've read recently. She got tipsy on pinot noir and ate too much of her pesto angel hair with blackened chicken—now, at the door to the room, she's regretting it. She feels nauseous from the wine, and she knows her breath is bad from the garlic.

Tom doesn't seem to notice; he's calm and a little giddy and keeps passing a hand over her ass, up under her dress. She wants to feel sexy, but she just can't, not with the thought of her dinner or her certainty that she has pesto in her teeth. Italian places are romantic in theory, but the pasta and the garlic and the rich sauces and filling wines are not conducive to carrying the romance past dinner.

Inside their room, Tom sets down the bottle of wine they brought back—some sort of cab sauv—and says, "Hot tub?" He has a slack-jawed smile on his face. "You promised."

Elle feels way too self-conscious to get into a swimsuit and way too full to get into any water, but she says, "Yes, let's try it out." She doesn't want to ruin their night—her fullness will probably subside, anyway.

Tom comes over to her and grasps the fabric of her dress down by her hips, then lifts it up over her head. She feels her stomach instinctively suck in, but Tom isn't really looking at her. He tosses the dress on the bed, and then he's taking off his shirt. "You looked so beautiful tonight, at the restaurant," he says.

Elle is warmed by the comment. "You're sweet."

"It's true."

She stalks over to her suitcase—trying not to look at the peonies—and digs out her bikini top, turning her back to Tom to change. She hears him rustling in his own bag, changing into his trunks. "I feel kind of full," she says, pulling on her bottoms. "My dinner was really rich."

"Me too," Tom says, but it's not with the same tone as Elle. He sounds satisfied. "The garlic butter on my steak pushed it over the edge. So good."

Facing him again, she says, "No, I mean I don't feel all that great."

He closes the gap between them. "Sounds like you need some more wine." He cups her face and gives her a long kiss—he also tastes garlicky, and it makes her feel better about herself. "This has been such a great evening," he says. "I have you all to myself."

She smiles. "Why don't you go start up the hot tub?"

He nods, grabs two water glasses that the B&B arranged on a side table, and works on uncorking the wine bottle. Once the glasses are filled, he carries them both outside, disappearing into the darkness.

Elle takes a deep breath. She can hear him throwing back the heavy cover of the tub, starting up the jets. She wants to want him, to feel more in the mood, but she just can't get past her queasiness. She thinks about other women, more confident women. Not Holly or Tom's ex-wife, but *all* the women. How does Elle stack up? The truth is she's far less charming and experienced than Tom, and she cares for him so much. Sometimes, she can't help but wonder why he's with *her*.

In the bathroom, she grabs the two heron towels, checks her teeth in the mirror, and then inspects her bare stomach—it doesn't look as bloated as it feels. A little more satisfied, she adjusts her top to show off more cleavage, then heads outside.

She can barely see the path, but by the time she arrives, her eyes have adjusted. The tub glows from blue underwater lights. Tom is already in, arms resting along the rim, a glass of wine in each hand.

"How is it?" Elle asks, setting the towels down on a little plastic chair nearby.

"So nice," he says.

Elle walks up the few steps to the tub and swings a leg over the side, into the turbulent water. At first it feels like nothing; then there's the sting of heat. She pauses, waiting for her body to acclimate, then slides in close to Tom. The water causes her extremities to tingle. For a moment, she closes her eyes. The only sounds are the jets, the hissing water. She can feel the fabric of Tom's trunks fluttering against her thigh. The line where bubbling water ends and the chilly air of the night begins shimmies along her collarbones. She still feels bloated, but she's not quite so tense anymore.

Tipping her head back, Elle opens her eyes. Steam rises up all around them, encompassing them in a cloud of humid air. High above its tendrils, the stars shine brightly in the clear sky. They are far away and vast tonight. Elle has the thought that this is the closest she—or anyone—will ever get to the stars. And for a moment, it makes her feel small. Immensely small.

Tom shifts beside her. She lowers her chin again, facing forward through the steam, and the movement causes a rush of blood in her head, temporarily dizzying. She suppresses a bloated hiccup. The blue lights in the walls of the tub shimmer under the frothing water. Her legs, outstretched beneath the surface, look alien. She stares at them, trying to regain some calm.

"What are you thinking about?" Tom's voice, though soft, seems to barrel through the softly hissing air.

"Just looking at the stars," she says. "They make me think about how insignificant we are."

"You and me?"

"Humanity."

"I always felt like they made humans seem significant. Like, of all the stars, this might be the only solar system with life. We're a needle in the haystack of the cosmos."

Elle can picture his logic but doesn't feel that way at all. "For me it's the opposite. Everything is so massive out there, so full of power. What makes us so special among the nebulas and the red giants and the white dwarfs?"

"Okay, you lost me. Dwarfs?"

Elle looks at him holding his glass by his shoulder, dark chest hairs flat against his damp skin, white swim trunks illuminated by the lights. She smiles. "I suppose I retained more than I thought from that Astronomy 101 class." She grasps the other glass and takes a sip.

Tom sits up and looks out across the black lake, up toward the stars. "I don't know about giants or dwarfs, but I do know your dad is up there."

Elle nods. She doesn't tell him that she doesn't think her father believed in a heaven—he was more likely to believe that once someone was dead, they were dead. Back to the earth to feed the flowers. Nonetheless, she is touched by Tom's sensitivity, the care behind his words. She loves him for having this conversation at all.

"No matter what's actually up there or what it all means, they *are* beautiful," Elle offers.

"You're beautiful," Tom replies, setting his glass down.

In spite of the fog of the wine and her pensive mood, Elle forces herself to scoot closer. Tom clearly notices, his hand coming to rest high up on her thigh, a finger drawing loops on the sensitive skin near her bikini line. She tries to be in the moment with him, focusing on the motions of his finger, staring at her blue legs beneath the surface of the roiling water. Her stomach still feels oily and heavy from the food.

"The hot tub is nice, isn't it?" Tom's words are muffled by the hum of the jets.

Elle stares at his mouth, slightly open, and says, "Yes."

He moves in and kisses her deeply, enthusiastically. Splaying her hands across his back, she thinks to herself, *Just enjoy it.* Tom pulls her closer, one hand on her hip, one hand on the back of her head. Their mouths slip over each other's with lips and tongue and the occasional bump of teeth, and she allows herself to become immersed in the sensation, the sensuousness of the water and his touch. The chill of the night air on her exposed skin coaxes her to get even closer to Tom, fall deeper into his hold.

Then his lips are on her neck, hands tugging at the ties of her bikini top. Elle pulls back a little—they're not the only people staying here, and she doesn't want to be exposed—and without resistance, his fingers sink to her hips again. He's still fervent, still apparently lost in the moment.

But maybe she's being too shy, too careful. She's always been that way, never hopping the fence during recess to explore the field beyond her grade school playground, never getting into boys' cars during high school, never drinking too much at college parties. She recalls her mother's advice: "Don't be inattentive." She thinks of Holly's hand on his arm, Miranda's tan line on his finger. Is Elle being too prudish, too careful? What's so wrong about two adults in a fairly private space fooling around a little? The B&B probably expects some of that to happen.

Slowly, still kissing him, Elle reaches back to untie the knot at the base of her neck. Tom doesn't seem to notice until she pulls back, letting the strings fall to the water. Her nipples tense from the sudden cold, so she slips below the surface a little more. But then Tom is urging her up again, wanting to look. His hands move up her sides, thumbs stroking under her breasts. Then he cups them, lips meeting her cleavage. Elle is glad to please him. She feels only a faint twinge of regret in the back of her mind.

Looking into her eyes, Tom says softly, "You didn't have to."

"I wanted to."

"I love your breasts."

"Men love all breasts."

"But yours are the best," he says.

"They're kind of small."

"They're perfect."

Elle resists the urge to cover them, to retrieve her top. She finishes off her wine.

"The steam, the water, the lights," Tom continues. "You look like a sea goddess."

Elle laughs. "I think you're a little drunk."

"It's still true," he says.

Perhaps Elle should slip off her bottoms too. No harm in skinny-dipping, and she knows he would like it. She's done enough to ruin their weekend; she wants to be playful for him, wants to be the kind of woman he's proud to spend his time with. She looks into his eyes and thinks about their love. He makes her want to be more daring, more fun. His ability to bring out her wilder side is part of the reason she loves him—isn't it?

She loops her fingers through the ties at her hips and tugs.

"Oh, you don't have to do that," Tom says.

"I want to," Elle repeats.

Pulling back, sobering up, he says, "No, now I feel like I pressured you. I pulled at your top, and now you feel like you have to." He reaches for her hands, but she moves away slightly, giving him a playful smile.

"You don't have to, sweetheart," he repeats.

"I said I want to," she whispers.

He sits back, the knuckles of his right hand pressed into his mouth. Tugging on her bottoms, she slips them off, all the while watching his face. She lifts them above the water, completely off, and tosses them over toward her top, which is floating in the opposite corner of the hot tub, twisting in a mini whirlpool. She bites her lip. Tom's hand moves from his mouth up over his head, fingers sliding through his short hair, and pauses at the base of his neck, elbow pointed upward, head tilted like he's not sure how to respond. Elle feels almost empowered by her effect on him. He likes it, and she's pleased.

"Well?" she asks.

"Well what?" he says.

She spreads her arms a little. "Well, what do you think?"

"I think you're great," he says, coming closer. He runs a hand down her side, leans in for a kiss.

She pulls away slightly.

"What?"

She nods at his swim trunks. "It's only fair . . ."

He grins, untying his drawstring. He tosses his trunks over to the corner with her bikini. Then they meet again, kissing, grabbing, tangling together, the water circulating all around. Elle feels sexier than she ever has—she's never done anything like this. Tom sits back, and she straddles him, kissing his jawline, his neck. Then a thought enters her mind, about the logistics of sex underwater, the potential for irritation from the chlorine. And how many people have been in this hot tub before them, couples on their own romantic weekends?

Tom, still wrapped up in the moment, tips his hips a little, a hand at his base, ready to slip inside her.

But Elle stops him.

Her mind blares—this isn't fair to him, to get this far when clearly he didn't mind her staying dressed, her being tame. But she has to stop;

she can't do it. The thought makes her feel guilt ridden and overheated. Head spinning, she can feel the sting of bile in the back of her throat. Her stomach clenches, gurgling.

Tom sits up. "Elle?"

"I . . ." She trails off, trying to suppress a heave.

Surging out of the water, Elle leans over the cold rim of the tub and throws up, panting, her ribs pressed against the plastic. Moaning, she only has time to catch her breath before there's another sour heave; below her, the steaming liquid hits the pine needles and splatters the plastic stairs. She throws up twice more before she can finally shift her position, buckled over the side of the hot tub, her naked body exposed to the cold nighttime air.

Tom rests his hand on her back, rubbing gently.

Spitting repeatedly, Elle finds herself mumbling, "I'm sorry; I'm so sorry."

"It's all right, sweetheart. It's all right." Grabbing their towels, he says, "Let's get you inside."

~

Sunlight streams through the curtains: late morning. Elle is wrapped up in Tom's arms, heavy with sleep. Her eyes are watery, her mouth sour. Carefully, she shimmies out of his hold. The air in the room is chilly, and her skin prickles as she walks to the bathroom. Closing the door, she looks at herself in the mirror, her hair crispy in places where her vomit dried. Otherwise, she looks fine, not even a hangover—but then again, she threw up most of it. Clenching her teeth at the thought of Tom seeing her so sick, Elle flips on the light and the fan and turns on the shower water.

She pulls out her travel soap, shampoo, and conditioner from the series of ziplock bags she packed them in, then steps into the shower. Adjusts the nozzle to a softer pressure, wets her hair, lathers. God, what she would give to do last night over. To not compare herself to other women; to not make a fool of herself. Tom was so sweet, so gentle, no expectations, just love—why did she think he'd be anything but? Alone in the shower, she appreciates the chance to breathe. To wash her hair twice. To vow to let this be a new day.

Urging her embarrassment out of her mind, she runs through a few options for things they could do: hike, rent a boat for the lake, window-shop in town, check out a local museum. She wouldn't want to spend the day with anyone else but Tom. She promises herself she'll be better to him. More outgoing. More upbeat. And she'll drink less. She would never forgive herself if she screwed it up.

Elle's eyes are closed as she rinses the soap from her hair—she startles at a rush of cold air. It's Tom, getting in.

"Hello, gorgeous," he says.

She wipes her eyes and opens them—Tom is naked with her, standing just out of the stream of water.

The comment makes her smile. "Really? After last night, you're still attracted to me?"

"We've all been there." He lifts up the conditioner, and she nods, grasping the bottle, squeezing some into her palm.

"I'm so sorry," Elle says, running the conditioner through her hair. "I feel terrible for ruining our night."

"Don't. With the lights and the water and the nakedness—you looked so sexy. I just hope you didn't feel forced into it."

Elle shakes her head.

"I hope you know you're sexy to me no matter what."

"Until I throw up all over everything." What's worse, she realizes, is that the innkeeper will find it.

He steps into the water and starts soaping his body with the B&B's complimentary bar. "Forget about that part." He wraps her in a slippery, wet bear hug.

"I love you," she says, grateful for him.

"I love you too." After another few moments of washing, he asks, "What's the plan for today?"

"I'm not sure," she says, still feeling humiliated. She considers washing her hair a third time. "There are lots of possibilities."

"And?"

She steps into the stream again, rinsing off. "Would you rather go into town or go exploring outside?"

"Definitely outside," Tom says.

"Well, there are some boat rentals. We could hang out on the lake?"

"Have a floating picnic." Tom gives her butt a playful squeeze. "Pack a lunch, eat in the boat?"

She loves his enthusiasm, his confidence. It makes her feel better. "Sounds like a perfect day."

September 7, 2015

Nearly four weeks after Elle found out

"And when were you married?"

Elle sits across from the attorney Angela recommended. His office is on the fourteenth floor of a big building downtown, and she wishes she'd worn something more professional than shorts and a black tee. Not that she looks sloppy, only that all the women in the office are wearing skirts and heels and blouses, and Elle has that feeling of being an outsider, and it makes her uncomfortable. The lawyer wears a nice-looking suit, and he tips back in his leather office chair with a notepad.

"We were married April eighteenth, 2009," Elle says in a small voice.

"And do you know the name of your husband's lawyer?"

She didn't think to ask—does he even have one? "I'm not sure," she says. "Do I need to ask him?"

He waves the question away. "Don't worry about it right now," he says. "Do you have any children?"

"No."

"That'll make things easier," he says. "Now, what about assets?"

Listing assets is like listing memories. They celebrated their newly bought house by sharing a pizza, surrounded by boxes. They test-drove a sports car and went through the Starbucks drive-through like it was theirs before finally settling on the Accord. And Tom narrated the features of their new 401(k) from his laptop in bed while she stared at the ceiling and played footsie with him under the covers.

Every asset she remembers cuts deeper. *They're just things*, she reminds herself, but as the lawyer takes notes, each scratch of his pen across the page feels like a knife scratching against her skin.

July 31, 2006

Over nine years before Elle found out

They've only been dating a few months, and now Elle is afraid she's pregnant.

She's sitting in a doctor's office staring at a copy of *Elle* from three months ago. She had made the appointment two days ago. This morning, she woke up and forgot to eat. She slipped into clean sweats and a plain tank and then drove white knuckled until she spotted the brick building, fed a parking meter, and picked up the first magazine she saw in the waiting area. Thumbing through, she doesn't read a word.

Ambient music plays overhead; it makes her think of lush botanical gardens filled with koi ponds and cherry blossoms. She hears the click-clack, click-clack of the receptionist typing. Elle glances around the room at the ugly light-pink-and-green chairs and the other people waiting. An elderly man sits across from Elle, reading a hardback. There's a Hispanic woman with her son sitting to Elle's left. Despite a plastic horse clutched in the boy's small hand, he's squirmy, and the mother is clearly struggling to keep him patient. She whispers to him, grabbing his arm as if to physically hold him down while he bops from side to side. Suddenly Elle feels hot and squirmy herself. She can't look away from the boy.

Setting down the magazine, Elle searches for a better distraction. Bending forward, she rifles through her purse for a stick of gum. She would have sworn there is a pack inside, but her purse is filled to the brim with junk, so she can't find it—when was the last time she cleaned out her purse? She sets her phone on the glass magazine table, digging deeper into the crumb-filled bottom of her bag. But before she can find any gum, her phone is buzzing, the vibration on the glass tabletop jarringly loud, an assault on the quiet room. Startled, she snatches it up and answers.

"Tom," she says, keeping her voice low in an effort to not disturb the others.

"Hey, sexy," he says, and the word makes her jaw clench. "I'm having lunch—just wanted to say hi."

"Oh," she says. "Well, hi."

"Hi." A pause. "What are you doing?"

"Errands."

"Like?"

"Oh, boring stuff. Grocery store. Gym." Elle hesitates, not wanting to lie. "I'm at the doctor's right now."

His voice comes back urgent. "Is something wrong?"

"No." She falters, deciding on, "A checkup."

"People our age don't just go in for checkups," Tom says. "What's wrong?"

Elle glances at the boy, who is now sitting backward on his chair, little legs folded so Elle can see the bottoms of his sneakers. He's leaning back as far as he dares, hands grasping the armrests so he doesn't fall. His mother appears tired.

"I probably shouldn't tell you over the phone, Tom," Elle says, still distracted by the boy. Each time he tips back, her heart catches. She imagines his fingers slipping, his head cracking against the glass coffee table.

"Oh, God, well, now you have to," Tom says. "I'll worry all afternoon."

Elle lowers her voice, concerned the other patients might eavesdrop. "I'm late."

Silence, growing longer. She flexes her abs to see if she can feel the baby in there, a knot of pressure where there wasn't one before. She knows it's silly, but she can't help it. She can't tell if she feels a difference.

Finally, he asks, "Did you take a test?"

"Two," Elle says. "One positive, one negative. But I'm late. So I made an appointment."

"Oh."

Glancing at the boy, Elle sees him just in time as a hand slips, but before he falls, his mother grips his arm and yanks him back into his chair. She leans in close, whispering sharply in Spanish. The boy frowns.

"Elle?" the receptionist calls, and Elle glances up, nodding.

"They're calling me in," Elle tells Tom as she slides her purse onto her shoulder.

"My last class gets out at nine," Tom says. "Will you come over to my place and tell me the verdict?"

"Yes, sure," she says, and she hangs up.

~

Elle takes the stairs two at a time, heading up to Tom's third floor apartment. She's had a skip in her step all afternoon; she celebrated the doctor's good news with a caramel Frappuccino, sipped idly in the sun. Relieved and refreshed, she's wearing Tom's favorite perfume. At his door, she knocks three times before walking inside, not bothering to hide the smile on her face.

He's in the kitchen, dishing out two plates of spaghetti. When he sees her, he sets down the sauce pot and walks over, his face a mixture of emotions: a wrinkled brow of concern, a frown of distress, eyes glittering with—what? Hopefulness? Excitement? His strange and unreadable demeanor pokes a hole in her high.

He kisses her cheek in a brief greeting, holding her shoulders. "So?"

"Not pregnant," Elle says, the words coming out breathy and sweet.

For a moment, Tom is just silent. His hands fall to his sides, and he turns back to the kitchen.

"She said I'm probably late because of stress—nothing to worry about," Elle continues, trying to read his now-blank expression.

Grabbing two forks, he carries the spaghetti plates over to his small dining table, where a candle has already been lit. Elle follows him, taking a seat. The food smells delicious.

"I know it's a little late for dinner," Tom says.

Elle glances at the clock on his oven, which reads 10:05 p.m. "Yeah, I already ate," she says, "but you know I can't resist your spaghetti."

His smile is faint, a consolation.

"Is something wrong?" Elle asks. "Long day?"

Tom shrugs, chewing.

"Well, what?" Growing frustrated, she says, "I thought you'd be happy. Not pregnant! We dodged a bullet."

He sets down his fork, raising his eyes. "I know we've only been together for a little while," Tom says finally. "It's just, I don't know, somewhat of a bummer. I love kids."

Tongue tied, Elle sits there, waiting for him to say more.

"I don't mean to freak you out," Tom continues. "I spent all afternoon thinking about the what-if, that's all."

He takes her hand, which rests numbly on the table. She resists her urge to recoil, to run. *Kids? Now?* With today's news, she can't imagine having any other feeling than relief.

"Obviously this is better," Tom says. "I'm glad it's negative. This relationship is really, really new. I know that. But I'm glad this came up." He takes a breath. "I want a family someday, Elle. Not now, but someday." He squeezes her hand before letting go, picking up his fork once more. "I hope I haven't scared you."

Elle doesn't know how she feels. She picks up her fork, too, taking a bite. He makes all his spaghetti sauce himself, and she can taste the freshness of the tomatoes, the hint of balsamic vinegar. The candlelight flickers across his face, illuminating his kind eyes and soft lips. His stubble is a shadow along his jaw, and she imagines the roughness against her neck. She hasn't thought about kids, really. Not lately, anyway. She always assumed she'd cross that bridge when she came to it, her maternal instincts kicking in sometime around when she hit thirty. Sometime in the future.

"I've scared you," Tom says, interrupting her reverie.

"No," Elle says, meeting his eyes again. "No, not at all, Tom."

"You just aren't ready."

"Well, no," Elle says. "I mean, we aren't even married."

"Yes, that's true," Tom says with a chuckle. "I'm sorry—I'm getting way ahead of things."

"It's all right."

"It just got me thinking, you know? It wouldn't have been ideal, but I wouldn't have minded. That's all I'm saying."

"That's good." Elle feels her body relax, but not all the way.

"Don't worry, I'm not going to rush us into any—"

"Tom," Elle interrupts, and he smiles. Twirling her fork in her noodles, she says, "I'm just glad you like me enough to think about it."

September 7, 2015

Nearly four weeks after Elle found out

"He did not."

"He did," Elle says. She ran into Angela in the hallway outside the divorce lawyer's office, and the two of them are having a late lunch in a small steak house off the main lobby.

The ruffles on Angela's blouse lift and fall when she leans forward. "Owen seriously told you to get a Hollywood wax?"

"Or shave," Elle says. "We were talking about Tom, and he was being actually almost sweet, and then he starts going on about how all the younger girls are going hairless."

"How insensitive," Angela says, forking up some of her salad.

"I'm not *that* old, am I? I mean, I never thought midthirties was *old*."

"Of course it's not," Angela says. "Did you tell Bonnie about all this?"

"Oh, yes."

"She thought it was funny, didn't she?"

"Of course she did," Elle says.

"You don't agree?"

"It was awful!" Elle says, laughing. "But also funny, I guess. *God*, are all young guys pricks?"

Angela nods. "Pretty much."

"Anyway, thanks again for putting me in touch with the lawyer. He seems knowledgeable."

"Best in the business." Angela looks at her plate and then back up at Elle. "Are you still seeing Owen?"

Elle shrugs. "I haven't seen him since the other night."

"Has he contacted you?"

"A few texts. I haven't responded."

"He sounds like a bum," Angela says. "Good in bed, though?"

Elle feels as though she might blush. She takes a sip of her wine. "He's energetic." Her words come out less enthused than she intended.

"But he's no Tom."

Elle nods. Angela is right. She'd grown accustomed to the familiarity of having the same man, knowing him, knowing what to do and when, knowing how to get them both there by the end. She'd thought she'd forgotten what it is like to be with Tom, as it's been so long—but Owen has shown her just how engrained Tom is in her, how even after a dry spell, she still can recognize the missing nuance of her husband.

April 10, 2006

Over nine years before Elle found out

They've decided to spend the whole day in, sleeping and reading and making love. It's raining outside Elle's tiny studio apartment. Her cream-colored sheets look almost gold from the light of a warm spring sky coming in through the curtains. With his arm around her, Tom gently runs his finger up and down her shoulder. Naked, Elle can feel the coolness of the cracked window reaching out toward her exposed skin: her thigh, shoulder, cheek. She leans into Tom's lips. The day is slow and lovely.

Letting out a long sigh, Tom says, "Now what?"

Elle shrugs. "Again?"

A small smile tugs at the side of Tom's mouth. "Okay, but I'm going to need some kind of nourishment first."

Elle does a mental inventory of her kitchen: eggs, yogurt, milk; bread and cereal; coffee, juice; some blueberries and peaches in the freezer. Then she has a thought, her mind moving into the depths of her pantry, filling a recipe in her mind. As usual, she probably has enough ingredients. Baking is the only thing missing from this perfect day.

"I know what I'll make you," she says.

"No baking," Tom says, reaching for her as she slips out from under the covers.

"I'll be fast."

"We're supposed to be relaxing," Tom says.

"Baking helps me relax."

"If you keep baking for me all the time, I'll get fat."

"But I love baking for you."

Her back to him, eyes on her pantry's stock, she hears him sigh out his surrender. Turning slowly, Elle ducks into her apron, nothing underneath. "What if I bake like this, in my *napron*?"

Tom smiles, resting his hands behind his head. "All right, fine. Carry on."

Elle wiggles her hips as she plugs in her mixer.

Lovers' Lazy Morning Coffee Cake

Preheat the oven to 350° and wiggle your hips once again for your lover, who is watching you from nearby. You might turn on music—something upbeat and fun—or simply talk, your words flowing over the zing of your old mixer's motor. Beat 1 cup of butter and 2 cups of sugar until just incorporated. Don't scrape down the sides of your bowl or overmix at any stage—this coffee cake is low key and bakes better if the batter is lumpy. Add 2 eggs and a big splash of vanilla, beating, and then slap in 2 cups of sour cream and beat for a little while longer.

Wiggle your hips again as you bring out 2 cups of flour, a heaping tablespoon of baking powder, and salt. Sift those and mix in on a low speed until lumps form; then increase the speed and mix another few seconds. Grease and dust a 12-inch round coffee cake pan—or a 9-inch pan and a few ramekins. Scrape the batter out of your mixing bowl and into the pan, leaving at least an inch of space below the rim. There will be sugar-butter lumps on the sides of the mixing bowl, but those make the coffee cake even better, so scrape them in too. Give your lover the bowl and spatula to lick, but only after you've had some yourself; this is the best-tasting batter you'll ever have.

Ask your lover what flavor of topping is preferred; there are endless possibilities. Peach and fresh ginger. Mixed berry. Apple, cinnamon, clove. Cardamom and pear. Lemon plum. Frozen fruit is best, due to the way it thaws in the oven. Perhaps your lover chooses blueberries and peaches—those are what you have on hand. Spread them over the top of your coffee cake evenly, leaving 1 bare inch around the outside edge.

Bake it until it rises; it'll grow tall as the topping sinks into the middle, taking at least 60 minutes. Check it now and then between intimate conversation, inserting a toothpick into what looks like a soggy middle. It'll come out clean long before the top looks brown and done. Don't overcook it; it's best moist. Make love while it cools in its pan. Serve it warm with coffee or at night with ice cream.

Inverting the cake onto a cookie sheet, Elle eases the pan upward and replaces it with a large plate. Sandwiched between the sheet and the plate, Elle flips the cake over once more, revealing it upright on the plate. A few edges are crumbly, but otherwise it looks lovely. The peaches and blueberries sank well into the middle, and the crust is cracked and sweet. Dusting it with powdered sugar, she hears Tom rustling the covers, his bare feet on the hardwood. Then his body is behind her, his fingers brushing her hair off her neck, his lips meeting her skin just below her ear.

Drawing out the O's, Tom says, "That looks so good."

"I'll cut you a piece," Elle says, leaning back into him.

His hand comes up to cup her breast under her apron. He hits a ticklish spot, and she squirms away, a squeal stirring the back of her throat. He eases up, moving to stand beside her as she cuts into the coffee cake. It's still crumbly, steamy, saggy, not having had enough time to cool, but she serves it up anyway. As she slides it onto a clean white plate, Tom reaches into her apron again, and again she squeals.

"That's it," she says, pointing toward the bed. "Go."

"But—"

"Go."

He drops his hands and mock pouts back into bed. Elle smiles to herself, her apron crooked.

After deftly serving up another piece, she grabs two forks and stalks back to bed. When she hands over Tom's piece, he immediately takes a bite. Settling beside him with her back against the headboard, Elle revels in the way his eyes widen and his cheeks pull back. He takes another two bites before pausing to say, "This is amazing."

Elle nods, trying a piece herself. It turned out well, fluffy and sweet but not too sweet.

"You sure you like it?" she asks, eating another forkful.

Tom bobs his head.

They eat in silence for another few minutes, and then Tom takes their dishes to the kitchen. Slipping into a T-shirt, Elle gets back under the covers and grabs the TV remote from the nightstand. When Tom comes back, he wraps his arms around her before she can hit the on button.

"Thank you," he says.

"You're welcome." Her heart flutters; there's nothing like hearing that her baking is good.

He squeezes her tighter, and the room falls silent. She hears the whooshing of cars outside on the street below. Moments tick by, and then, barely audible, he whispers, "I love you."

It's the first time he's said it to her, and the words make her dizzy. She replays them in her mind as her heart thumps against her breastbone. "Really?" she finally says, looking into his eyes. She watches as they crinkle into a smile.

"Of course."

"Say it again?"

He laughs. "I love you."

"I love you too," she says, kissing him briefly. "You really do?"

"I really do."

The idea settles in her mind, and it makes her feel warm, full. "It's not just my baking?"

"Well, that doesn't hurt."

She gives him a playful push, and he gathers her up into his arms, even closer. "But it's *you* I love. The baking is a bonus."

Elle nods against his chest, clamping her eyes shut. She breathes in his scent, and it makes her heart pound even harder. Her cheeks feel flushed. "I love you more than baking," she says, and she means it.

September 12, 2015

One month after Elle found out

Owen wore her down. After a week of texting, Elle has agreed to meet him for dinner. He suggested a trendy Mexican place in Greenwood, a place she's actually been meaning to try (when it opened earlier that year, she asked Tom if he wanted to go, but he was busy that night—oh, had she only known *why* at the time). A real date with Owen is a terrible idea—it's not like she wants something serious with him—but after he insulted her, he begged and begged for the chance to apologize in person, and she couldn't say no. It's not like she has any other plans for Saturday night, anyway.

Stepping in from the crisp evening, Elle is impressed by the classy yet rustic decor. Intricate wrought iron dividers section off the bar; the main dining area is arranged with worn wooden tabletops, which are uniformly spaced and adorned with orange cloth napkins. Panels of detailed blue-and-yellow tiles decorate the walls. Bronze light fixtures dangle cylindrical glass lampshades, emitting seductive light. The whole place smells like roasted peppers, cilantro, and lime—a welcome scent to her hunger.

Elle is ten minutes early, and so she brushes past the hostess to wait at the bar. She's not sure if Owen thought to get a reservation, and thanks to light traffic, she has time for a drink before he shows up.

"A scratch margarita, please," she says to the bartender, who acquiesces.

She watches him make it, pulling bottles of yellow juice and tequila from hidden shelves beneath the bar, his lean, tattooed arms working deftly to salt the rim, rattle the cocktail shaker, and garnish with a lime. She spots an octopus ring on his middle finger as he slides her drink toward her.

"Thanks," she says.

He tips an imaginary hat. "Enjoy."

Playing softly through overhead speakers is a slow Latin guitar song. Elle sways a little to the music, watching other diners share chips and guacamole, swirl wine, and tip their heads to eat their gourmet tacos. Elle is strangely nervous—a tingly, light-headed nervousness. Elle hasn't been on a date for nearly ten years, and it makes her feel like an insecure college student. Only now she's an insecure adult, and the tequila seems only to make it worse.

She wishes Tom had taken her here. He would've liked the strong drinks, the proximity to home. He would've wanted to walk the street afterward; she would've ducked into the neighboring ice cream shop, the smell of sugar cones wafting out the open door. Had she come here with Tom, she wouldn't have sat at the bar beforehand, because they would've driven here together. They would've already been seated, already nibbling on chips.

"Elle?"

Owen's sandy hair is a little tousled from the wind. He slides onto the barstool beside her. "Am I late? I thought we said six."

She shakes her head. "I got here early."

He glances at her half-finished drink. "I see that."

He's wearing jeans and a T-shirt, which seems a little casual compared to her maxi dress, and it makes her feel so much older than him, or at least more responsible. It's a nice restaurant, after all.

As if to fill the awkward silence, Owen says, "You look nice tonight."

"Thank you," she says.

The hostess arrives, holding a notepad. "We have a table ready."

Elle picks up her drink and scoots off her stool, following the hostess to a narrow two-person booth toward the back of the restaurant. Owen slides in across from Elle and orders a margarita, and then it's just the two of them, alone and face to face for what Elle realizes is the first time (at least vertically). She notices he has freckles, a little dusting over the bridge of his nose. How had she missed that detail before?

"So . . . did you have a nice week?" he asks.

"Fine." Elle drops the lime into her margarita. "You?"

"Work sucked," Owen says.

"Where do you work?" How does she not know that already?

"I'm a security guard," he says. "Lately, they have me at the American Eagle downtown."

For a moment, she's a little impressed. She imagines him in a uniform, helping the public. "That sounds cool."

"It's not."

"Oh?"

The hostess delivers his drink and some chips, and Owen glances up at her. "Thanks." Then he returns his gaze to Elle. "It's a lot of standing around, really."

"It's not dangerous?"

Crunching a chip, he shrugs. "When I first started, they had me at a convenience store in south Seattle. *That* was scary. But American Eagle? Nah."

"You don't like it, then?"

"Hell no," Owen says. "It's really boring. Mostly just standing around, watching people shop."

"What do you want to do, then?" The question makes her sound a teensy bit like his mother, and she cringes.

Not seeming to notice, he sighs long and hard. "Oh, I don't know. Maybe something in marketing or customer service?"

"So no police academy?"

"Security's a temporary gig," he says. "Honestly, I thought I'd meet women doing it."

"You don't?"

"Nobody like you," he says.

Elle finishes her margarita, squirmy from the serious remark. She eats a chip, then another, and then thankfully their waitress arrives to break the ever-lengthening pause.

"Sorry for the delay; we just got super busy," she says, gesturing toward a big crowd seated in the center of the small place. "Have you had a chance to look over the menu?"

"I haven't," Elle says.

"I can come back."

"I hear the tacos are amazing," Owen says, looking at Elle. "Want to just do that?"

Glancing at the menu, Elle spots a taco listing of about ten different varieties. She asks the waitress, "What do you recommend?"

"I love the fish-and-mango street tacos."

"Let's do those," Elle says.

"I'll take the verde carnitas tacos," Owen says, handing the waitress his menu.

The waitress smiles. "And you're all set on drinks?"

With the context of this dinner—Tom's affair, sleeping with Owen, the strange age gap—Elle says, "I'll take another."

The waitress nods and shuffles away, swinging by the big table to take their orders too.

Thankfully, conversation with Owen meanders after that. Their tacos arrive quickly, and the waitress's recommendation was spot on, the mango pairing well with the flaky fish, crumbly cheese, and green cream sauce. Between bites, Owen asks about Elle's bakery, and she's met with enthusiastic *yum*s and *wow*s when she explains her favorite recipes. It's nice, for once, to have a captive audience, even if she has to ignore the circumstances that brought them together tonight. As she talks, she loses herself in the descriptions of the food, the stories of dropped pies and botched special orders and other funny happenings over the glorious years owning her own bakery.

Owen surprises her when he says, "I'll have to stop by sometime."

She doesn't want him to stop by. In fact, she doesn't really want this to continue at all, even if it has gone surprisingly well tonight. Before she can tell him no, however, she hears a buzz in her purse and pulls out her phone.

Tom: *At the grocery store. Need anything?*

The rosy bubble of this enjoyable evening is shattered with that stupid, mundane text. How can she be on a date with another man—a much younger man, whom she has no future with—while Tom is buying groceries? She feels suddenly so foolish, so shitty for thinking Owen could be a realistic escape from her failing marriage.

She texts Tom back, *No*, and returns the phone to her purse.

"Who was that?" Owen asks.

"Nobody."

"Your husband?"

"I'm not sure what he is anymore." Tom already did the damage, but if Elle is truly on a date, she's in the wrong, too, a little, isn't she? Having an intimate dinner with another man? Isn't this exactly why she's angry with Tom? Firmly, she reminds herself that *Tom* is the one who broke their vows. He's the one who severed their marriage, and she can't sever it twice over by seeing someone else. Owen is a symptom of Tom's behavior.

Owen frowns slightly. "You're not divorcing?"

"I'm seeing a lawyer," Elle says.

"But does that mean—"

"Let's not talk about Tom." Elle wonders if the waitress will bring the bill soon; their plates clutter up the table, dirtied by dribbles of meat and sauce. Their empty margarita glasses are sweaty with condensation from melting ice cubes.

"Right, okay. Listen." Owen leans forward. "Thanks for coming tonight."

She's ready for the night to be over. Despite dinner being pleasant enough, the reminder of Tom has made her overheated and shameful and flighty. "It's fine."

"No, I messed up the last time we spoke, and I'm sorry."

"I appreciate that."

"I like you, Elle," Owen continues. "We have fun."

"Yeah."

"I'm glad we met."

"Yeah," she repeats, unsure of where he's going with his train of thought.

"You're great." A pause. "And I don't mind about the shaving thing," he says, much too loudly. "It was only a suggestion."

Elle clenches her teeth. "I don't want to talk about it."

"I just mean I don't mind a little hair, you know?"

Elle winces and glances around, afraid someone might hear this painfully uncomfortable turn in conversation.

"It doesn't make you less sexy—"

"Owen," Elle says harshly, cutting him off. "Stop talking."

"What?" he says. "I'm trying to apologize."

Before she can respond, the waitress arrives with the check, and Elle digs through her purse—too slow, for Owen is ready with his card. The waitress bustles away before Elle has a chance to protest.

"You didn't have to pay," she says.

"Sure I did. I'm a gentleman."

She almost laughs. What an absurd statement after what he said just moments ago. Surprisingly, she finds herself warming to him again. He's harmless, if a little clueless, and she likes the way his T-shirt is bunched around his biceps—or is that the tequila talking?

After the bill is paid, Owen guides Elle out to the sidewalk. The sun has set, and the wind is chilly on her bare arms; she rubs the goose bumps with her hands.

"Well, thank you," she says to Owen.

He nods. "Those tacos were bomb."

"Good suggestion."

Owen steps a little closer and brushes the hair away from her face. Leaning in, he almost kisses her, but then her phone buzzes again, and she pulls away.

It's Tom again: *You home?*

Without responding, she drops the phone back in her purse. "Sorry about that."

"It's cool."

He kisses her. He tastes like red onions. For a split second, with Tom still on her mind, she imagines it's him she's kissing. Only Owen feels different against her mouth, worse somehow. It's a mere moment, but it changes everything.

When they part, Owen asks, "So would you like to come back to my place tonight?"

The question grates at her. Not only does it cheapen his apology, but it makes her wonder: How involved does Owen want to get with her? All that and Tom's texts tangle her thoughts.

She says, "No, I don't think so."

"I thought—"

"I can't do this," Elle says. "I just—I can't do this."

Owen frowns in a wounded sort of way. "But your husband sounds like a jerk."

"It's not him." This wasn't the way to get back at Tom. Meeting Owen has only made her feel worse. "I didn't intend for this to get serious."

"I thought we had a nice time tonight," Owen says. "Didn't you?"

"I'm sorry." She turns away, heading toward her car.

Owen calls after her. "Is it something I said?"

She doesn't answer, can't possibly answer. There's no way she could explain to him what it's like to still have Tom infiltrate her thoughts. No amount of revenge sex or taco dates or awkward pillow talk or poorly said apologies could ever get Tom out of her head. It has taken Owen to teach her that fact, but with an unfair consequence. It's better if she simply walks out of Owen's life—right?

In the car, Elle digs her phone out of her purse and replies to Tom's text: *On my way.* She blows her nose on an old Starbucks napkin. She breathes out through pursed lips, her cheeks puffed, emitting a low whoosh of air, until her whole chest feels empty. As she pulls out of her parking space, her cell screen lights up with a questioning text from Owen, which she ignores.

When she gets home, Tom's car isn't in the driveway, but new groceries are stocked in the fridge. It's all the usual things: her favorite coffee creamer, his favorite sandwich bread, eggs, and more. She spends the rest of the evening alone. Tom doesn't return until long after she's climbed into the guest bed. She's been tossing and turning, but within minutes of his keys clattering on their kitchen countertop downstairs, she falls asleep.

$\sim$

The following day, in the late afternoon, Elle and Bonnie go for a walk in Discovery Park. It's a sunny day, and despite the hour approaching dinnertime, joggers in skimpy outfits run alongside their dogs, and families seem far from packing up their children. Frisbees are thrown, and sunbathers fill up the grassy hillside near the bluff, catching rays before the season turns for good.

Elle and Bonnie take the trail to the beach, walking at a brisk pace. Overhead, huge cumulus clouds shift slowly, making odd shapes.

"I still can't believe you saw him again," Bonnie says. "After how terribly it went the last time."

"He insisted," Elle says. "But I shouldn't have gone."

"Was his apology not sincere?"

"He seemed sincere enough, only . . . I don't know. It was almost like he didn't understand why it bothered me."

"So you're not going to see him again?"

"No way." Elle smiles as they pass a couple heading in the opposite direction; she waits until they're out of earshot to continue. "It felt like it was becoming more than just casual."

"And you only want casual?"

"I'm still married, Bonnie," Elle says.

"And if you weren't?"

Elle considers that, then shakes her head. "He's a kid. I'd feel like his mom."

"Hot," Bonnie quips, then bursts out laughing.

"It's really not funny," Elle says.

She hoots. "I disagree."

"Come on. I mean, what would you do?"

"Well, you know I never liked him. And as you said, you're still married, so that's messy." She slows down, lingering by a break in the trees right next to the bluff. "Knowing you, you'll need time to truly get over Tom."

Elle can't imagine getting over Tom. She's not sure she wants to either. Staring out at a container ship sliding through the distant water, she asks, "What if it were you and Charlie?"

"If it were me and Charlie, I would've already downloaded Tinder." She picks up the pace again, heading downhill toward the beach. "And his mistress would be dead."

A little startled by how black and white Bonnie makes it seem, Elle forces out a little chuckle. She shouldn't have asked—not considering the uncomfortable encounters she's had with Charlie herself.

She recalls going to a barbecue at their friend's house once. Bonnie and Charlie were newly engaged. A bunch of couples were there, kids squealing through the sprinkler set up in the backyard. The adults lingered in patio chairs and by the grill, watching Bonnie quarter turn the steaks (she knew her way around a mixer but was even better around a grill). Elle went inside to replenish her iced tea. The house was chilly and quiet. Perspiring from the afternoon heat, she patted her chest with a napkin. When she turned around, Charlie was there.

"Hot?" he asked.

Embarrassed that he'd seen her dabbing her cleavage, Elle glanced out toward Tom, who was retrieving a beer from a cooler. "Are the steaks almost done?" she asked.

"You'll have to ask the grill mistress," Charlie said. "If you need to cool off, you can use the sprinkler."

She didn't know what to think of his comment. Was it a joke? A come-on? She never found out. With a little chuckle, Elle rushed back outside.

How would Bonnie react if she learned of Elle's awkward encounters with Charlie? The bar, the barbeque—they weren't the only instances. Would Bonnie be so black and white then?

"Of course, Charlie wouldn't cheat on you," Elle says now, albeit a little nervously.

"I know," Bonnie says. "I'm sorry I can't say the same about Tom."

As they come out of the trees, the low sun is blinding off the water. They make their way down to the beach, stepping over logs and rocks until they reach hard-packed sand. The tide is out, and little rippled pools have formed; she can smell the salt, cleansing to her palate. Stones dot the otherwise smooth beach. Despite a **No Dogs** sign back by the trailhead, two black Labs run loose, splashing through the shallow seawater after a neon-pink ball. Their owner, some fifty yards away, wanders closer, gripping a long tennis ball flinger. The dogs dart back, ready for another long throw.

A chilly wind whips up off the water; Elle sniffles, her nose running from the brisk walk down. With the hulking bluff behind them, it's just the sun and sand and ocean. Elle feels the prickle of melancholy in her veins, but she's grateful to be outside.

"When did things get so complicated, Bonnie?" Elle asks, squinting in the direction of her friend.

Bonnie drapes her arm across Elle's shoulders. "Things always have been."

"I guess," Elle says. "Thank God I have you."

"Likewise," Bonnie says.

A ball skips into the water close by, and the dogs dart past, nearly knocking Elle off her feet. Their owner yells, "Sorry!" Elle and Bonnie merely laugh, watching the slightly smaller dog leap into the waves, the ball wedged proudly in its mouth.

September 16, 2015

Four and a half weeks after Elle found out

Elle plunges both hands into the waist-high flour container, cool powder enveloping her skin. Wrist deep, she revels in the softness of it, just for a moment. It was a long day, a hot afternoon, especially for the season. Mindy is closing the front while Elle and Bonnie prepare some dough for the next morning in the back room. Over the hum of the refrigerators, Bonnie has a stereo playing an old Shania Twain CD. Elle doesn't care for country, but Bonnie is singing along, and it's fun anyway, that end-of-the-workday oomph filling Elle's bones, making her head buzz.

She lifts a double palmful of flour and spreads it over the metal table that takes up most of the small back room. Without hesitation, Bonnie plops a ball of cinnamon-roll dough in the middle of the flour and begins rolling it out.

Bonnie sings along to the music, and her bangs lift and fall across her face with each stroke of the rolling pin. Her voice drops into a hum as she turns the dough on the table, silk between her fingers. "I make it look good, don't I?" Eyes still on her task, Bonnie shakes her shoulders.

"What?" Elle realizes she's been staring.

"I know I'm a marvel to watch, but would you make yourself useful and do the filling? I'd like to get out of here on time—I have a date with the hubby."

With a touch of sarcasm, Elle says, "Yeah, yeah," but when Bonnie looks up, Elle smiles.

Evening closings are how she and Bonnie became best friends, with the music and the dough, talking about their men. After business hours in the back room is where Bonnie first announced she was getting married, and the two of them ended up drinking all the cooking brandy. It's where, every year, they pull an all-nighter making sixty-plus special-order pies for Thanksgiving. It's where Elle promoted Bonnie from employee to partner. It's where Bonnie once tried to work while on pain meds after having dental surgery and fell asleep on the floor while Elle was taking out the trash. And it's where Elle told Bonnie about Tom's affair.

With the mixer plugged in and its bowl locked in place, Elle heads into the walk-in for some butter. As the door closes behind her, the outside world disappears. All she can hear inside is the refrigerator itself, the fans rotating rhythmically, chilly air prickling her flour-gritty skin. Elle takes a deep breath in—until the cold burns the base of her lungs—then lets it out. She should be having more fun with Bonnie, but instead she's been spacing out, feeling down about Tom. She wonders what he's doing—thinks, bitterly, that maybe he's with the other woman. In reality he's probably at work.

Staring at the box of butter, her arms covered in goose bumps, Elle pictures Tom at work: the tutoring and online-education company he built early in their marriage. Wearing his suit, sitting at his desk (the other woman probably likes his suits as much as Elle did when he first started wearing them). Maybe he's texting the other woman; maybe he's going to meet her soon. There's a nice happy hour place not far from his building, where Elle has met him on more than one occasion—maybe they'll meet there. She'll get a lemon drop, and he'll have a beer and tell her about his day. The woman won't know what he's talking about when he mentions their systems issues, when he complains about the regional tech support manager, Brian, or when he admits that today, just this once, he smoked a cigarette because things were just that stressful—but Elle would. She knows everything about Tom. To think that all those little things she's learned about him over the years are now useless . . . what a waste.

Bonnie opens the door to the fridge, hands white with flour, ponytail in disarray. "Are you making the butter yourself in here?"

Elle hears Shania singing a song about a woman who can do it all. "Just lost in thought." Grabbing a brick of butter, Elle walks over to the microwave.

"Tom," Bonnie says.

"I found a receipt for a bouquet of flowers." She stops, her fingers coming up to rest on her lips, blocking a sob. "I'd forgotten, distracted with the lawyer stuff. But I found it again in my pocket this morning."

Bonnie turns the music down. "I'm guessing they weren't for you."

"No."

"Do you think they were for—"

"Who else would they be for?" Her voice is sharp.

"This is why you need to move on."

"He's still my husband," Elle says. Her back is to Bonnie.

"Is he, though?" Bonnie asks. "Can you still call him that after what he—"

"Like your marriage is so perfect," Elle snaps.

"What is that supposed to mean?"

Struck with sudden guilt, Elle can't bring herself to look at Bonnie. Her voice softens. "I'm sorry. It's just—you don't just stop thinking about a person." She unwraps the butter, places it in a bowl.

Bonnie's tone is forgiving. "You don't need to torture yourself with it either."

She's right, but Elle can't seem to get her head above water long enough to think clearly. Each thought of Tom is a riptide able to sweep her away: *He's still seeing her.* "I don't know what to do, Bonnie. I don't know what to do. I still—" She wipes her forehead with the back of her wrist.

"You're considering staying with him." A pause. "I thought you were seeing a lawyer."

"I am—I did. I just—" She shakes her head, presses the "4" and "5" buttons on the microwave, sets it at half power, then hits start. Elle watches the butter in the bowl turning under amber light. She waits for Bonnie to question her, to tell her what a mistake it would be to stay with him, but instead Elle feels her friend's arms wrap around her.

"You need to get out of the house," Bonnie says. "Get some space so you can think."

Elle nods, looks at Bonnie's wide, freckled face. The shadow of brown eyeliner along her lashes is smudged in places, but her blue eyes look bright and big. "You're right," Elle says. "As usual."

Bonnie grabs Elle's shoulders and gives them a squeeze. "Stay at my house for a few days—you can pack your things once we're done here, and I'll make the guest bed."

A twinge of concern pulses through her belly, and it's not just for Tom. Elle has managed to generally avoid Bonnie's house—or rather her husband—ever since their uncomfortable first encounter. Social functions are easy—even when Elle was maid of honor for their wedding, she and Charlie barely spoke—but living with him for a few days? She won't be able to avoid him. The thought of it makes her sweat—yet at the same time, staying in her own home doesn't feel like an option anymore.

"What about your hot date?" Elle asks.

"Charlie will understand," Bonnie says. "The three of us will have a nice evening at home. Hell, I'll have him pick up some wine on his way home from work." She pulls out her phone.

Before Elle can protest—or even suggest she stay in a hotel instead—the swoosh of a text being sent emanates from Bonnie's phone.

"Are you sure you don't mind my intruding?" Elle asks.

Bonnie, back to rolling dough, says, "Nonsense."

Swallowing her worry, Elle retrieves her butter from the microwave—it's perfect, not completely liquid but very soft—and plops the yellow blob into the mixing bowl. Adding brown sugar, she starts up the mixer, beating the ingredients until they're smooth and fluffy. "What will Tom think when I'm not there tonight?"

Bonnie looks up from her task. "Have you been sleeping in the same bed?"

"No," Elle says. "I've been sleeping in the guest room. But I still see him around the house, here and there."

"Do you talk much?"

"It's like living with a stranger. The most we've said to each other in the past few days has been about coffee creamer."

"He'll notice," Bonnie says. "He's a man, but he'll notice when you're not there."

The idea of leaving makes Elle feel weak—is she really *leaving* her husband? It's not that simple—yet she finds pleasure in the thought that he'll miss her. That he'll wonder where she is, if she'll return to him, who she's with. That perhaps he'll worry about whether she's all right.

She'll have to figure out Charlie when the time comes.

"Why don't you come to our house around seven thirty or so?"

Elle nods. "Yes, that sounds good."

June 2, 2015

Two months before Elle found out

The Sunday farmers market was exploding with raspberries, and Elle couldn't resist. Two large flats, the berries early-season firm, first to be ripe. Two days since buying the berries, and already there are fruit flies hovering over the green pulp flats; they can't keep away either. Elle picks up a particularly large raspberry, perfectly formed, and pops it into her mouth. A little sour. She inspects the flats and finds another one, this time not so perfect. It doesn't hold its shape so well, sagging over her index finger when she picks it up. A few of the globules are torn, wrinkled, dull in color. And it seems hairier than the other berries. Elle sucks it off the tip of her finger. Just right, the taste tart but not green, sweet but not so overly ripe that it's heavy in flavor. The sad-looking ones always taste the best.

It's Tuesday, and Elle is home from the bakery. Tom is at work—she hasn't seen much of him lately, anyway; they've been caught in a dry spell, which she tries to forget at this moment. She has the house all to herself. The oven is already preheated, the cookie sheet prepped with buttered parchment. It has been nine years since her father died, and Elle is making scones, as she always does on this day in June, the anniversary of his death. Her scones were his favorite.

Turning toward the sink, Elle shakes the little red purses into a strainer and flips on the tap. Adjusting the head to a light sprinkle, she tosses the berries in the strainer. She then lays out a double layer of paper towels and spreads the berries out evenly over the puckered, swirling white pattern. Juice from the raspberries blots the paper towel; she leaves them there to dry.

Next, she pulls her ingredients from the upper cabinets, paper flour bags and sugar bags dusting the counter in white. Bending down, she grabs a large silver bowl, a glass measuring cup, and a set of silver measuring cups from the lower cabinets. Then she stands back. She always does this. A necessary step. Her tools, ingredients, and berries arc across the splay of her large butcher block counter, the center of the surface clear and open for flour, for kneading. This is her religion. She knows the recipe by heart, as she knows many, like scripture, engrained into lines on her palms, repeated so many times that it has become a part of her.

Her father never wanted to watch her make the scones. "I don't want to interrupt," he would say, and then he'd go out in the garden, his own version of a temple, to prune or weed or just breathe. And then her timer would go off, and he would come back in, dirt darkening the lines in his hands and flour lightening the lines in hers. Together, they would wait for the scones to cool, and then, without even washing his hands, her father would peel one off the parchment and break it open. An explosion of sweet steam. He would swipe each half with butter, yellow mounds melting almost instantly. A smile. A pat on her shoulder or a kiss on her cheek or both. Then back to his garden.

Standing before the counter, a June breeze coming in through the window above the sink, now Elle smiles. "This is for you, Dad," she says aloud, into the open space of the kitchen. She hasn't written this one down, but perhaps this year she will. Inhaling, she catches the scent of the berries, the flour, even the metal tools. Exhaling, she begins.

Father's Scones

Preheat oven to 350°; prepare a cookie sheet with parchment, plenty of grease.

Start with the lemon. Wash it, dry it, zest it, and set the zest aside. Cut the lemon in half. Your kitchen will smell like lemon, sweeter than you last remember, always. Now juice your lemon, either with a hand juicer or with your palms. I prefer palms, cupping one half of the lemon in my right hand, then placing the palm of my left hand across my right fingers and bringing my palms together. When you do this, think of a person you miss—your husband who hasn't been home much, your father who passed away—and push that longing into your lemon. If you're using a hand juicer, twist each half over the dome until your wrists hurt. All those lemons in your life put to use. Set the juice aside.

Next, combine 2/3 cup of sugar, 4 cups of flour, a few heaps of baking powder, and salt in your silver bowl. The feel of the flour might remind you of white bedsheets when you first get in, silky and cool on your bare skin. Add the zest.

It is time for the cream, organic, with a blockage of fat at the top of the carton, the consistency of whipped butter. Pour out the cream, reveling in the brief pause before the liquid breaks through its own barrier, rushing to fill your glass vessel. Fill the cup a little past the red 2 ½ line and keep the carton out; you may need more if the dough appears parched. Pour the cream over the dry ingredients, almost yellow in comparison to the bleached flour. Use your hands. Immerse them in the cold liquid. Scrape your fingers along the bottom of the bowl, lift up, repeat.

It becomes sticky fast, tangling with your fingers until you have trouble moving them at all. Your forearms will grow tired. There's a point at which you consider abandoning the dough altogether, but as we are all told in hard times, continue on. In another few kneads, it will become tame. Cradle it up like a child. Each time it's turned, it almost breaks apart— almost. Against your intuition, you have to trust that it'll hold together.

Now. Now it is ready.

Set the bowl and dough aside and flour your surface. Use a lot of flour; allow it to fill the grain of your butcher block counter. Look out the window and imagine seeing that person you miss—hold on to their image. It brings with it the nostalgia you'll need to finish the recipe.

Remove half the dough from your bowl and place it on the floured counter. Flatten it with your palms and shape it roughly into a square, about 1 inch thick. The more perfect the square, the better, but don't bother with measuring it out. Imperfection is a virtue in baking; the crooked scones are always eaten first, more welcoming, sweeter.

Set the square aside and repeat the squaring-flattening process with your other ball of dough, leaving this one in the center of your surface. Better yet, pinch up the sides a little, maybe a half inch, creating a square trough. You are almost done.

It's time for the berries. 3 cups or so. In the sling of their paper towel, lift them and pour them onto the square trough of dough. Arrange them in an even layer, ensuring they cover every inch of dough, especially the corners. Sprinkle them with lemon juice, a bold handful of sugar. Now lift your first dough square and lay it on top of the berries. Roll your rolling pin, from the center outward, once toward each corner of the berry sandwich. This will crush the berries, releasing their juice into the dough. Use your bench scraper to reshape, to help fuse the edges so you can't see any berries peeking out from the edges of the dough slabs, like tucking away memories for another day.

Using your scraper like a blade, cut the big dough-berry square down the middle, then across. You now have four equal squares. Cut each of those in half, then across. Cut each of these 16 minisquares once diagonally. Arrange scones on your prepared cookie sheet, not too close—they will double in size. Berries will fall out as you tediously move the scones from counter to sheet, your fingers and dough stained red. Cram the berries back in their dough pockets, but don't get obsessive about it. That person you've loved and lost would probably appreciate the crooked scones. They're always the best ones.

Elle slides the scones into the oven and sets her timer for twenty, knowing they might need longer until their tops are golden. When she turns around, Tom is standing on the other side of the island counter, holding a bouquet of peonies and a plain white envelope.

Elle's throat closes. She reaches up to brush her hair off her forehead, notices her hands are a mess of flour and raspberry juice, and refrains. She has barely seen Tom all month. Her face grows hot.

"Sweetheart . . ." she says. It's all she can get out. Things have been uncomfortable between them these past few months, with hardly any conversation, both of them distracted and growing apart as the days race by.

"Did you think I would forget?" he says.

She shakes her head, urging her eyes not to fill with tears. She can't remember the last time he made a gesture like this.

"What kind did you make?" he asks.

"Raspberry," she says.

For a moment, they stand there looking at each other from across the table, which is littered with ingredients, her dough-crusted bowl, and the scraper.

"You got off early," Elle says, circling the table toward him.

He sets the flowers down on the edge of the counter and hands her the card. "I know."

For the first time in a long time, Elle settles into his arms. Tom brought the smell of his office in on his coat—like paper and carpet cleaner—but she doesn't care. The oven ticks. Nestling her face against her husband's collar, Elle imagines her father out in the garden, waiting for her to call him inside.

September 16, 2015

Five weeks after Elle found out

Elle isn't sure what she'll need. Bras? Check. Panties? Check. Eyeliner, mascara, foundation? Check. Toothbrush, hairbrush? Check. All her drawers in the dresser she shares with Tom are open. Tom's sock drawer and T-shirt drawer are closed. Elle is sitting on the bed in a pair of leggings and an oversized T-shirt, unsure of how long she'll be at Bonnie's. It's not like she won't have a chance to stop home for something she forgot, but still, Elle doesn't want to forget anything. Disappearing from Tom for a few days will be a good thing—best to disappear completely.

She throws her things into a carry-on suitcase, grabs her pillow from the guest room. Should she leave him a note? No. Let him wonder.

Downstairs, she slips her binder of recipes into her suitcase, then makes sure the stove is off and that Velcro's bowl is overflowing with kibble. Stroking his striped and slender back, she hopes that staying at Bonnie's won't make things complicated; she and Charlie have never spoken of how they met, and she's not sure how he'll react to having her there. They've managed to generally avoid each other, not talking unless they have to and even then only discussing the weather. During double dates—Elle and Tom, Bonnie and Charlie—they never spoke beyond hello, the men falling into conversation separate from the women as soon as they ordered their dinners.

As the cat slaloms between Elle's ankles, her palms begin to sweat again, and her mind circles back to Tom, who is probably out with the other woman right now. Yes, despite the potential awkwardness, it will be good for her to escape for a while. Gritting her teeth, Elle wipes her clammy hands on her pants and pats Velcro's head once more.

The last thing she does is turn on the porch light, as she's done so many other times for Tom when he's worked late. If it's not on, he'll trip over the uneven path to the door in the darkness; he'll curse, and Elle will hear him from the kitchen while she's making dinner; he'll tell her he will fix the goddamn path stones this weekend; and then he never will.

Elle shakes her head, clearing her mind of the familiar scene. By the door, her hand hovers over the light. Maybe she wants him to trip when he gets home; maybe he doesn't deserve her courtesy. Maybe he won't even notice either way. She flips it off. He doesn't deserve her thoughtfulness. She opens the door, steps through with her suitcase and her pillow. But before she closes it behind her, she reaches inside and flips the light back on.

∼

The road ahead of Elle is blurry with her tears. At seven fifteen, rush hour is ending. Gripping the steering wheel, she is free.

∼

Elle pulls into Bonnie and Charlie's driveway at 7:29 and takes a moment to compose herself. She uses a Starbucks napkin to dab under her nose; she reties her ponytail. The liberation she felt on the drive over is slipping away, leaving her drained. She could sleep for a week and still not feel rested enough, but maybe Bonnie will let her stay in bed that long in any case. With one more swipe of the napkin along her eyelashes, Elle pulls her keys out of the ignition, grabs her purse from the passenger seat, and climbs out of the car.

By the time she's retrieved her suitcase from the back seat and locked up, Bonnie is on the porch, and Charlie is nearly to Elle's side, ready to carry her bag in for her.

"Welcome, Elle," he says, grasping the handle of the carry-on.

She gulps hard. "How've you been, Charlie?"

"Oh, same old," he says. "Bonnie has your room all ready—she even broke out the nice sheets."

Inside her pocket, Elle grinds her keys against each other—but she tries to keep things light. "Bonnie owns nice sheets?"

From the porch, Bonnie says, "The package listed a thread count and everything."

"Well, I'm officially impressed," Elle says, walking past Charlie and up the porch steps to her friend.

Locked in a half hug, the two women lead the way into the house. Inside, the TV is on, and the whole place smells like fettuccini alfredo.

"I made extra, in case you're hungry," Bonnie says to Elle, pointing at the big pot on the stove. "And Charlie forgot the wine."

"What?" Elle says in mock anger, glaring at him.

Charlie's already in the recliner, the Mariners playing. "We still have beer."

"Not even close to the same," Bonnie says.

Charlie waves her off, letting out a loud *gah* when the announcer says, "Steee-rike!"

Bonnie turns to Elle. "Can I fix you a plate?"

Somewhat relieved by Charlie's preoccupation, Elle feels a wash of comfort slip over her. The food, her best friend's company, and finally a place to stay where Tom isn't around the corner—it all adds up to a long sigh. "Yes, please," she says, feeling the tension in her shoulders ease for the first time in weeks.

~

They've finished off the beer and moved on to some of Charlie's "special occasion" scotch, a half-empty bottle of Johnnie Walker Black. In the background is a baseball game between two teams Elle doesn't recognize, a game that already happened and of which Charlie already knows the outcome. They're talking and laughing, and they drink every time the pitcher adjusts his cup. Elle's stomach is full from the food, and she likes the feeling, the idea that she can still genuinely enjoy herself; for the time being, she has allowed herself to forget the complications surrounding her.

Soon enough, though, it's late, and Bonnie stands up. Her pajama top is a little crooked, her hair mussed. "Bed," she says.

Elle gives her a hug. "I should go too."

"Oh, c'mon, Elle. Finish the game," Charlie says, his words a little slurred.

Her eyes dart from Bonnie to Charlie and back again.

Bonnie shrugs. "Suit yourself." Her feet scuff along the carpet as she walks away, down the hall, disappearing into the dark part of the house.

"I'm tired," Elle says, but she feels as though she's anchored to her seat. Why would Charlie want her to stay?

He doesn't respond, just sips his scotch. The game breaks to commercials, and a lull falls over the living room. It's just her and Charlie, a situation they've avoided for so long. Elle curses herself for not leaving when there was an opening; now she's stuck. She *is* tired. But now she has to finish the game. If she gets up, Charlie will think she's avoiding him. Of course, that's true. And again, her mind grapples with why he would want her to stay.

A few minutes go by in relative silence, and then Elle stands and takes her plate into the kitchen and gets herself a glass of tap water. As she comes back into the living room, the screen shows the players on the field, a windup and pitch.

Charlie mutes the TV. "Elle," he says, "do you remember when we met?"

Her breath catches in her chest. Why now? Why talk about it now? She thought it was behind them after he and Bonnie married, but the awkwardness always remained. Since then, Elle always thought she'd keep the secret buried and *thought* he was on the same page—but apparently not. With her mind blaring, Elle nods, sets her glass on the coffee table.

"Have you ever talked—"

"No," Elle interrupts, anxious guilt flooding her cheeks. She glances toward the hallway where Bonnie disappeared.

"All right," he says, turning the sound back on.

Elle hears the crack of ball on bat, but her attention is fixed on her best friend's husband. *Why do you ask?* she wants to know, but instead she says, "I'm tired."

He takes a sip of scotch, eyes on the TV. "I'm sorry about everything. Tom doesn't know what he's missing."

The implication of his words makes her flinch. "Good night," she says, and she disappears into the guest room before he can say another word.

September 17, 2015

Over five weeks after Elle found out

Elle wakes up with her face plastered to the pillow, dry drool crusted on the cotton pillowcase. Late morning streams through the thin curtains, showering the room in a soft, pale light. The day looks gray. As she lifts her head and swipes a hand over her face, her temple pounds with the weight of sleep. Her mouth tastes stale, and she feels overheated in Bonnie's guest bedsheets, the comforter fluffy and cozy but altogether too hot. Yet there's something sweet about waking up late, a pleasantness to how heavy her limbs feel and even the echo of a headache behind her eyes.

Sitting up, Elle swings her legs out of bed and shoulders into the robe Bonnie left out for her. If she were home, she would be listening for Tom, holding her bladder to avoid bumping into him in the hall. A ripple of sorrow pulses through her. This was her first night at Bonnie's. Is he thinking about her? Did he notice yet that she isn't home?

Now, she listens for Bonnie and is comforted by the thought of not having to avoid anyone in the hall—or maybe she should. Her conversation with Charlie last night slides into her thoughts, and rather than leaving her room, Elle finds herself listening yet again. Nothing. She opens her door and peers down the hall, expecting to hear someone, but again, there's nothing. Elle tiptoes out the door, feeling as though she's trespassing in her friend's home. Reaching the end of the hall, she realizes that Bonnie must be at the bakery. Thursday. And Charlie must be at work.

Her shoulders relax, concern draining from her thoughts, at least for now. With her mind clearer, she realizes how hungry she is and heads into the kitchen. There's a note on the counter:

Elle,

Enjoy your day off. I'll be home at six, Charlie too. Bubble bath in our bedroom, plus magazines. Pancake mix (not sorry) in the pantry. Make yourself at home.

XO Bonnie

Elle looks around and adjusts her robe. When was the last time she had a day off like this? Too long. Tom crosses her mind again, but she urges herself to think of other things. Today is a gift from Bonnie: the bakery covered, a place to stay. And right now, pancakes sound fabulous—even if they are from a box. She reads the note again, and Bonnie's *not sorry* makes her smile.

Opening the pantry, the baker in her wants to make the pancakes from scratch—they would be so much better—but Bonnie has few baking ingredients; she likes to leave her work at work. And anyhow, Elle *does* find a nugget of guilty pleasure in the ease of using a mix. Trying a few cabinets, Elle finds a pan and a bowl and gets started.

Lazy Lonesome Pancakes

Is it even worth writing this down? Follow the box's instructions: 1 cup of pancake mix, 1 cup of milk, 1 egg. An extra splash of oil so they get crispy around the edges when they cook. The trick with any box batter is to leave it lumpy. Overmix, and your pancakes will be soggy; take your laziness to heart and neglect the "recipe." Don't even use a whisk—a fork is fine.

But if you're a true baker, you'll make the box pancakes your own: a dash of vanilla, because you can. Cinnamon too. And while you're digging around in an unfamiliar pantry, if you find chocolate chips, throw in a handful. If you find fruit in the fridge—some old strawberries—slice them up for an extra-special topping. You might be lazy, and you might be lonesome, but these extra touches will make your pancakes lovely. And pancakes are meant to be lovely.

Heat a skillet, grease it, pour the batter, and you know the rest.

All in all, it takes her longer than she would have hoped to make them, not knowing where everything is in the kitchen, but with the TV on and a stomach full of pancakes, Elle starts to feel a little better. Glancing at the clock on the DVD player, she realizes it's almost noon. Elle takes her dish to the sink and heads upstairs. She considers checking her phone—has Tom called?—but resists, heading straight for the master bedroom for her bath.

When she opens the door, there isn't much to see: a bed, the sheets rumpled from sleep; two bedside tables with lamps, books, Kleenex; and a chair with laundry on it. Yet Elle feels as though she has opened a window into Bonnie and Charlie's private life. This is where they stay up late talking, where they argue, where they make love. Elle's own bedroom with Tom looks so similar, so why is Bonnie still with Charlie while Elle is an outsider in her own home? Feeling as though she has done something wrong—though she hasn't touched a thing—Elle pads into the bathroom.

On the counter among some hair products, toothbrushes, eyeliner, and men's aftershave, Bonnie has left a half-used bottle of tropical bubble bath, a candle, and three magazines. Turning on the water, Elle lights the candle and pours in a good amount of the peach-colored soap. While the tub fills and foams, she disrobes and looks at her magazine choices: *Cosmopolitan*, *Women's Health*, and *Pastry & Baking*. Picking up *Pastry & Baking*, she steps into the water. It's hot but welcoming. Toes tingling, she breathes in the scent of the bubble bath, a mixture of coconut, passion fruit, and other tropical ingredients. Almost cheaply sweet, but it doesn't hinder Elle's sense of contentment. She thinks to herself that this is perhaps as relaxed as she could ever be, given the circumstances.

Flipping the magazine open to the table of contents, Elle is startled by the sound of the front door—or what she imagines is the front door, the clang of the latch opening, the clatter of the door closing. Sitting stiffly, Elle sets down her magazine. Silence. She can hear the bubbles in her bath, a faint crackling as they dissipate. The edge of the water tickles along her chest with each careful breath. Burglary? A robber wouldn't walk in through the front door. It was the front door, right? She looks down at the bubbles, an aerated mountain disintegrating bit by bit. Should she get out? Her gaze lifts to her robe, hung on the back of the door—it seems so far away.

Footsteps again, faint, grazing over carpet, getting closer; she holds her breath. Sinking deeper into the water, Elle feels suddenly very vulnerable. Naked. In a tub. Protected only by the thinning bubbles, which now only barely cover her breasts, her belly, her thighs. Through the door, she can hear the rustling of papers, the shifting of laundry.

Elle grips the edge of the tub, ready to get out. Then the door opens.

Elle's knees instinctively jerk toward her torso, and she tries to cover herself with the magazine. Water splashes; bubbles waft into the air. It takes only a moment for Charlie to realize what has happened, his face going from creased to wide eyed, and then the door slams shut, a series of *sorrys* filling the tense air.

Mortification congealing in her chest, Elle sits there for a moment, wet magazine turning to pulp in her hands, the water settling. She wants to sink under the surface and never come up again.

But she *has* to say something. Her voice lifts through her own discomfiture. "Charlie?"

From the other side of the door, his voice returns muffled. "Elle?"

Resting the sopping magazine on the edge of the tub, Elle steps out and, still dripping, puts on her robe. She cracks the door open. He's sitting on the bed, shoulders hunched, a hand sliding over his crown, his face, falling to his lap.

When she comes out all the way, he looks up and says, "I didn't see anything."

Elle tightens the belt of her robe. "I thought you were at work—I should have locked the door."

"I forgot a case file."

Elle feels a droplet of water sliding down her leg. She doesn't know what else to say.

Charlie's eyes are still on her. "You have some bubbles in your hair."

She reaches up and, sure enough, feels the crunch of bubbles under her fingers. She can't help but laugh, and then Charlie laughs, and then the room falls silent again, and he says, "I'm sorry. I really didn't mean to walk in on you."

"I didn't think you did," Elle says. She shifts from one foot to the other, realizing she's made the carpet damp beneath her feet.

Charlie rests his elbows on his legs, staring at his clasped hands. "And—I should have said this a long time ago—I'm sorry about the way we met."

The top of Elle's esophagus constricts.

"I want you to know I've always been faithful to Bonnie."

"Oh, Charlie, I—"

"No, you're her best friend. I don't want you to think ill of me," he says. "I think I made you uncomfortable last night—and I—I wanted to apologize then, but I chickened out."

Elle sighs. "Well—thank you. I'm sorry too."

He bobs his head, then sits up. "I should head back to the office."

"Sure." She crosses her arms. "Did you find your file?"

He picks it up off the bedspread, waves it in the air. "Sorry to ruin your bath."

She shrugs. "Maybe I'll go for a walk."

He bobs his head again, then walks out the door, down the hall. She listens for the front door to latch again, then the sound of a car door, the engine rumbling.

Alone once more, Elle looks back into the bathroom. There's water on the floor, the issue of *Pastry & Baking* falling apart where it rests on the porcelain edge of the tub. While she cleans up, she can't help but think about Charlie's words. *I've always been faithful to Bonnie.* The tenderness with which he said it. And she knows he's telling the truth. And she wonders why Tom couldn't do the same.

January 7, 2006

Over nine and a half years before Elle found out

There's a kitchen shop in the U District like no other, a hole-in-the-wall place that Elle discovered years ago and hasn't told anyone about, like a secret guilty pleasure—all hers. With her bakery opening in a little over a month, Elle has come in for some last-minute supplies. A few frivolous serving plates, an extra set of measuring spoons, a bench scraper, and a new blue-checkered apron. All things she either didn't need or could have bought from her catalogs, but she wanted to treat herself with a trip. It's a Saturday night, and she has nothing better to do than buy baking supplies; on her way home, she'll probably pick up a pizza to eat in front of the TV, alone. She has worked hard these past few months, getting the bakery ready, so why not at least enjoy herself and pick out something nice?

Arriving at checkout, Elle fumbles the delicate dishes out of her arms and onto the counter. The owner—a sunny woman with deep laugh lines and silver-blonde hair—starts ringing her up, wrapping the dishes in gray paper. "Did you find everything you needed, Elle?"

"Always. Thanks, Laurie," she says, unzipping her purse.

At that moment, the door jingles, and a man walks in, beads of January precipitation clinging to the shoulders of his wool peacoat. He ducks into an aisle, and Elle goes back to thumbing through cash and punch cards for her credit card. With her mind wandering back to her bakery, Elle recalls the one thing she actually did *need* from here. "Oh, shoot, I forgot pie weights."

Laurie smiles. "I'm sure you know where they are."

Elle nods. "I'll be right back."

After hurrying past a wall of Bundt pans and springforms and cake molds, Elle arrives at the pie-weight section. She peruses the various ceramic and steel beads, like looking at malas, wanting to linger but urging herself to decide quickly so as not to keep the shop owner waiting. She settles on a container of large Mrs. Anderson's Ceramic Pie Weights and darts down a different aisle toward the front counter. The aisle she chooses—where she earlier selected one of her cake plates—is where the man stands, the only other customer in the shop at nearly seven in the evening. He's studying a mug set, looking confused.

Elle pauses. It's not like her to stick her neck out, but the atmosphere and her cheery mood cause a dash of friendliness to stir inside her. On a whim, she says, "Looking for something?"

He shakes his head, not looking up. Great—now he thinks she works here. She should say something else—something better—but she can't think of anything. Suddenly Elle feels as though her fleece jacket is strangling her, holding in all the heat.

"Are you looking for a gift?" she asks. Not better. Not better at all.

This time he does look up, and she notices that his eyes are gray blue. "Yes," he says, and his breath seems to catch. "It's my mother's birthday tomorrow."

His voice—it's gentle, deep, a little gravelly, like he just woke up, like he's talking to her in bed—and he barely glanced in her direction. She's lured in by his voice. Staring at a series of black freckles on his neck, collarbone, leading down into the folds of his jacket, she can't bring herself to move on. Elle hasn't felt this unexpectedly intrigued by a man since her brief but passionate affair with an exchange student sophomore year—the happenstance of it makes her head whirl.

"Just under the wire." Elle clutches her pie weights a little tighter.

"It'll be late no matter what—I have to mail it to New Jersey." He sets the mugs back on the shelf.

"Oh," Elle says. "What does she like? If it's late, it better be good."

He sighs. "I'm not sure, really. I just know she's a good cook." He faces her more squarely. "Any suggestions?"

Elle looks down at her hands. "What does she like to cook?"

"I always liked her stews, but she rarely made them. Took too much time."

Elle nods, thinking. Then she has an idea. "Follow me."

She leads him through the store, toward the back, where the appliances are kept. She's not sure why she's helping him at all, only that she's glad she is, that his company makes her heart patter like crazy, and she wants to be near him as long as she can. She hears his footsteps behind her as she leads him down the aisles. What is she doing? This is so unlike her that she feels as though she's in a trance, as though she's not herself at all under the spell of this *stranger*.

Arriving at the back wall packed with panini presses and waffle irons and hand mixers, Elle points to a simple Crock-Pot up on one of the higher shelves. He reaches for it, and she admires his height, the shadow of stubble on his jaw. He is perhaps only a few years older than she is. Her fingers curl into her palm. As he eases it off the shelf, observing the package, he says, in that incredible voice, "A slow cooker?"

"This way she'll have time for stew," Elle says.

Above his straight nose, his eyebrows crease. "I'm not sure she actually *likes* making stew."

Shifting on her feet, embarrassed by the whole thing, Elle struggles for words. "How about, with the card, you tell her to use it the next time you visit? That you love her stews but wanted to take the work out of it."

Again, his eyes rest on her. He nods, his face breaking into a smile. "Oh, she'll love that," he says. "Yes, promise a visit. Good idea. I'll take it."

Together, they walk up to the counter, and Elle tries to subdue her nerves, clenching her pie weights, chewing on the inside of her cheek.

When they arrive at the counter, Laurie asks Elle, "Did you get sidetracked?"

Before Elle can come up with a response, Laurie turns to the man. "One moment, sir, while I ring her up."

"Wait, you don't work here?" he asks Elle.

She shakes her head.

"Well, I hope you get commission." He turns to the owner. "She just sold me one of your Crock-Pots."

Turning toward her, Laurie says, "You did? That merits an employee discount."

Elle lets out a breath of laughter. "Laurie, it's no big deal, really."

"Consider it a thank-you," she says, swiping Elle's card.

Elle glances at the man, and he grins. "There. You helped me; now I helped you."

The owner rings him up next, and Elle lingers, putting away her card slowly, shuffling her bags as if she can't figure out how to carry them. When he's finished, they walk out together into the frosty air. It's just after New Year's. Pavement skies. Black ice. There are few people out on the street, and the wind nips at Elle's face, penetrating the confidence and ease she found in the store.

Feeling suddenly very self-conscious, Elle says, "I hope your mother likes her gift," then starts for her car, slowly, cursing herself for being chicken, but what did she expect to happen?

And then as the evening settles around her, and all she can hear are her own footsteps, and she's sure she just blew it, sure she'll never see the man again, she hears that voice riding over the cold to her ears—"Miss?"—and she turns around. Her quick and sudden high dips when she sees him reaching out with a receipt. "You dropped this," he says, and she's disappointed but not surprised that's all he wanted.

But as she takes it from his hand, their fingers brush, and for a moment she's enwrapped in the fantasy again—and then it continues on when he says, "Tom."

For a moment she's not sure what to say, his touch like a shot of warmth to her very core. She remembers her name. "Elle."

The breeze picks up, bringing with it the sharp sprinkles of an icy rain. "Nice to meet you."

She nods. "You as well."

"And thanks for the help," he says, lifting his bag.

"No problem." She turns away, feeling shy now and defeated—if only she were more outgoing, she might have been able to show more interest. With the wind lifting and the rain coming on stronger, blowing her hair back, she finds it even harder to walk away.

And then his voice again. "Do you smoke?"

She turns, finding him closer to her than she thought. "I—" Elle smoked a handful of times after lovemaking with her foreign exchange student, an act somewhat carnal and wildly outside her normal character. It was something she gave up when he gave up on her. Now, Tom's offer seems almost suggestive. "It's been a while," she says.

Pulling out his pack, he leads her into the indented doorway of a closed shop nearby, just as the stormy weather moves in for real. With a few clicks of his lighter, Tom lights up. Elle sets down her bags and receives a cigarette from his fingers, places the end between her lips, and bends forward, taking a long draw of the flame. She fills her skull completely before breathing out the smoke.

Their closeness in the doorway, sheltered from the rainfall, combined with the memory of her previous cigarettes has Elle light headed. Warmth spreads through her shoulders and thighs, the scent of sex almost detectable inside the burning of her nose. She leans against the cobwebby frame and directs a long exhale over her right shoulder, out into the street. To her left, Tom taps some ash into the slush on the sidewalk, his eyes focused somewhere outside their close quarters. A melancholy feeling creeps up inside Elle and winds like a vine through her ribs. What are the chances that this man will become something other than another cigarette?

Maybe she shouldn't have taken his offer instead of simply moving on—the nicotine has her mood turned upside down.

"Elle," Tom breathes, and she's back in the hopeful moment. Reimmersed in his baritone. "Is that short for something?"

"No," she says. "Though my mother used to call me *mademoiselle* when I was little. I suppose that's what my name alludes to." She takes a pull, lets it out. "I like Thomas."

He gives her a sidewise glance. "No one calls me Thomas."

She offers a mischievous smile. "I do."

"No, you don't," Tom says, nudging her with his shoulder.

The tip of her cigarette flares in the darkness of their private nook. Outside, the wind surges, willing them closer. "Thomas," she whispers. "Thomas."

She tips her head back laughing, and then he's bending toward her, and then their noses touch, and his hands fall gently onto her waist. And in that moment, like the spark between their lips, she gets the sense that her life has changed, the taste of him, this stranger, as sweet and familiar on her tongue as honey.

September 17, 2015

Over five weeks after Elle found out

Elle pulls into a parking spot down the block from the bakery. After cleaning up the mess of water in Bonnie's bathroom, she couldn't stay in the house any longer. The sun has come out, the clouds clearing to reveal a bright, chilly sky. As she walks along the sidewalk, the sun feels warm bouncing off the shop windows. Elle checks her phone: one missed call from Gina, but nothing from Tom. She's not sure whether to feel relieved or sad.

Approaching the bakery, she's glad to see a handful of people crowded inside. Almost closing time, and people are eager to snatch up the last of the pastries, cookies, or other treats. Elle feels a pang of concern, hoping a bear claw is left, and quickens her pace. Of course she knows that the bear claws usually sell out first—hers is an empty wish—but her excitement is amusing. Even now, after all this time, her heart still flutters at the prospect of pastries. She feels like a little girl again.

The bell on the door jingles when she walks in—how strange to come through the front door in daylight, when usually she's stumbling in through the back before dawn. No one notices. There are a few customers ahead of her, ogling the cases, some pointing, some whispering to each other about their selections. Mindy is quick and efficient at taking their orders. Elle is pleased to see everyone cheerful, the line shrinking smoothly.

Before Elle has even reached the front of the line, Bonnie comes out, sliding half a cake back into the cold case, handing over a single-slice box to a customer waiting off to the side.

When Bonnie spots Elle, she says, "Oh, no, you don't. This is your special day off. Get out of here!"

Elle raises her hands in surrender. "I'm just here for a bear claw."

"At two o'clock?"

"I know, long shot."

"Well, hold on. I might have one in the back." Bonnie winks and disappears into the back room.

Elle steps to the side, allowing the next customers to approach the counter, and smiles at Mindy briefly before she takes their order: two berry turnovers and the last cinnamon twist.

Bonnie comes back out with a bulging pastry bag. "Your bear claw, miss."

"You had one back there?"

"I was going to bring it home to you."

"You're the best," Elle says. "And you know I haven't been a *miss* in years." She won't be a *Mrs.* anymore soon either.

"Well, I can't call you *ma'am*."

"Wow, this *is* a special day."

Bonnie grins. "Did you have a nice morning? Pancakes? Bath?"

Elle looks around, making sure she isn't in anyone's way. She inches closer to the side. "Pancakes were good—so little effort."

"See? Sometimes it's nice to bake from a"—she lowers her voice until it's barely audible—"box."

"The word makes me cringe."

Bonnie laughs. "And the bath? Did you take a bath?"

"Well, Charlie stopped by."

"Yeah, he came in here on his way back home. Said he needed a file."

Elle's throat starts to close again, so she blurts, "He walked in on me."

Bonnie's face goes blank for a moment, and Elle thinks maybe she shouldn't have told her.

"In the bath?" Bonnie says, brow creased. Then she disintegrates into laughter. "Poor Charlie! I bet he was so embarrassed."

"Poor Charlie?" Elle's shoulders relax a little. "Poor me!"

"I'm sure he was much more embarrassed than you were," Bonnie says. "What did he do?"

"He closed the door! And apologized—a bunch." Elle stares into her friend's freckled face, a twinge of sorrow nudging her side. Bonnie's first instinct was to *laugh*. No jealousy, no concern. *Poor Charlie*.

"So what are you going to do the rest of the day?"

"Eat this," Elle says, lifting her pastry bag. "And, I don't know, go for a walk? Window-shop?"

"Good. I want you to relax," Bonnie says. "No baking—I saw that you brought your recipe book."

"I can't help it."

"If anything, work on getting that behemoth published. But otherwise, relax."

Before Elle can respond, a group of five crowds inside, and Bonnie lifts her gaze to them. Taking their orders, Bonnie waves to Elle as she heads out the door.

Out on the sidewalk again, the breeze touches her face, welcome after the heat in the bakery. She checks her phone. A text, but not from Tom.

Owen: *Free tomorrow night?*

Something similar to angst flutters in her chest. A booty call? They haven't spoken since their dinner, and she thought things were clearly over. She wants them to be over. A onetime thing turned into a few-times thing, a too-many-times thing. A way to get back at her husband, but what is there to get back? Revenge doesn't work when the other person doesn't give a damn.

A few kids brush past Elle, and she realizes she's been standing in the middle of the sidewalk. She steps off to the side, thinking. A dirty feeling trickles over her, and she wishes she'd never gone home with Owen. What had she been thinking? She could blame the liquor, but that wouldn't be true. She had *intended* to go home with someone—and that's why it's so shameful. Maybe she's being hard on herself, but she can't shake the feeling that she did something wrong.

A typing bubble pops up on her screen—he's saying something else—and that anxious fluttering starts up again. The bubble disappears, and her anxiety worsens. She gets in her car. Whatever he says, she'll refuse.

With a whoosh her phone receives his next text: *Dinner again? Sorry, busy.*

Setting her phone on the empty passenger seat, she puts the key in the ignition and pulls out of her parking spot. Elle is blocks away from the bakery by the time she realizes that she had meant to take a walk.

~

After going through a coffee drive-through, Elle turns onto the highway. She's not sure why, other than a desperate curiosity, a clawing and instinctual urge that she can't dissuade. She's put her phone on silent to hush any more texts from Owen. The road noise is too quiet, so she turns on talk radio, but she doesn't really listen. Her mind is elsewhere, on Tom again. Every spare moment: Tom. She can't even stay away for one day. She's like an addict.

She munches on the bear claw, flakes of dough sprinkling her lap. Traffic is slowing, and she brakes, coming to a full stop. It's the afternoon rush. *Crap*, she thinks. Should she take the next exit and turn around? He's probably going to get drinks with the other woman this afternoon. Thursday happy hour.

The car in front of her crawls forward, and Elle removes her foot from the brake pedal. She glances down, brushing the crumbs from her lap. When she looks up again, the car in front of her has stopped. She slams on the brakes, and her seat belt locks. She inhales a tiny piece of dough and descends into a fit of coughing. Did she hit them? They're moving forward again, slowly, and she can't see any damage on the clean white bumper. The tickle in her throat intensifies, tears coming to her eyes. She takes a sip of her coffee. The person behind her honks, and she eases on the gas again but keeps a two-car distance between her and the person ahead of her.

Maybe she should turn around before she gets into an accident. But no, she's almost there. With an eye glued on the traffic, she finishes her bear claw. She wonders what kind of drink the other woman prefers. Tom used to poke fun at Elle's tastes—always toward the sweeter side. He prefers bitter, the more the better. The mistress probably agrees. They probably laugh about Elle's refusal to drink cocktails that don't include simple syrup. They probably think Elle is a pansy for letting any of this happen in the first place.

It takes another twenty minutes to get through the clogged-up downtown exit. There's an uncovered parking lot across from Tom's building, one of those lots that charge an obscene twenty-five dollars per hour. She backs into a space along the far wall, mostly hidden from view by the other cars. The building looms high above, a great big wall of windows, mirroring the blue of the sky. At its base, a series of steps flanked by giant planter boxes leads up to a revolving door. Elle tries to see inside, but the windows are tinted.

A pair of suited-up men walk out, chatting, their watches glinting in the sun. A homeless man is nestled into a crook in the neighboring building, a mass of dirty blankets and duffle bags. Many people hurry by in either direction, trying to make the crosswalks before the lights turn red. An older woman pushes through the revolving door, looking stylish with white hair and a trim pantsuit. Another pair of men exits behind her, talking.

Elle sips her coffee. Bonnie wouldn't approve of Elle waiting outside Tom's building, and truthfully, she doesn't really approve of it herself. Is this what she has been reduced to? Stalking her own husband? Yet no matter how many times she counts to three, ready to drive away, she just can't put the car in drive. Tom could walk out at any moment.

Elle waits another ten minutes. People mill around. Someone parks not far from her and pays the ungodly rate, returning to his car to slide the ticket onto the dash before locking up. She finishes her coffee, pops a mint in her mouth, and stares, practically willing Tom to come out. It's a little early for work to be over but the perfect time for happy hour. His mistress probably meets him here all the time, right?

Her suspicions are piqued when an attractive redhead pauses outside the building. She's wearing a pencil skirt and a blush blouse stretched over big breasts. A pang of adrenaline shoots through Elle's chest like a shot of whiskey. Her heart beats faster, and she bites down on the mint, little cool flakes exploding over her tongue. The woman glances at her phone, leaning against one of the planter boxes. She's waiting for someone. Elle is certain she's waiting for Tom.

Elle gets out of the car. What is she going to do? For a moment, she has the urge to run at the woman. She imagines his mistress jumping back with a start, one of her heels breaking on the uneven sidewalk, her phone shattering on the concrete. She imagines pulling at that red hair, yelling, getting hauled off the other woman by random businessmen on the street.

Of course, she doesn't do any of that. The sun beats down. Maybe she'll talk to the woman instead, ask her if she knows she's a mistress. Maybe Elle will show her face when Tom comes out, just to force him to realize how much he's hurt her. More likely, though, she'll do nothing. What can be done, at this point?

Elle gets back into the car, feeling foolish and embarrassed and small. Seemingly on cue, a man walks out of the building—not Tom— and gives the redhead a quick peck. They walk off together.

Almost let down, Elle puts the car in drive.

Traffic is worse on the way back to Bonnie's house, giving her plenty of time to feel awful about driving to Tom's office in the first place. Has she really stooped to this level? Is she truly this pathetic? She feels like a ball of yarn, completely unraveled.

~

As Elle parks in Bonnie's driveway, her phone buzzes. It's not Owen *or* Tom: it's her mother, just in time to make her feel even lousier. It has been three months since she talked to her mother, and she never returned her mother's last call, so she answers.

"Hello?"

"Darling," her mother says. "I'm sorting through some old things and wanted to know—do you want your father's old photo albums? I'm purging, and I just don't have room for them anymore."

Staring at the face of Bonnie's garage through the windshield, Elle says, "Purging?"

"I'm selling the house. Didn't I tell you?"

Elle should want to know more, but the house is large and has seemed empty since her father died, since her mother let the gardens overgrow. Elle doesn't have enough room in her heart to feel sad about yet another thing. "You didn't tell me," Elle says, keeping her voice light. "But that's great—it's time you downsize."

"Yes, yes. Anyway, do you want the albums? I won't have room at my new condo, and I'm not wasting money on storage."

A bee swings in front of the car and lands on one of the wiper blades, its legs thick with pollen. Elle watches it from behind the wheel, its tiny body swaying in the faint breeze. "Sure, I can take the albums."

"All of them?"

"Yeah, Mom, just mail them."

"Tom won't mind?"

The question knocks the wind out of Elle; her mother doesn't know what's going on. She looks for the bee, but it must've flown off. "No, he won't mind." She wonders about her own photo albums. What will she do with their wedding album? The photos from their trip to France two years ago?

"All right, well, will I be able to mail them in one big box?"

"Yeah, sure," Elle says, staring. Tom wouldn't want their albums, but neither would she. Throwing them away would be too undignified for perfectly good albums. Her mother is right, though: storing them is pointless too.

"So how's my mademoiselle?"

"I'm all right, Mom."

"And Tom?"

"Fine, I think."

"You think?"

"We've been . . ." Elle hedges. ". . . quarreling."

"About?"

She'll have to tell her mother eventually. "He cheated on me, Mom. We might be separating. I don't know. I'm staying at Bonnie's right now."

"Oh," her mother says, but it's not laden with disappointment as Elle expected. It's the sort of *oh* Elle would say if someone told her that they dropped a strawberry on the bakery floor. *Oh, better pick that up before someone steps on it.*

"Well, are you okay?" her mother asks.

It surprises Elle. No judgment, no criticism? "I'm all right."

"I hope you're staying strong."

With irony, Elle thinks of her afternoon, her trip downtown. "I'm trying, thank you."

"I'm not sure the women in our family are cut out for marriage."

If Elle has been feeling warm from her mother's unexpected kindness, she goes cold now. "They aren't?"

"Well, look at your aunt Susan. And Grandma. Single women are common in our family. It's in your blood, Elle."

"But you were married."

"That doesn't mean I was cut out for it," her mother says. "I thought about divorce before."

"You what?" Elle feels the old wound of her father's death in her chest, deflating her lungs. With her mother's words, it grows worse.

"The cancer," she says, as if it were obvious. "I thought about divorce earlier, too, when we argued, but it always faded. The cancer made me think seriously."

Horrified, Elle wants to know, "But why?"

"Well, it wasn't easy for me either, dear. The chemo. The hair loss. The puking. I'm not a nurse, but suddenly I had to be one. I didn't like seeing your father that way; he was no longer the strong man I married."

"But did you not still love him?"

"People in love get divorced all the time," her mother says. "You do what's best for you."

"What about all those times you spoke of decorum?"

"You've always been an independent woman, Elle. Too much for your own good. I just wanted you to see the people around you."

Her mind is swirling. "You didn't divorce Dad."

"I knew I'd miss his company, so I stayed." Her mother pauses, and there's some shuffling on her end of the line. "Do you think you'll stay with him, dear?"

Elle finds her eyes watery, Bonnie's garage shifting into a blurry gray shape. "It's not as simple for me, Mom."

"It's never simple, Elle," her mother says. "It's life."

∼

That evening over dinner at Bonnie's house, Elle tells her, "My mom called."

"Oh, God. Are you all right?"

Elle laughs. "Fine. It was actually . . . I don't know."

"Did you tell her about Tom?"

Elle nods. "She was strangely . . . transparent."

"Wow," Bonnie says, glancing at Charlie. He's bent over his dinner, chewing. He looks up, clearly unsure of what to say.

"She kind of made me feel better. And worse. But mostly better."

"Wow," Bonnie says again, taking a bite of her salad. "She's a changed woman."

"Actually, I think she's the same. It's just a side I'd never seen before. Like, for the first time, we were speaking woman to woman, not mother to daughter."

Bonnie nods, taking another bite. "I'm glad to hear it, then."

Changing the subject, Elle also tells Bonnie and Charlie about Owen's texts. Over the next hour, the bath doesn't come up—but then again, Bonnie doesn't seem to think anything of it, so why would it? She doesn't tell Bonnie about her trip to the city, either—her best friend definitely wouldn't approve. So Elle allows Owen to become the main point of interest. Elle and Bonnie chat while Charlie sits there, eating his food, laughing occasionally at Bonnie's offhand comments: "What is he thinking?" "Just ignore him until he gives up."

Elle can't help but feel sorry for Owen; she doesn't want to lead him on, and ignoring him seems too cruel. Better to be up front. But she hasn't said anything else to him, and he hasn't texted back either. The truth is that she has no idea how to handle the situation; she hasn't been single for nearly a decade, and she's tempted by Bonnie's easy way out.

Elle goes to bed with the feeling that she'll hear from him again, and the idea of that kind of awkward confrontation makes her stomach churn. As the minutes pass, Elle lying awake in the darkness, her mind orbits back to Tom. Gravity. She tries to conjure up the image of his face or the way his hands feel on her skin. It's a struggle. She can remember Owen better than her own husband, and the thought makes her sad. Does Tom still remember her? Does he recall their spare kisses on sleepless nights? The tickle fights of their early years? His wraparound hugs while she stood before the mixer in their kitchen? So many touches, lost to this marriage-shattering shit he's put them through. She can't bear to think of him touching the other woman in the same familiar ways.

Elle turns on her side, staring through the curtains into the dark tangle of tree branches outside the window, the faint light of a streetlight glimmering as the breeze rattles the leaves from tree boughs. She closes her eyes, trying to remember him, unable to get a clear image, anger and love and everything in between swelling deep inside her, like embers still alive after the fire is thought to be out.

December 31, 2007

About seven and a half years before Elle found out

Parties always make her anxious, a twisting of excitement and worry. Tonight's party is worse, though. Elle and Tom are heading to a party put on by one of his buddies from college—they all knew Tom's ex-wife, Miranda. They went to school with her, partied with her, watched her walk down the aisle where Tom waited at the end. They don't know Elle, and to them, she's probably just "the new girl." Or maybe even "the rebound." And sometime tonight, during the introductions and the drinks and the New Year's well-wishes, someone might call Elle *Miranda*. And how could she respond or recover after that?

For now, it's still early, only four p.m., and Elle has plenty more time to worry and also a cake to bake. Tom's grading papers on the couch—she kicked him out of the kitchen. Her grandmother's recipe: "An adult chocolate cake," Althea used to say. Dark, unsweetened chocolate. Coffee mixed in. And Kahlúa. The texture fluffy but dense where it counts. It's one of those cakes that's richer than it appears, where a small piece seems inadequate until halfway through eating it, and then the fork slows down, and that last bite may or may not be left on the plate. Elle's father called it deadly every time his mother-in-law took over the kitchen.

Elle looks toward the living room and sees the top of Tom's head, hears the fluffing of pages like bird wings, a calculated flourish. And his red pen, out of view, but she recognizes the sound of it, the purposeful scratching. She has interrupted many red comments on student papers—for Tom's attention, a kiss, or more.

He catches her looking and smiles. "Are you baking or spying?"

Elle shrugs. "Baking."

"*Sure*," he says, not convinced. "Come here, sexy."

Elle flattens the folded, cocoa-stained recipe on the counter, then walks across the carpet to Tom. "Yes?" From behind the couch, she leans toward him, and they kiss upside down.

"I missed you," he says, "all the way over there."

This is only the second holiday season since her father passed, and Tom has been extra attentive. Through the awkward Thanksgiving with her family, her touch of melancholy during Christmas with his family. Even on the good days, like on December 27, when they had their own private Christmas together, or today. Leaning over the back of the couch, her chest constricts with joy.

"You missed me?" Elle says.

"Yeah," Tom says, setting down his red pen.

Elle meets his lips for another kiss, this one deeper, his tongue slipping into her mouth. And then her world is tipped, and he pulls her over the couch, and she's suddenly in his arms. This time when her chest tightens, the sensation travels all the way down into her belly.

She laughs against his mouth. "Smooth, but I really need to make this cake."

He kisses her again, and then they break apart. "It better be a damn good cake."

"It is," Elle says. She gives him one more peck before heading back into the kitchen, walking slowly, knowing he's watching.

"You're such a tease."

"You're the one who told me to come over."

"You know I can't resist you when you're wearing your apron."

"My *napron*?" Elle plugs in her mixer, and they make eye contact. He smiles. "I love your *napron*."

"And I love your red pen."

Adult Chocolate Bundt Cake

This cake is perfect for parties, and you need a party spirit when you bake it. Turn on some music, let go of your anxieties, put on something comfortable, and preheat your oven to 275°—yes, really, 275°.

Butter your Bundt pan generously and dust it with cocoa powder. The cocoa will get everywhere, and it stains, so wear an apron and accept the mess. You can clean later.

Have a sip of Kahlúa; then heat 1 ¾ cups of strong coffee and ¼ cup of liqueur on low for a few minutes. In the meantime, combine 2 cups of flour, 1 teaspoon of baking powder, and a dash of salt. Sift. It's essential that this recipe has no lumps, so be gentle with the drys after sifting. Once finished, have another sip of Kahlúa, turn up the music, and add 2/3 cup of semisweet chocolate and 1 cup of butter to the coffee/liqueur mixture. Stir until it's as smooth as jazz. Add 2 cups of granulated sugar, have another sip of liqueur, and stir until dissolved. Remove from heat, and allow the chocolate mixture to cool for approximately the length of your favorite song. Dance while you wait. Don't be nervous. Then transfer the chocolate mixture into your mixing bowl.

Add the sifted flour, powder, and salt—a half cup at a time—to the chocolate, beating between each addition. Once smooth, add 2 eggs and a teaspoon of vanilla, and beat for another half song.

Pour the batter into your prepared Bundt pan and bake for 1 ½ hours—that's right, 1 ½. The cake is ready when it pulls away from the side of the pan and is springy when touched. Take it out, let it cool for 10 minutes, and then invert the cake on a plate. Leave the pan over the cake until it's completely cool—this will seal in the moisture and give you time to clean up your mess or listen to the rest of your CD.

The cake is good with powdered sugar, but only dust it once the cake is completely cool—or even once you get to your party—to ensure the sugar doesn't soak in and disappear into the cake. It's also good with homemade whipped cream or even a simple ganache. Tailor the topping to the party. Warn people that it's more rich than they think, but overserve anyway, and don't fret when they don't finish their slices—it's never because they didn't like it.

Elle decides to dust it with powdered sugar. Festive. Tom comes up behind her while she's placing a large red bow in the center of the cake and kisses her ear.

"How much Kahlúa did you have?"

Elle shrugs, focused on her task.

His lips move to her neck. "I don't want you falling asleep before midnight."

"I won't," Elle says, facing him. "Why so lovey dovey today?"

"What, I can't be lovey dovey?"

"No, you can," she says. Now that the cake is done, her nerves flare up again, and she kisses Tom once more, trying to relax.

"That looks good."

"The cake?" She turns around again, his hands resting on her hips. "Yeah, it turned out well."

"Now what?"

Elle looks at the clock. "Now I get ready. Chris said eight, right?"

"Eight," Tom confirms. "But that's not a hard deadline."

"What's gotten into you?"

"I just think it's going to be a fun night, that's all."

~

They arrive at eight fifteen, but only because Elle decided at the last minute—when she noticed the powdered sugar kept fading into the cake—to make whipped cream from scratch. She wants it to be a hit. She'd rather be *the baker* than *the rebound*, and it's embarrassing when *the baker* brings something that isn't devoured immediately. If it's less than amazing, then come the whispers, the side comments: "This reminds me of a recipe my friend makes." "I could've made *that*." Or worse: "What does Tom see in her? Her baking isn't even all that special."

Elle stands on the sidewalk, the crisp December wind biting through her tights, and clutches the cake plate a little tighter. It feels precarious under the foil, gripped by her quivering hands. Crimping the edges, she watches Tom grab the bowl of whipped cream from the back seat and lock up the car.

"Ready?" he says.

Elle nods.

"You look beautiful."

"Thanks, sweetheart."

His hand comes to rest on the small of her back, the other one-handing the bowl of whip, and rather than making Elle feel comforted, a stitch of worry makes her palms tingle. The foil on the cake plate crunches under her grip.

"So who's going to be there?"

"Well, Chris." Their shoes echo on the frostbitten sidewalk. "Andy and Melissa. A few others from college. Plus a bunch of Chris's work buddies from Amazon."

"And they all knew *her*?"

His voice softens. "Yes, but now they'll know *you*."

Elle gazes up at the apartment building, her breath white against the dark sky.

"It's going to be fun, Elle." He guides her toward the door.

Stepping inside out of the cold, Elle sighs. There's a man in the lobby reading a book. He doesn't lift his head as Elle and Tom walk toward the elevators.

With a ding the doors close, and Elle says, "This is fancy."

"More so than I thought. He and Jack bought it recently—I haven't seen it yet."

She stares down at her shoes, black suede, scuffed. Twinkles of frost speckle their surface, melting into the material as she watches. Her stomach sinks with the upward glide of the elevator, and she works to steady herself and the cake as it comes to a halt.

"You're sure I look upscale enough?"

Ding.

"You look incredible," Tom says.

They make eye contact and smile as the doors open. Again, his hand lands on her back, the other one holding the bowl of whipped cream. This time, though, Elle *does* feel a little comforted. She thinks to herself how much she loves Tom, a slow-burning ember in her heart, and right when she's about to tell him, he says, "Can you hear the music?"

Tom leads the way out of the elevator. Elle listens, and yes, she can hear the music, a faint thumping at the end of the hall. Elle glances down at the cake as she walks, stepping carefully.

"How many of your college friends will be there?" she asks.

"Chris made it sound like a lot." He glances at her. "Don't worry; they're harmless."

"I want them to like me," she says lightly, but she feels uneasy. She would rather be eating ice cream and watching the ball drop on TV with Bonnie, but the thought makes her feel bad—she also wants to be with Tom, having fun.

"Are you having a case of the *introverts*?" Tom asks playfully.

They approach the door, and Elle hears the boisterous chatter of voices, people there already. She doesn't want to bring up his ex-wife or her insecurities. "Maybe a little."

Tom stops and gives her a kiss. "You look great, the cake will be a hit, and they'll all love you."

Her shoulders relax a little, and she shifts her fingers underneath the cake. "Okay."

"Apartment five twenty-two," Tom says, pointing.

Following him toward the door, the burgundy carpet scuffing under her heels, she takes a deep breath. Scolding herself for blowing things out of proportion, Elle glances down at the cake, telling herself that it will indeed be popular—and so will she. But while she's musing, they're suddenly at the door much quicker than she thought, and she walks straight into Tom, and then she's falling, and the cake is slipping from her grip, and she sees the **522** on the door right before she crashes straight into it, cake splattering against the crème-colored paint. Tom isn't there in time to catch her; her palms and knees take the brunt of the fall. Legs curling under her body, with cake all over her hands, the bottom of her dress, the door, and the welcome mat, Elle's eyes brim with tears.

Tom's there, his hand on her elbow, helping her up. "Are you all right, honey? Are you all right?"

Before she can answer, the door opens outward, nudging Elle in the shoulder. A blond man in a blue button-down pokes his head out.

"Tom, you made it," the man says, and then, as he swings the door out farther, his face scrunches. "What happened? Oh, shit. Did I do this? Did I open the door right into you?"

Before Elle can say no, Tom says, "Oh, c'mon, man, at least wait five minutes before you pick on my girlfriend."

Chris shakes his head. "I thought all apartment doors were made to open inward—you'd think the fancy-pants designers of this building would have a clue."

"You'd think," Tom says.

Chris claps him on the shoulder. "Gah, I'm so sorry! Elle, right?" he asks. "Chris. Here, let's get you cleaned up."

With Tom's hand still on her elbow, Elle steps over the mess and follows Chris through the large, airy apartment, clusters of people pausing their conversations to look right at her. Her palms are stinging, ankles trembling. She can barely walk straight from the shock of the fall. Tom's grip on her arm is strong. This is a disaster.

Chris leads them down a hall and into a bathroom, flips on the light. "Here you go," Chris says. "I'll clean up the mess at the door. Again, I'm so sorry." He disappears down the dimly lit hall again.

Tom closes the door and guides Elle to sit on the toilet. "Are you okay?"

Elle shakes her head, eyes filling with tears. Tom hands her a tissue, and she dabs under her lash line.

"If it's any consolation, I thought you stuck the landing."

His comment makes her let out a breath of laughter.

"A perfect ten. The other competitors don't stand a chance."

"I tripped before he opened the door," Elle says. "It's not Chris's fault at all."

"I know," Tom says.

"Why'd you let him think it's his fault?"

Tom shrugs. "It's less embarrassing for you that way," he says. "Chris won't care. If anything, he'll just be nicer to you tonight."

Elle's not sure what to think, what to say. Ankles still shaky, she stands up and kisses Tom, a long kiss. It makes her feel better—*he* makes her feel better. When they part, he brushes the hair out of her eyes.

"I really wanted some of that cake," Tom says.

Her lips purse. "I can make another."

"Just for me?"

Elle nods, turning on the sink. "Anything for you." She washes the cake off her hands, then gets to work dabbing her dress with a wad of damp toilet paper.

Tom slides his hand down her side, over her ass. "Anything?" He squeezes.

"Mm-hmm." His attention makes her cheeks flush; she can see it in the mirror. A wipeout, covered in cake, and he still thinks she's sexy. The idea makes her whole body buzz with warmth.

She sits back down on the toilet to examine her knees, which now, out of the fray, have started to hurt. She wads more toilet paper and dabs her tights. They're torn, a few beads of blood forming on the bare skin of her right thigh.

"I'm bleeding," she says, and Tom kneels in front of her to get a better look.

"Does it hurt?"

"Not too bad," she says.

He opens the mirrored cabinet, finds a bottle of peroxide, and applies some to her knee with a tissue. Elle flinches, her scrapes fizzing, but the sting quickly subsides.

A knock disturbs the muffled background of music, reverberating through their enclosed space. "Everything okay?" Chris calls in. "You two better not be boning in there."

"So what if we are?" Tom opens the door, and Elle follows him out, not quite ready, but she can't stay in the bathroom forever. Chocolate-free, she still feels wholly embarrassed, hyperaware of the music thumping and the chatter just down the hallway.

"I'm so sorry about your cake," Chris says. "It looked so good. I had to actively resist eating some right off the floor."

Elle finds herself smiling. "Dang," she says.

Chris leads them through the clusters of people, some dancing, most just standing and chitchatting with drinks in hand. In the kitchen, a few people are mingling near the alcohol, and Chris clears a path through. "What'll it be?" The counter is cluttered with bottles of wine, whiskey, vodka, soda, juice, and more.

Tom says, "Beer? Amber."

While Chris grabs one from the fridge, Tom pours Elle a Solo cup of red wine. He hands it to her, and she takes a big sip right away, reveling in the heat it spreads throughout her chest, the bite of the tannins on her tongue.

"Better?" Tom says.

Elle takes another long sip. "Getting there."

"Elle, I'd introduce you to Jack, but he went out for ice."

"Later," Tom says.

Chris nods. "He'll be even more upset about the cake. He's a chocolate fan."

Elle purses her lips. "Next time we visit, I'll make another."

"And I'll stay clear of the door." Chris chuckles.

They mingle in the kitchen awhile, chatting with Chris about his work at Amazon and the growth of the company. Tom only briefly mentions his work at the college, how tiresome it has become for him. Twenty minutes go by, and Jack comes home, introduces himself, tells them about med school, and then moves on as well. Elle focuses primarily on her wine, pouring another cup, the conversation gone in a blur. Soon, Tom leads her into the main room, where he sees an old friend whom Elle has never met. Her muscles seize at yet another introduction but quickly ease again with another sip of wine. No one has called her Miranda yet.

"Rav," Tom says, giving the man a hug. "This is my girlfriend, Elle."

He shakes her hand. "Ravi. Nice to meet you." His eyes rest on her a moment before darting back to Tom. "*This* is your girlfriend? She's way out of your league."

"Oh, I know," Tom says, squeezing her close. "Rav was my roommate freshman and sophomore years."

Her head starting to swim from all the wine, she tries to remember what Tom has told her about Ravi. "The architect, right?"

Ravi dips his gaze at Tom. "You told her about me?"

Tom waves him off, and Elle asks, "Have you designed any buildings I would recognize?"

"My biggest project so far is designing a few of the new Bellevue College buildings."

"Wow," Elle says, but before she can say more, another woman comes up, wearing a short, silver sequin dress. Compared with the other woman, Elle feels altogether ragged. Her tights ripped, her palms scuffed, her makeup smudged.

"This is my fiancée, Brandy," Ravi says. "Brandy, this is my old roommate, Tom, and his girlfriend, Elle."

Brandy shakes their hands, a charm bracelet on her thin wrist jingling. "You're the baker, right?" she asks Elle.

A little surprised, Elle says, "Yeah, did you see my big entrance?"

"No? Ravi told me that his old roommate was dating a baker. That's so cool," she says. "I can't bake to save my life. Burn everything."

"She makes great toast, though," Ravi says, and they all laugh.

More conversation, and then Tom and Elle peel away so Tom can grab another beer. Walking closely through the crowd—which has now doubled since they arrived—Tom says, "See? No one cares about what happened."

The room wobbling just a little from the wine, Elle says, "I guess you're right." The fall. Her tattered appearance. The cake ruined. With the alcohol, the whole thing begins to seem like a cartoon, slapstick.

So what about the cake? So what about Tom's first marriage? She's supposed to be having fun. And Tom's right: no one seems to care—about any of it.

"You want more wine?"

"No, I should slow down."

Tom grabs a beer from the fridge, opens it, and then guides Elle back into the main room to talk with more people. Elle spots Andy and Melissa, who they've had dinner with before, and she heads right to them, comforted by the familiar faces. Tom peels away for a bit, but Elle's ankles aren't so wobbly anymore, and she talks to Melissa for a long while, venturing to the food table together to munch on cheese and crackers and grapes between giggling about how similar Tom and Andy are, always grading papers.

"I swear, if he could, he would write on *me* with that red pen of his!" Melissa says.

Elle bobs her head. "Tell me about it."

"I'm eager to see where this tutoring thing takes them."

Reaching for more cheese, Elle says, "What's that?"

"Tom hasn't told you? They've been talking about starting an online tutoring business."

She feels her brow crease. "Tom hasn't said a word." Suddenly self-conscious about being out of the loop, Elle pops the cheese in her mouth.

"Maybe I ruined a surprise," Melissa says.

Before Elle can shrug it off, Tom reappears. "Want to dance?"

Elle looks out across the dimly lit room. Many people are dancing now, and as she considers it, someone turns up the music. "Oh, sure," she says, and Tom grasps her hand and whisks her away.

The music is loud in the center of Chris and Jack's living room. "Melissa said something about a tutoring business," Elle says into Tom's ear.

Embarrassment spreads across his face, lips pressed together, eyes searching some distant corner of the room. Squirmy, he waves off the topic. "Oh, it's just an idea we're humoring. Probably a pipe dream fueled by my thirties."

She shakes her head, trying to be encouraging. "It's normal for you to want to do bigger and better things, especially now." He didn't take turning thirty-two last month very well, and Elle knows that the faculty drama at the college hasn't helped.

"I didn't want to bother you with it."

"It sounds interesting," Elle says. "You should've told me."

"You're right." He touches her cheek, his own expression softening. "I forgot how supportive you are."

"I want to hear more about it later," Elle says.

"Then you will."

The music swells, and they let the matter disintegrate. He dances with his hands on her waist, holding her body close, rocking her to the rhythmic drums of a song she doesn't recognize but likes. She feels the bass in her chest with each beat, a little wild, a little sensual. They're in their own private world, dancing together. She thinks of Tom's care in the bathroom earlier, letting Chris believe it was his fault. Tom's support all the time, really. Early mornings at the bakery, tired afternoons. She's glad to have the chance to support him too. Staring into his eyes, feeling his breath on her face, the music reverberating between them, she can't help but feel at ease.

It's getting late. Everyone has liquor in them now. She laughs as Tom spins her in a circle, wiggles his shoulders. Silly. More songs dash by. She begins to feel sticky in her tights; Tom has rolled up his shirt-sleeves. Elle realizes how uptight she's been feeling. Long days baking with not enough time for fun.

"Are you having a good time?" he asks.

"Yeah," she says. "I'm really glad I came."

"Me too," Tom says, and he kisses her cheek.

Soon, the lights flicker, and someone yells that it's almost midnight. Chris is handing out tall plastic champagne glasses filled with bubbly. Someone has turned down the music and turned on the TV, a newscaster talking with the Space Needle in the background. Elle glimpses the clock in the corner of the screen: 11:56 p.m. She looks around for Tom and sees him making his way through the crowd toward the kitchen. Chris hands her a glass of champagne and a confetti popper. The room crowds around the TV, inching closer, shoulders bumping. Elle peers around and spots Tom coming back with a bottle of water. Thank goodness. He hands it to her, and she drinks half. He drinks the rest. Chris passes by, and she realizes Tom doesn't have a champagne glass. She says so to Tom.

"I'll share yours," Tom says.

11:58 p.m.

Tom settles behind Elle, his hands wrapped around her stomach. The image on the TV is panning over the mass of people clustered underneath the Space Needle. The room falls quieter by the second, and when the clock strikes 11:59 p.m., Tom whispers in her ear, "Elle."

Her heart is thumping in her throat from the dancing, the excitement. "Yeah?"

"We're approaching another year together."

"I know. It's great," she says.

"You're so talented and sexy and smart and sweet," he says, lips grazing her neck, his voice becoming low, serious. "And I can't imagine my life without you. I want to start 2008 off right. Start the rest of our lives this new year."

Elle turns her head toward him, realizing what's happening. Body quivering, heart pounding wildly in her chest like the beat of a dough mixer, she turns around. "Tom?"

He sinks to one knee as the countdown begins.

"Elle, I love you."

The newscaster and everyone in the apartment yell, "Ten . . . nine . . ."

"I want to spend the rest of my life with you."

"Eight . . . seven . . . six . . ." A few people in the room notice what's happening and turn away from the TV, staring right at Elle and Tom. "Five . . ." He pulls a black box out of his pocket and opens it. Elle glances from the cushion-cut ring to his face. Her hands come up to cover her mouth.

"Will."

"Four . . ."

"You."

"Three . . ."

"Marry."

"Two . . ."

"Me?"

"One!" The TV erupts with applause, with "Happy New Year's!" but everyone in the apartment is silent now, waiting for Elle's answer.

Flooded with a rush of heat, emotion, dizzying surprise, she says, "Yes! Yes, of course!" Tom stands, and the room fills with cheers, with congratulations, with laughter. Elle rushes into his arms, kissing him, burying her face in his collar, listening to the sounds of the fireworks on the TV, the newscaster's voice welcoming Seattle into 2008.

"Can I put the ring on your finger?" Tom says, arms coming to her shoulders, easing her away from his embrace.

She holds her hand out, wrist shaking uncontrollably. He slides the cool silver onto her finger, the ring glistening in the TV light. Before she can kiss him again, Tom's friends are crowding around, shaking his shoulder, clapping his back. The women circle Elle, wanting to see the ring and squealing when they do. It feels heavy on her finger. Someone says, "At least a carat," and maybe it's Brandy, but Elle isn't sure in the commotion. Her head is swimming, and she wishes she hadn't drunk so much. Had she known, she wouldn't have. Still, her body is awash with heat, tingling, unbelieving. She goes to Tom's side again, and he wraps his arm around her waist. She can't stop looking at him, the smile on his face, wide and eye crinkling.

"Did you know?" he asks.

"I had no idea."

"I thought the night was ruined with that cake," he says. "But I couldn't wait any longer."

"What cake?" Elle says.

September 26, 2015

Over six weeks after Elle found out

She can't help it. When Bonnie and Charlie go out to run errands together, and Elle is left sitting on the couch, again, she can't help but think of home. She's been gone for over a week now, and no calls. No texts. Nothing. Is Tom trying to give her space? Or does he simply not care? Elle can't bear to think the latter is true, not after nine years, not even after the affair. It can't be possible that all his feelings for her are gone. Transferred so easily to someone else.

Elle closes her eyes, not wanting to admit to herself that perhaps she *does* still love him. Among the anger and hurt and shame is a small piece of something still there, like a pristine photograph amid the wreckage of their marriage. She bends her knees up under herself and checks her phone again, but still nothing. Not even a text from Owen, which admittedly is a relief, if not also a little disheartening. He texted another few times throughout the week, usually when she was at the bakery, and no matter what, she averted him: *Can't, early morning tomorrow. I'm so busy this week. I have to work, sorry.*

Elle sighs and takes a sip of her tea. An issue of *Women's Health* rests on her lap, but she has yet to flip it open. She resists checking her phone for the third time in the past ten minutes, time crawling, forcing her to feel each wave after wave after wave of various emotions, the worst of which is a dreadful uncertainty: Why isn't she good enough? What does the other woman possess that Elle does not? Do his friends know? Is she a laughingstock at his office? A part of her doesn't want to know, doesn't want to find out.

Standing, Elle walks into the kitchen to refresh her tea, which has gone cold for the second time this afternoon. With her elbows on the counter, hands wrapped around her mug, she rests her head on the granite. Down the hall, Bonnie's dryer rumbles. Elle listens for a few seconds, noting the ticks in random sequence, probably a button tumbling against the metal drum. Then she has a thought: clothes.

Elle walks back into the living room, leaving her tea to cool in the kitchen. She picks up her phone and texts Bonnie: *Stopping home for more clothes, be back later tonight.*

With the whoosh of the text being sent, Elle rushes into the guest room. She puts on a sweater, grabs her purse, and smooths her hair in the mirror before leaving. There's a skip in her heart as she closes Bonnie and Charlie's door behind her.

~

Tom's car isn't there. Not that she expected it to be, just that she hoped.

Opening her door, Elle shakes the thought from her mind. Hoped for what? That he'd be home, rose petals in the doorway, chardonnay on the counter, telling her it was all a joke? No. The truth is that she doesn't know what she was hoping for, other than perhaps just to see him. See him and what, though? She likes to think that if he were home, she would yell. But they've done enough yelling, and she isn't even the yelling type.

Elle unlocks the front door, opens it slowly. Inside, their house has an empty chill to it. Flipping on the light, she realizes that things are just as she left them. Velcro runs up, purring, rubbing against her leg.

She bends down, scratches behind his ear. He meows, a long, high note, stretched out as if to say, *Where have you been?* Then another, sharper meow before darting into the kitchen. Elle follows him to find that his bowl is empty. A few broken kibbles rest at the bottom of the blue porcelain. Sharp guilt spurs her side at the thought of the cat going hungry in the midst of Elle and Tom's feud. She's comforted when she spots the guts of a mouse just inside the cat door—at least he wasn't *completely* without food. She taps the edge of his water bowl with her toe and sees that it, too, is low. Setting her purse on the counter, Elle opens the pantry and grabs Velcro's food. He erupts in a series of meows, hushing only when his bowl is completely filled again, teeth crunching on his fresh feast.

As she puts the bag of cat food back in the pantry and goes to replenish Velcro's water, Elle's attention turns back to Tom. Where is he?

It doesn't take her long to check the rest of the house, searching for a sign of him. No ties hung over their bedpost, not even a used cup in the kitchen sink. The thermostat is as she left it, turned down, which explains the chill that suggests the absence she doesn't want to admit: that he hasn't been home since she left for Bonnie's ten days ago.

Elle sits down in their living room, and Velcro, full bellied and purring, hops on her lap. It's four p.m. She strokes his peach-colored coat, running her fingers over each dark striation down his back. Hair clings to her black pants, but she doesn't think much of it at this moment. What she wants to know is where her husband went.

He's probably with the other woman, staying at her place. While the thought sickens her, she realizes another level of wrongness to it: ever since she confronted him about cheating, he's actually been home *more*. But after her being out all night with Owen, who knows? Maybe Tom *is* at his mistress's place after all. Every thought she cycles through leads her back to utter uncertainty.

Elle checks her phone, considering texting him, when she notices she has a message from Bonnie, from an hour ago: *No, don't go. You left to get distance. Don't ruin that.*

Elle texts back: *Already here. Tom is gone . . . ?*

Bonnie's response is instant: *Huh?*

It doesn't take Bonnie and Charlie long to get there, their car still full of groceries. Elle explains his absence, why she thinks it's strange.

"He would've at least stopped at home, and he would have fed Velcro," Elle says.

Her best friend nods, half hugging Charlie.

"I want to stay here tonight," Elle says. "Just in case he stops by."

"No, Elle. The whole point of staying at our place is so you can clear your head. Sitting around here worrying about Tom isn't going to help that," Bonnie says.

"I'll worry about him anyway. At least here I can make sure the cat doesn't starve."

"Look, I know you don't want to hear this, but, Elle, he's probably somewhere with *her*, assuming you're here taking care of things. He up and left."

"Just like I did," Elle retorts. "He was home all the time before I went to your house, more than usual. And now nothing?" Elle shakes her head, feeling worked up. She has a funny feeling in her chest that something is off.

"Elle," Bonnie says, but she doesn't finish her thought.

"I appreciate you taking care of me, Bonnie, but I want to stay here tonight," Elle says.

Bonnie looks up at Charlie and then back to Elle. "All right. I won't stop you."

"Thanks."

"We should get going; the ice cream is probably melting," Charlie says. "If you need anything, call us."

"I'm fine. I just want to be here in case he comes home," Elle says.

"You're such a worrier," Bonnie says. "He doesn't deserve you." She gives Elle a hug. "Love you."

"Love you," Elle says.

She follows them out onto the porch, waves as they drive away. Turning back inside the house, Elle looks at Velcro sitting on the couch. "Where is he?" she asks him.

August 13, 2015

One day after Elle found out

When he admits he cheated, the next thing Elle asks is, "How long?" How long has her husband been sleeping with the other woman? She knows the answer already, but she wants to hear him say it.

Evening cold clings to his body: the chill of dying summer. Elle, suddenly sure he was just with the woman, stands and gets as far from the man who was once her husband as she can without leaving the bedroom.

How long?

"Four months?"

He says it like a question, but it is not one. She says it as a way of comprehending: "Four."

They stand there in tense silence, listening to the bedside clock ticking.

Elle asks, "Did you tell her you were already getting a divorce, that you'd been 'separated for months'?"

"That's low."

"Well, what do you want me to say, Tom? It's not like this is a new deal for you."

"I've been faithful for eight years, Elle."

"And we've been together for nine."

September 26, 2015

Over six weeks after Elle found out

Nine p.m. and nothing, but what did she expect? Elle hasn't seen Tom for eleven days, and if he left, there's no reason he would come back home tonight, the one night she's there waiting for him. She wants to be angry or not care, but she can't help but worry. Nine years. Things are different now, but has he really changed that much? Has she? Elle knows her husband. Despite everything, he would've at least told her he was leaving.

Unlike she did.

Elle's been sitting on the couch with Velcro watching *How I Met Your Mother* reruns, laugh tracks set to misunderstandings flashing by on the screen while she eats cereal with half-and-half because there's no milk. She isn't really watching, though. Of course not. She keeps checking her phone as if something's going to change within the next ten minutes, or five, but it has been hours and, really, days now of nothing. Elle clenches her teeth against the prospect of something actually bad happening to him. As much as she would like to not care what the hell he's out doing, she can't help but feel concerned. He's probably with *her*, but the possibility that he's not, that maybe he's gotten into a car crash or a mugging or *something*, keeps Elle shifting in her seat. She checks her phone. Maybe she should text him?

She imagines Tom at the other woman's house, his phone lighting up. What would he say: "It's my wife"? Or "ex-wife"? She imagines the phone buzzing in the back pocket of a mugger, or on the side of the road among broken glass and black tire marks.

Her phone dims, and she taps the screen to wake it up. She types, *Are you okay?* then deletes it. She types, *We should talk*, then deletes it. She types, *Where are you?* and hits send.

Fidgeting in her seat, she stares at the screen on the cushion next to her until it goes dark. Her cereal has gotten mushy. She stands up and, the belt of her robe dragging on the floor, places her bowl in the sink. The next episode is starting; she can see it from the kitchen. Velcro is tiptoeing along the back of the couch, uprooted when she got up. She can't stand the idea of sitting back down. Instead, she opens her cabinets and takes a quick mental inventory. Enough ingredients for a small batch of her favorite cookies. Baking will make her feel better, get her mind off things.

Checking the time once more—it has been four minutes—she slides her mixer away from the wall, into the middle of the counter. Next, she retrieves her book of recipes on her laptop, only to realize that this one is not in there. She's never written it down. Perhaps tonight, while they're baking, is a good time to do so.

And by the time she's done, maybe Tom will be home.

Double-Chocolate Comfort Cookies

Impulsively check the clock; remind yourself that you're baking these cookies to take your mind off something. Measure out 1 cup of semisweet chocolate chips, eat a few, and then melt the rest. Eat another handful, straight from the bag, while you watch the glass bowl spin for 2 minutes on half power inside the microwave. Don't let the dull hum make you antsy; don't blame yourself if it does.

Preheat the oven to 350° and check the clock again. It has only been 2 minutes. Deep breath. Turn your attention toward sifting 1 cup of flour, ¼ cup of cocoa powder, 1 teaspoon of baking powder, and ½ teaspoon of salt. Set aside.

Cream 5 tablespoons of butter. Allow the rhythm of the mixer to enchant you. Stare into the bowl, the rich, creamy scent wafting up at you, until the butter is pale and fluffy. Add ¾ cup of light brown sugar, ¼ cup of granulated white, and become entranced once again. Don't allow yourself to grip the table or clench your fingers into your palms, as much as you think that might help; rest your hands flat on the counter and focus on the baking.

Your mind will inevitably circle back around to what you're supposed to forget, so at that time, whisk. Add 2 eggs to the mixing bowl and watch those beat in. The mixture will become looser, more orange. When you add 1 teaspoon of vanilla and 1 teaspoon of espresso powder, the batter will take on a speckled brown tint. Revel in the intoxicating smells, now sweet and earthy and familiar. When you add the chocolate, the batter will take on a scent of warmth, of comfort. You'll feel a little better. Don't let your self-awareness take you again down that dark path of unease. If you feel it looming, turn off the mixer and scrape down the sides of your bowl. Be thorough. Add the sifted drys; beat until well mixed.

At this point you'll have a real, recognizable chocolate dough. Have a taste. It'll present itself as an explosion of chocolate, *but more than that, something deep and complex, full bodied in flavor. Appreciate the sugars' grit, the disintegration of the dough on your tongue. Salivate. Have more. Scrape down the sides of the bowl and mix a little longer, adding some chocolate chips for texture. Listen to their metallic rattling as they bang against the sides of the mixing bowl, prominent over the rev of its motor. Then, using a spoon, portion the dough into golf balls and space on a parchment-lined cookie sheet.*

They'll bake for only 10 minutes—yes, 10. Whatever it is that's upsetting you might try to prod at your mind during this time. Lick the mixing paddle, the spoon, the inside of the bowl if you have to. Clean up your mess. Write down a recipe. 10 minutes. It will go by quickly if you keep busy.

It's likely that the timer will still startle you when it goes off. Open the oven and check the cookies—do they look under-cooked? Good. Set them on a cooling rack and let them breathe. They'll firm up as they cool. When they're no longer hot to the touch, have one. You might need a fork. They look like cookies on the outside but will resemble brownies toward their middles. They're good with ice cream or plain, room temperature or heated up. You can even freeze them for later occasions, thawing them in the microwave whenever you need a hit. Go with whatever makes you feel better. The most decadent, the most indulgent, or maybe just the least effort.

~

Elle sets her plate aside, licking chocolate off her lips. She forces herself not to look at her phone. Worry still consumes her, getting worse by the hour, like dough rising, each guilty or panicked or angry thought like a grain of yeast, escalating things. Again, she considers calling him, or anyone, but she tells herself to wait another day. She looks around for Velcro but doesn't see him. Probably on the bed, getting hair on the matelassé. Glancing at the TV—which has now switched to some sort of Christian programming—Elle grabs the remote and turns it off. She considers leaving her phone downstairs but can't bring herself to do so. Slipping it into her robe pocket, she checks to make sure the oven is off and turns off the downstairs lights.

She climbs their stairs in the dark, having memorized the contours of this house they've lived in now for seven years. The railing glides under her palms, worn smooth from use. A few of the steps creak under her weight, a soft gasping she has learned to expect and appreciate. There's satisfaction in knowing something so well—and knowing some-*one* so well. Like a recipe by heart, every step, every ingredient, every taste. So familiar that it feels a part of her, as soon as her fingers dip into flour or reach skin. Each knead like an argument, each release a kiss, until something has been made out of practically nothing, a string of separate ingredients mixed together like a courtship until they make one whole, grown stronger by each trial, each compression under two palms.

Elle finds herself standing in the doorway of their bedroom, swaying on her tired legs, thoughts of baking rocking her side to side, heart beating like a KitchenAid. She hasn't slept in their bed for weeks, having made the guest room hers after the night she confronted Tom. Their bed is how Tom left it, unmade but with the covers pulled up over the pillows as she's nagged him to do so many times. *Don't leave the covers back, or Velcro will get hair in the bed.* Sure enough, the cat is curled up at the base of the bedspread. When she approaches, he lifts his head and starts purring, pushes his crown into her hand. He was always Tom's cat, choosing her husband's lap over hers every time—despite the fact that Tom got Velcro for her. She scratches behind his velvet ears, his wide yellow eyes staring up at her, slowly blinking.

Circling to the other side of the bed, Elle counts the change on Tom's nightstand. Forty-eight cents, plus the top of a broken golf tee. Also on his nightstand, pushed between the lamp and the wall, is a stack of books: mostly nonfiction, probably ones he has to review for work, thick and dense looking—plus the book of poems. She slips the poetry out of the stack, hoping to find a bookmark, but there isn't one. Placing it back on top of the pile, Elle runs the edge of the blanket through her fingers. She slips off her robe, peels back the covers, and slides in, the cold, untouched bedding enveloping her warm skin.

Tom's side of the bed. She flips the lamp off. Resting her head on his pillow, she can smell his shampoo: tea tree. She rolls over and takes another deep breath. The scent conjures up his image, the touch of his hands on her waist, the sound of his snores. She recalls the many nights he came to bed late, the many mornings she got out of bed early. She recalls him staying up to read, his breath on her neck when he switched off the light. Lying there awake, waiting for his hands to fall on her, breathing as if she were asleep until he rolled over and gave up.

Her chest swollen with emotion, Elle buries her face in his pillow. Things she thought she'd forgotten about him come roaring back, her throat closing, her eyes brimming against the pillowcase. Velcro pads along the bedspread, careful steps beside Elle's body until she feels his whiskers on her ear. She lifts her head and looks at his silhouette in the dark. He starts purring again. She looks at the clock to find that it's past midnight, checks her phone and then replaces it facedown on the nightstand, next to the change and the tee. Pulling the covers up to her cheeks, she wonders, *What happened to us?*

July 16, 2014

About thirteen months before Elle found out

In the arctic air-conditioning of the QFC on Holman, Elle and Tom are hungry and tired and searching for dinner. With him manning the cart, she walks ahead, a small list pinched between her fingers. Dishwasher soap, check. Paper towels, check. Cat food, check. Dinner, not yet.

"What about a rotisserie chicken?" she asks, wandering toward the deli.

Tom shrugs, unenthusiastic. "We could see if steak is on sale?"

"I looked; it's not."

He frowns.

Their grill has gone unused since they ruined chicken kebabs at the start of the summer. "What about hot dogs? We could grill them."

"That sounds good and easy."

"Hot dogs it is," Elle says, picking up the pace. She glances over her shoulder to see Tom right behind, pushing the cart. He smiles.

With Elle in the lead, they weave past other customers, arriving, finally, at the hot dog section. Staring down at the endless options—bun length, ballpark, beef franks, cheddar dogs—Elle searches for something familiar.

"What's the kind you like? Nathan's?"

"Huh?"

"What brand?"

He doesn't answer.

Elle looks up to see his eyes elsewhere, staring down the cold case toward a produce bin filled with melons. There's a woman there, at least six months pregnant, holding a cantaloupe to her nose. She sets it back down, reaches for another. Her long brunette hair falls across her shoulders as she tips forward, biting a red lip in concentration. She appears precarious with her big belly, leaning across the honeydews and watermelons.

Elle glances at Tom again. "So . . . Nathan's?"

"Sure, whatever."

Wariness seeps into her veins like ice water. "Tom? What is it?"

"That's Miranda." Pushing his way between their cart and the refrigerated case, he turns his back to her, picking up a pack of Nathan's ballparks. "Let's go."

But Elle can't tear her eyes away from her husband's ex-wife. She saw a picture once but has never met her in person. She's taller than Elle expected, almost Tom's height. High cheekbones and copper skin. Her blush-colored dress is as delicate as a jellyfish, silk ruffles flowing beneath the bulb of her belly.

Tom rushes their cart back down the aisle, heading for the checkout stands. For a moment, Elle is caught between them: Miranda, unsuspecting, and Tom, fleeing. He glances back, first at Elle, then past her. The ice in Elle's blood intensifies, chilling her lungs; she feels a pang of jealous discomfort. He turns away again, the cart squeaking against the linoleum. Elle watches him go, her legs anchored.

From behind, Elle hears a voice, light and sweet: "Tom?"

Her husband's shoulders hunch forward. He stops, pivots. At first, his expression is hard, then blank, then cordial. "Miranda?" he says, as if he's just noticed her, as if he hasn't just been running from the prospect of speaking to her.

"I thought that was you," she says, a little breathless, balancing her shopping basket on her hip.

Tom returns to Elle's side as Miranda walks up.

"It's me," Tom says, his voice strained. Then he adds, "And this is my wife, Elle."

"Nice to meet you," Miranda says.

"What are you doing in town?" Tom asks.

"Dad's selling his house, so we came to help him move." While she talks, Miranda idly touches her belly; her wedding ring stands out, heavy looking on her slender finger. "I forgot how much I missed the breeze off the water; Boulder has been in the hundreds."

"Jeez," Elle says. "Too hot for me."

"Me too," Miranda says. "I could melt. A good excuse for popsicles, though, which I've been craving nonstop."

Tom smiles, but it's forced. Elle touches his forearm, running her hand from wrist to elbow. "We still need bananas," she lies. The bananas are just a few produce stands over, an easy escape.

"How've you been, Tom?" Miranda asks.

"Oh, well enough." He gestures at Elle before touching her back, right between her shoulder blades. To Elle's relief, he adds, "Hungry."

"Still teaching?" Miranda presses, unable to take a hint.

"Actually, I run my own business now. We both do."

"Oh," Miranda says. "Good for you."

Tom asks, "Still accounting?"

Miranda glances at Elle. "Riveting, right?"

"I wish I were better with numbers," Elle says.

A pause falls over the three of them.

Elle looks at Tom, taking advantage of the lull. "Bananas?"

"Yes." To Miranda, he adds, "Give my best to your father."

"Good seeing you, Tom," Miranda says.

He nods, already walking away. Once Miranda has disappeared down another aisle, Elle grabs a bunch of five bananas, setting them in their cart. She looks at Tom, but his expression is tight and distant. The two of them head for checkout in silence. It isn't until they're at their car that he says, "What are the chances?"

Elle lifts a bag into the trunk. "I'm sorry."

Wordless, Tom wheels the cart back to the store while Elle settles in the passenger seat, her head ringing. Why does Miranda still bother him after all this time? Elle thinks about her own past romances, how she wouldn't mind seeing them now. Elle and Tom haven't even spoken about Miranda in years; she's a part of Tom's past that hasn't stung Elle in a long, long time. But seeing her pregnant and aglow—that's different. Elle is most concerned by Tom's strained reaction.

Elle watches Tom wheel their cart into the stack. As he does, Miranda comes out of the store with a single paper bag, filled to its brim, cradled in her arms. She says something to him, and he nods. He makes a gesture, wrist twisting, thumb pointing out toward the parking lot. She smiles and touches his arm, and Tom takes a step back, saying one more thing before walking away.

When he returns to the car, his jaw is still clenched.

"What was that about?" Elle asks.

"More small talk." He starts the ignition.

"Why'd you gesture over here?"

"I told her I had to go."

They have to cross traffic to get home, and they sit in silence on the edge of the parking lot, watching cars whoosh by, waiting for a gap in the endless stream.

"She's pretty," Elle says.

"Don't do that."

"Do what?"

"Compare yourself to her." He eases on the gas, falling behind a Subaru stopped at the light that'll lead them home.

"I just meant—"

"It's okay." He turns on the radio.

She's too distracted to pay attention to NPR. As he drives home, all Elle can think about is Miranda. And cantaloupe—it would've been a nice appetizer while their hot dogs cooked.

~

After dinner, Tom picks up a book. His jaw hasn't relaxed since QFC, and Elle hasn't been able to coax him out of his distracted thoughts. As she cleans up the kitchen, she glances in his direction.

"Did you like dinner?"

"Yes," Tom says.

"I always forget how good hot dogs are."

"Me too."

"They remind me of baseball," Elle says. "We should go to a Mariners game."

He lowers his book. "Do you need something?"

"No. Am I bothering you?"

"I just want to know if I should put my book down or not."

Elle continues wiping down the counter, her back to him now. The bananas they bought to escape Miranda rest beside the coffee maker. It turns out they already had bananas, the old bunch growing brown. "You can read," she says. "I'll make banana bread."

Too-Many-Bananas Bread

Why is it that bananas are green forever, ripe for a moment, and brown too soon? Whether you bought more bananas than you needed or forgot to eat them while they were ripe, this recipe will save you. We all have old bananas lying around; life is full of overripe conversations. Here's how to put them to use.

Mash up 4 brown bananas—a fork is simplest, but a food processor will save you time. Throw in a cup of sour cream, a cup of oil, 2 cups of sugar. Blend until the food processor squeals. Add 4 eggs and 2 teaspoons of vanilla. Blend once more, briefly. This isn't a hoity-toity recipe; it's a practical distraction.

Transfer the liquid to a mixing bowl. It'll take you all of 30 seconds to fold in 3 cups of flour, 2 teaspoons of baking soda, and a teaspoon of salt. If you're feeling gnarled by life, add walnuts. If you're feeling naughty, add chocolate chips. If you're in a heated mood, add both.

Grease 2 bread pans with cooking spray. Add the batter, sprinkle some nuts and chocolate chips on top, and throw both pans in a 350° oven. Bake them side by side for over an hour; pivot halfway through baking; toothpick test when they look close. When they're done, let them cool until you can handle them. They'll slip free of their pans with little effort; set one on a plate, let cool, cover with plastic wrap. Freeze the other for later. Look forward to morning, when you'll enjoy a heavily buttered slice. If you can't wait, have some right away.

~

Their bedroom is dark, save for Tom's bedside lamp. He's sitting up against a stack of pillows, reading. When Elle walks in with two plates, he looks up over the brim of his book, replaces his bookmark, and sets it aside.

"That smells . . ." He breathes in. "Yum."

Sliding into bed beside him, Elle hands him a plate. She gave herself the end piece with extra butter; his piece is a little bigger, dappled with a cluster of chocolate chips. "Feeling better?" she asks.

"What do you mean?"

"You've been weird all night," Elle says, nudging him with her elbow.

He takes a bite, loosing a pronounced *mmmm*. "I haven't been weird."

"Yes. You have," Elle insists. "It's Miranda, right? Were you caught off guard?"

Chewing, he says, "It wasn't seeing her that caught me off guard."

"Then wha—"

"It was seeing her *pregnant*."

"Oh."

"It's just—"

"I know." Of course. Of course seeing Miranda pregnant would've bothered him—it's why they broke up in the first place. Different opinions about families: that was their deal breaker. To see her married and pregnant . . .

Elle, feeling suddenly inadequate, takes a bite of the bread.

In a small voice, Tom says, "It just got me thinking again."

"Thinking?"

"About kids."

Elle swallows, the lump of bread seemingly twice its actual size. Her mouth goes dry. "Kids?"

"You know I've always wanted kids. I think now's the time." He turns toward her, his arm resting against the upright pillows, his other hand coming to rest on Elle's leg. "Work is good. Stable. The bakery is flourishing. We're ready, right? It couldn't be better timing."

"Oh, Tom, I don't know." She looks into his eyes, where a flash of something—doubt, sadness, desperation?—flickers and then is gone.

"I know it's scary," he says. "But isn't it wonderful too?"

Elle thinks about Miranda, the swell of her belly, the way she cradled it as she spoke. In that grocery store, she looked like the most natural mother in the world. She looked content.

A dreadful thought occurs to Elle: Did seeing Miranda today make Tom regret ending their marriage?

A dark feeling grips hold of Elle's heart. How can she refuse him? How can she tell Tom she's not ready? It would crush him—or he would leave her. No, refusing him is not an option. Maybe this is the push she needs to feel ready; maybe when it happens, she'll be glad.

"Okay," Elle says, barely audible.

"Okay?" Tom's face lifts into a grin like she's never seen, his eyes brimming. "We'll start trying?"

"Yeah."

"Oh, Elle." He gathers her close, and she's thankful—she doesn't want him to see the fear in her eyes. She doesn't want him to see that she has no happy tears to shed.

~

The next day is double date night with Bonnie and Charlie. Tom and Elle, running a few minutes late, find the other couple already seated in the back corner of the little Italian place. For a Thursday night, it's surprisingly full.

"Long time no see," Bonnie says to Elle.

She laughs. "You look nice."

They parted at the bakery only a few hours ago, both with frosting in their hair. Now, Bonnie wears a white blouse and jeans, and Elle a simple black dress. The men are in their work suits, though Tom left his tie at home.

"Sorry to get started without you," Bonnie says, taking a sip of red wine. "We couldn't wait."

"Long week?" Tom asks Charlie.

"Understatement," Charlie says.

The waiter appears. "Drinks for you two?"

"Whatever she's having," Elle says, gesturing toward Bonnie.

"Negroni," Tom says.

The waiter bows slightly and hurries off.

"How's the world of online tutoring?" Charlie asks Tom, and just like that, the men are in their own conversation. Tom launches into the story he told Elle on the way to the restaurant: more web-developer issues as they expand their platform.

"Tell me about the kitchen remodel," Elle says to Bonnie, taking a sip of her water. "Do you have a game plan yet?"

Bonnie's cheeks redden. "No plan, actually. Something came up."

"Oh, yeah?"

"Yeah." The pitch in her voice rises. "You know how my mother has been struggling?"

"Sure," Elle says, coaxing her to continue.

"Well, it's—" Eyes wet, Bonnie whispers her next words. "We need to put her in assisted living."

"Oh, Bonnie."

Tipping her head into her hand, Bonnie whimpers, "She's going to end up in memory care. I know it. There's nothing we can do."

Elle touches her friend's arm. "I'm so sorry."

"It's all right. It's all right," Bonnie says, dabbing her eyes with her cloth napkin.

A different waiter delivers Elle's and Tom's drinks. The guys are oblivious to the conversation on the other half of the table. They've moved on to Charlie's latest case; he's gesturing, cheeks pinched in a wry smile. As the waiter walks away, Bonnie sits up a little straighter, as if to shake the sadness off her shoulders.

"I'm sorry," Elle repeats, because it's all she can think to say. She can only imagine the sense of loss that Bonnie must feel right now, her mother still living but gone at the same time.

"No, *I'm* sorry. I shouldn't be tearing up at the table."

"It's okay."

"It's just fresh in my mind. I had to call the remodelers when I got home, so it feels official."

"Why didn't you say anything at work?"

"I didn't want to cry there either," Bonnie exclaims. "And—I don't know. It freaks me out, I guess. Losing memory. Losing your sense of self."

"It might not happen like that," Elle says.

Bonnie picks up her wineglass. "But it will. That's just how Alzheimer's works."

The men, absorbed in conversation, break into laughter. When Elle glances back at Bonnie, she's wiping her face, the redness already fading from her eyes.

"Let's talk about something else," she says.

"You sure?"

"I need to get my mind off things tonight." Bonnie glances over her shoulder before saying, "How about that awful woman today?"

"Oh, God, she was *evil*," Elle says, launching into detail about the tiff she had with a grumpy customer. "Who knew people could get so heated about scones?"

Soon, the waiter is back, and the four of them scramble to look over the menus. Once the food is ordered, the conversation meanders, and for a while, the four of them talk all together. Elle avoids eye contact with Charlie as usual, but even that feels effortless tonight. The food comes, and they feast. They order more wine, and the laughter intensifies. They stay late, and other tables empty. By the time the bill comes and the two couples throw their cards on the pile, the sky is dim and purple.

"Well, this was fun," Charlie says. "Too fun for a Thursday."

"Oh, it's early enough," Tom says.

There's a couple standing at the front of the restaurant, clearly waiting for takeout, and Charlie's eyes rove over the baby carrier held firmly in the husband's grasp. Following his gaze, Tom says, "Oh, wow, look how little."

"Brand new," Charlie says distantly.

The parents wear wrinkled T-shirts. The mother's face is pale, dark circles prominent under the overhead mood lights of the entryway. Elle gulps. She and Tom decided not to tell anyone they're trying—not that they've even had sex since the decision or done away with the birth control. Elle took her pill this morning. One more day of comfort.

Tom squeezes Elle's leg under the table, but she doesn't meet his eyes. Instead, she looks at the baby. Bundled into the carrier, it's sleeping. Is she supposed to feel something? What is she missing? She glances at Tom, who appears to be caught up in a dream. This can't be where Elle's life is headed—is it? For her, there's no yearning. In fact, she doesn't feel anything.

Elle is relieved when the waiter returns with their cards and receipts. The focus shifts to figuring out the tip, and the moment is over. When Elle looks back at the doorway, the couple with the baby is gone.

Outside, the four of them part ways with hugs and laughter and little waves as they walk in opposite directions back to their cars. Tom grasps Elle's hand, a warm breeze swirling despite the late hour. Their car is a few blocks down, and they walk slowly. For a moment, it feels like old times. Holding hands. Full from dinner. Looking up at Tom, she recognizes the spark she still has for her husband.

But then he says, "I'm so glad we're trying. Did you see that baby? That'll be us someday."

"Yeah, maybe."

"Maybe?"

"Oh, Tom, I don't know."

"You don't know?"

Elle sighs. If she tells him how she truly feels, the spark could go out. "Just don't tell Bonnie and Charlie, okay?"

"I won't."

"Bonnie's mom has to go into a home," Elle says. "She's having a hard time."

"Oh, that's too bad."

"Yeah."

"Are you okay, Elle? You seem off."

"I'm fine, just worried about my friend."

He stops, facing her on the street. "Are you having second thoughts about kids?"

"I don't know."

"You are, aren't you?"

Maybe she's overthinking it. Maybe as time goes on, her excitement will grow. Maybe when she's holding her own child, it'll be different. That's what everyone says, right? It's different when it's your own? Staring up at her husband, her heart swells. She refuses to break his heart now, when someday she might feel differently.

"It's the wine," she says, walking again. "It's making me sleepy. Did you enjoy dinner?"

"Always," Tom says, falling in step with her once more. He pulls her close, kissing the top of her head while they walk. "Did you have fun?"

"I did," Elle says, thankful for the change in subject.

September 27, 2015

Over six weeks after Elle found out

Maybe she should check his phone bill.

After she wakes up on Tom's side of the bed, the house still empty, it occurs to Elle that perhaps his absence can be explained by his phone records. At their kitchen table, she opens her laptop and signs into their online account. She scrolls through the endless data, the countless incoming 800 numbers and Seattle numbers, New Jersey for his family, then an area code she doesn't recognize: 720. It's from a week ago. What is that?

Poised on the edge of her chair, her back straight, Elle isn't sure what to expect when she dials the number. She glances around the empty kitchen. The little clock on the windowsill ticks. Does she want to know? She closes her eyes, weighing her emotions. Her concern for Tom outweighs her dread of calling a strange number from his phone record. *It's not like Tom to be gone this long*, a small voice in the back of her head says. The agony of not knowing finally drives her to hit the call button. She taps her toe as it rings.

"Hello?" A female voice.

"Hello? Who is this?"

"You called me. Who are you?"

"This is Elle Hutton."

"It's Miranda."

Miranda?

When Elle was a little girl, there was an earthquake at school, and the whole class hid under their desks, just like they'd practiced in drills. The whole quake lasted a mere two minutes, but it felt like her world was crashing down. Books fell off the shelves, and her pencil case rattled off her desk, splitting open on the linoleum right next to her. She closed her eyes tight, and even after the shaking ended, no matter how much her teacher tried to convince her that it was safe again, she held on to the leg of her desk and refused to let go.

Knowing that Tom called Miranda is the emotional version of that earthquake. Everything she thought she knew is tumbling off the shelves, and she's hiding under her desk, waiting for it all to be over. How can she ever come out after this?

"Hello?" Miranda says.

"Sorry to call you." Elle calculates how awful it'll be to tell Miranda the truth. Tom's absence makes the house seem twice as large. Her desperation keeps her from hanging up.

"What do you need?" Miranda's voice is kind, concerned.

"Well, I—Tom's been missing for a few days. I was going through his phone bill, and . . ." She trails off, her throat thick with shame. Miranda probably thinks she's delusional.

"Oh." A pause. "I don't know where he is."

"Why did he call you?"

Miranda doesn't answer. Did the call drop?

Elle asks, "You still there?"

"Yeah, I'm here. I'm in Seattle visiting my dad, actually."

Tom saw her—Elle is sure of it. Maybe he's with her right now. Why else would Tom call up his ex-wife? Growing red in the face, anger flaring, Elle asks through clenched teeth, "You're in town?"

"Yeah."

"But you don't know where he is?" Elle asks pointedly.

"I haven't seen him, if that's what you mean," Miranda says. "Why don't you meet me in person? I have time this afternoon."

Elle's stomach does a flip. "Oh, I don't know—"

"Carkeek Park?"

"You can't just tell me over the ph—"

"I think it would be better to talk face to face."

What does that mean? Elle fears the worst. What if Tom wants to get back together with her? Is it possible he cheated on Elle with Miranda as well? Elle quivers and grips the table to steady herself. This is probably the point at which she should duck under the furniture.

"How about two o'clock?" Miranda asks. "In the upper field."

Elle has no choice but to say, "All right." The thought of meeting Miranda in person, willingly, is downright sickening. But her need for clarity overcomes her reservations. It's time she got the whole story.

"All right. See you then." Elle hangs up. What on earth did she just agree to?

~

It's a busy, sunny afternoon, and Elle is forced to drive around the Carkeek Park loop twice before she finds a parking spot. Her hands quiver, and her eyes are watery from a hasty application of eyeliner. She blinks, searching the sun-scorched field for the brunette hair of Tom's ex-wife. Children and parents are scattered everywhere: by the jungle gym, picnicking, even cooking hot dogs near a stand of picnic tables. More still are down at the beach, watching a pair of kiteboarders skim along the water. Surrounded by joy and laughter, all Elle can think about is the hot ball of worry and anger in the pit of her stomach.

Getting out of the car, Elle wanders toward the field and finally spots Miranda. She's sitting on a picnic blanket with her legs stretched out in a *V*. Her daughter toddles in front of her, held up by Miranda's guiding hands. The girl squeals. A couple of dolls and a plastic horse are haphazardly strewn on the blanket. Near a fat beach bag are some snacks: Cheerios, a banana, a sandwich wrapper, and some Babybel cheeses.

Miranda doesn't seem to notice Elle until she's standing right in front of them on the grass. "Oh, Elle, hello," she says, letting her daughter flop down on the soft blanket. The kid doesn't seem to notice Elle at all; she crawls toward one of the dolls.

"Hi," Elle says, hovering awkwardly.

Miranda stands, coming to her full height, a little taller than Elle. Her long legs glisten in the sun. She's barefoot, her toes painted red. "A nice day for the park," she says.

"I suppose it is." Elle stands with her feet pointed toward the beach, not willing to face Miranda squarely. It's an outrageous thing: meeting her husband's ex-wife at a park, by a picnic blanket, while Tom is missing.

"Better enjoy the nice weather while it lasts, right?" Miranda continues. "Before six months of Seattle gray."

"Gray is better than Colorado snow," Elle says. "But that's just me."

Miranda's daughter points at a rainbow kite twisting in a strong updraft above them; she slurs a questioning sound.

"Kite," Miranda says.

Her daughter looks up at Elle and lifts the doll toward her. Hesitating a little, Elle stoops to take the doll from the girl.

"That's kind of you, Sadie," Miranda says.

Sadie turns her attention to the plastic horse.

Elle sets the doll next to its companion on the blanket and rises out of her squat. "She's cute." In truth, Sadie's presence is unbearable. Elle can't stand the strangeness of watching this child that could've been Tom's—*would* have been, had Miranda been willing to have a family while she was with Tom.

"She's a stinker," Miranda says with affection.

Abruptly, Elle says, "Can you tell me what's going on? I just—I don't have all afternoon."

Miranda's expression hardens; she folds her arms. "I know this is terribly awkward," Miranda says. "You're a nice person, Elle—or at least you seem nice. And I thought you should hear this in person."

Elle braces for the inevitable news: *Sorry, but Tom and I are getting back together.* Miranda is wearing a white button-down and navy camp shorts, and her pretty hair has a golden sheen in the sun. Her wedding ring is missing from her finger. Elle wants to scream.

"Well?"

Miranda frowns. "As you know, Tom called me. He said he needed the name of his divorce lawyer. He couldn't remember it. He was never good at staying organized about those sorts of things—well, you probably are used to that. But anyway, I'm so sorry to break this news. I thought he would've told you by now—"

"Wait," Elle says, interrupting Miranda's rambling. "That's it?"

"What do you mean?"

"The divorce lawyer—that's the only reason he called you?" Elle knows she should be upset to learn that Tom also contacted a lawyer, but given that she thought he and Miranda were back together, it pales in comparison. The hot anger in her stomach dissipates, leaving only a smoldering resentment.

"Well, yeah."

"So you really don't know where he is?" This meeting was pointless.

"No, of course not."

"But you're not wearing your ring."

Miranda reflexively looks down at her hand, and then her eyes meet Elle's. "You thought he and I . . ." She shakes her head. "I forgot the ring at home is all." Her brow creases. "So you knew about the lawyer?"

"Well, no," Elle says. "But I have one myself."

She sighs big and deep. "I thought this would be news to you." Miranda laughs, a nervous chirp. "I was so afraid. How awful would that have been?"

Elle nods, not nearly as amused. She stares at Sadie, who is happily prancing the horse across the blanket's edge. The sun beats down on the three of them, and Elle realizes she forgot to put on deodorant.

Miranda says, "I even brought some mini macaroons. I know, it's stupid, but I figured I'd want something sweet if I were hearing this news from my husband's ex-wife."

Elle looks at her. "I'll take a macaroon."

"They didn't turn out the way I would've liked."

"I'll still take one."

Acquiescing, Miranda hunches over and digs through her bag. She pulls out a Tupperware and opens it up. Inside, the little toasted mounds are nestled amid parchment.

Elle steps closer, catching a whiff of Miranda's perfume, botanical and fresh. She selects a mini macaroon and takes a bite. It's chewy, coconutty, light. A hint of vanilla masks the fact that the batch was a tad overbaked. The top is crisp, though, adding a pleasing dimension to the texture. They would be delicious dipped in dark chocolate.

Elle has the sudden urge to weep. Where is Tom? If he's not seeing Miranda again, where could he be? She devours the macaroon as a way of hiding her emotion.

Miranda brushes a strand of hair from her face. "Is it okay?"

"Wonderful, thank you," Elle says, her voice muffled. "It's kind of you to have made them."

Miranda shrugs. "I feel like baked goods make everything better—especially a situation as strange as this one."

Elle bobs her head, reaching out for a second macaroon. Sadie has the same idea; she reaches up with eager, chubby fingers. Miranda compromises by opening a baggie of Cheerios; she drops a handful onto the Tupperware lid and lowers it onto the picnic blanket. Sadie pinches a Cheerio between her index finger and thumb and slides it into her mouth.

"Sorry to drag you all the way down here for news you already knew," Miranda says. "I just couldn't bear the thought of telling you over the phone. I know I'm probably the last person you want to see right now."

To be polite, Elle says, "The macaroons made it worth the trip."

Miranda smiles.

They each nibble one more macaroon in silence; nearby, a couple is unloading two toddlers from an SUV. Elle's mind keeps circling back to Tom and that dreadful unknowing in her gut.

"I'm sorry you two are having trouble," Miranda says. "Speaking from experience, I know it sucks."

Elle isn't comforted by her words; instead, they make it all feel worse. Elle has gathered nothing from this painfully uncomfortable meeting. Tom is still missing, and Miranda is still gorgeous, and Elle still feels deeply, terribly insecure over this whole mess. Miranda's kindnesses and macaroons hardly matter to Elle's anguish.

Elle brushes the crumbs off her fingers. "I should get going."

"I didn't mean to insert myself in your relationship," Miranda says in a rush.

"It's fine. I just—I'd like to get home now."

"Do you want any for the road?" Miranda asks, holding out the Tupperware.

Elle ignores her question. Instead, in a moment of boldness, she surprises herself by asking, "How did you know? I mean, about wanting Sadie?"

"What?"

"How did you know you were ready? Tom said—"

"Oh," Miranda says, understanding. "The family thing." She shrugs. "To be honest, I grew into it. Too little and too late for Tom, but that's in the past."

Elle glances down at Sadie. The child doesn't make her heart pitter-patter; she doesn't feel any longing for her own. She's more interested in Miranda's macaroon recipe than the little girl playing with dolls on the picnic blanket. Little does Sadie know, when she was just a baby bump, she set off something in Tom; Sadie has been disrupting Elle's life since before she was born.

Miranda continues, "I realized I'd regret *not* having a baby more than I would ever regret having one."

For the first time, Elle considers her own sense of regret. She can't imagine ever feeling a gap in her life that only a child could fill. Everything she wants can be found elsewhere: in family, friends, career. She sniffles, resisting tears. She mutters, "Sorry. I know it's a personal question."

"It's all right," Miranda says, not seeming to notice the wetness in Elle's eyes. "Why do you ask?"

"I haven't grown into it," Elle confides in a small voice. She glances at her shoes. "Probably too much information."

Miranda touches her arm, causing Elle to look up despite her tears. "I hope things work out for you, Elle," she says, surprising her.

Not *I hope things work out for you and Tom*. Or *I hope your marriage works out*. Just *I hope things work out for* you. Miranda's words rattle around in Elle's head all the way home.

~

Heading back from the park, Elle stops at the grocery store for more wine and some macaroon ingredients—perhaps she can recreate Miranda's recipe? When she arrives home, Tom still isn't there, and Elle's worry comes back with a vengeance. To distract herself, she texts Bonnie, who assures her that the bakery is running smoothly; in the process, she ignores a text from Owen that merely reads, *Hey*. She longs for contact from Tom, which makes her feel stupid because he doesn't deserve her concern. Yet here she is, worrying. Again, she occupies herself by baking.

Miranda's Macaroons

Recreating a recipe is a guessing game that hinges on taste and prior knowledge. Previous recipes will tell you that macaroons require coconut, egg whites, and sweetened condensed milk. Taste will tell you that vanilla is involved, and personal experience will suggest that chocolate is a worthy addition. Buy enough ingredients to experiment, set aside the time to try and fail and try again, and you might end up with this: one 14 oz can of sweetened condensed milk, 2 egg whites for hold, and 6 cups of finely shredded coconut. Mix into a big, sticky mess—just like life, isn't it?

On second thought, the mixture should be lumpier. Add another cup of coconut. The condensed milk is making things runny, so add a 3rd egg white as well. There—better. Splash in some real vanilla extract; then bend low and breathe in. Can you smell the vanilla notes? Is there balance between coconut, milk, and extract? Splash in a touch more vanilla for good measure. That's it.

A pinch of salt will help with that balance. Preheat the oven to 400° and move your oven rack to the top. Using a kitchen spoon and clean fingers, form balls no larger than silver dollars. They'll look like pale little haystacks; throw them in the oven and wait until they turn brown—but watch that they don't blacken on the bottom. While you wait, melt some dark chocolate in the microwave with a touch of heavy cream. Once they're out of the oven, dip the finished macaroons halfway into the chocolate and let it harden. Feel a sense of baking prowess and accomplishment when you taste them.

Here's something life doesn't give you: a recipe. You have to make it up as you go along, adjusting accordingly.

~

Elle takes another sip of merlot from her second glass and checks her phone, though she knows no one has called. Only just now has she thought to check the iPad, but it's missing from the drawer, probably in Tom's possession since she found out. She settles back on the couch; Velcro is fast asleep on the opposite side. It's nearing eleven p.m. again. The weird late-night programming has come on, not Christian this time but infomercials with sweaty nonactors advertising products that no one would need. She takes another long sip of wine.

Flipping through the contacts on her phone, Elle considers calling Chris, but she saw on Facebook that he's in Disneyland with his family, and besides, she hasn't spoken to him in years. She considers calling Tom's office, but it's Sunday. She considers trying Tom again, but no, he would have answered if he could and wanted to. She considers checking his phone records again, just in case she missed something glaring, but she knows she didn't. She considers calling the police—how soon is too soon to call the police? And what would she say?

911. Her finger hovers over the call button.

Again, she imagines her husband in the other woman's bed. He probably just doesn't want to answer his wife, his almost ex-wife. His *crazy* ex-wife, if she calls the police. She doesn't want to be someone's crazy ex-wife.

But then she thinks about his phone on the side of the road while ambulance lights disappear in the distance, and maybe the police can help or would know what she should do.

"911, what's your emergency?"

She hangs up.

Setting her phone on the cushion beside her, she pours herself more wine and takes up the remote. With a click, the channel turns to more sitcom reruns. *Friends* this time. She never liked *Friends*.

She dials Tom's work and leaves a message. "Hi, this is Tom's wife, Elle. I'm calling to see if anyone there knows where he is. Call me back whenever you get this."

She hits the end button and stares at the screen. To her surprise, it lights up almost immediately and starts buzzing. She startles and bumps her wine, the glass wobbling and then toppling; burgundy liquid spreads over the coffee table, running onto the floor. Rushing to the kitchen for some paper towels, Elle answers her phone, pinning it between her ear and shoulder, her hands shaking. A calm voice comes through as Elle tears off a handful of paper towels and hunches over the spill. "Hello, this is Melanie. I'm a dispatcher with the SPD North Precinct. It looks like we got disconnected. What's your emergency?"

Sheepishness grips Elle's lungs. She pauses, clenching her wad of towels, kneeling over the mess.

"Hello?" Melanie asks.

Elle stumbles into her words. "No emergency. I—I misdialed. I'm so sorry."

"You sure you're all right, ma'am?"

"Yes," Elle says, forcing her voice an octave higher. "I'm fine."

"All right, ma'am. Have a nice evening."

The line clicks before Elle can say, "You too."

She sets her phone on the dry part of the table and presses the paper towels into the carpet. Her pulse is deafening inside her ears, and she's breathing hard. She lifts her glass off the floor and sets it on the coffee table next to the almost empty bottle. With the rush of adrenaline subsiding from that embarrassing call, Elle buries her face in her hands. This is getting out of hand. Now her concern has caused her to inconvenience the *law*. That dispatcher is probably irritated beyond measure at Elle's stupidity. Even third graders know not to call 911 and hang up without saying anything. She just hopes that a real emergency wasn't missed because of her antics.

Once most of the wine is sopped up, sitting back on her heels, Elle takes up her phone again and navigates to Tom's contact. He's the one she should have called, not the police. She taps his name on the screen, but he doesn't pick up: "Hi, you've reached Tom Hutton. If this is business related, please call my office at 360-206-5555. Otherwise, leave a message, and I'll get back to you ASAP."

Just his voice makes Elle want to melt into the carpet like the wine. Wrist quivering, holding the phone to her ear, Elle says, "Tom, this is your crazy ex-wife calling. Where are you? I hate that I'm worried about you. Call me back and put me out of my misery."

She hangs up, wanting to throw up—from the message, from the merlot, from the dispatcher, from the stain on the carpet. She bites her cheek to distract herself from it all. Crawling onto the couch, she closes her eyes. Repeating his voice mail message to herself, Elle wishes her head would stop pounding.

August 12, 2015

The day Elle found out

It's all on his iPad. Every last word. Elle didn't intend to snoop—she was looking for some photos Tom had taken of her baking, for a press release—when a message popped up: *What are you doing later?* The contact was simply *V*. So she opened it, and there they were. Texts upon texts.

She's sitting on the couch in their living room, late-afternoon sunlight streaming in, their wood floorboards patched in blinding orange gold. The iPad lies before her, open to the messages. She closes her eyes, dizzy, sick. She's a fool. *A fucking fool.* Of course he's been cheating. Her mind runs over the past few days, weeks, months. He's been distant so long she stopped noticing. Staying out late, less and less affectionate by the day. When was the last time they made love or even just kissed with tongue? Why hadn't she seen it? Why hadn't she suspected a thing?

She pores over the messages, unable to look away. Thumb scrolling over the screen until her joint aches. Her eyes fill with tears. It won't do her any good, but she has to read on, conversations running together: *Meet at the usual place, eight? Yes, can't wait. Come over. Last night was fun. I miss you, busy later? Can't tonight, I told my wife I'd be home.*

Thinking about you today, xo. Thinking about you too. Come to my place, I have a surprise. Hot last night, you made my week. Missing you, drinks? I'll leave work early.

The texts go all the way back to April—not even two weeks after their anniversary—and Elle reads every last one. By the time she's done, her cheeks are raw from the tears, her eyes wide, glazed, stinging. The room around her is fuzzy, her mouth stale. Betrayal slithers between her ribs, cold and probing. She has never felt so embarrassed or livid, emotion burning in her chest and constricting her neck.

It's one thing she never imagined he'd do. Is she naive for thinking so?

If their life together were a recipe, it would be this: tablespoons of late nights talking, a dash of fervent fingers across skin, and too many *I love you*s to count. Date nights and nights in and days spent in the sunshine or getting caught in the rain or sneaking cigarettes at family functions, and their wedding day. His homemade spaghetti sauce followed by her coffee cake. Their cat, Velcro. Their Greenwood home. Trust, laughter, tears, and pure joy, kneaded into one by years of togetherness. All that: shattered like a glass bowl, the person she thought she was scattered across the floor.

The iPad's screen dims. She imagines the two of them having sex, white sheets, his hands running over the woman's tan, flawless skin. In Elle's mind, the woman is a redhead. While she despises the idea, it won't leave her thoughts. She wants to know what the woman does for a living—something sexy, like a yoga instructor?—and then she doesn't. It doesn't matter what the other woman does; the only thing that matters is that she's doing Elle's husband. Looking down at her hands, her thighs, Elle wants to know what about herself isn't good enough. Her hair is limp, her breasts small. Maybe she isn't warm enough, outgoing enough. Not fun enough, after all?

Stop it, she thinks. Her *enough-ness* can't be it, yet that is all that comes to mind.

And Tom, how stupid can he be? His iPad synced with his phone. Did he want her to find out? Of course not. She's almost angry he didn't hide it better.

Elle wipes her eyes with a tissue and locks the iPad. She slips it back into the side table drawer where she found it. Standing up, she smooths her T-shirt, pulling it over the elastic of her pajama shorts. She might have enough ingredients in the house to make something. Maybe jam.

September 28, 2015

Over six weeks after Elle found out

With the light streaming in through the windows of their living room, Elle sits up. Late morning. Her limbs feel as though they're filled with pie weights. She checks her phone, half expecting a change, but there's only a text from Bonnie. *You all right?* Elle types, *Fine. How's the bakery?* and tosses the phone toward the other end of the couch.

Since Elle has been home, Bonnie has covered the bakery—according to Bonnie, Elle shouldn't work in the midst of all this stress and anger. *Take a few days.* How many? At first it felt like necessary time off, but now Elle can't stand it—just the weekend alone, and she's already baked two batches of cookies. Now, lacking any flour under her fingernails, Elle feels as though she's trapped in an endless state of waiting; without the bustle of the bakery to occupy her, the absence of Tom is magnified.

She assesses the room, the coffee table littered with dishes: a container from the leftovers she had for dinner, a plate with the remnants of another chocolate cookie, a wineglass with a dry red stain in the bottom, the bottle not far off. Already, a fruit fly circles the scene. Elle feels stale in her clothing. Recalling her embarrassing message on Tom's voice mail, she again thinks about who she might call. It's Monday, so why hasn't his office called back? Why hasn't Tom?

Suddenly, she just can't take it any longer. The stagnancy of the day—even just minutes after waking up—is torture. Eleven hours since she called him, and well over a week since she's heard from him at all. It's an emergency. It must be.

Elle picks up her phone and dials.

"911, what's your emergency?"

"I—I think I want to report a missing person."

The dispatcher on the other end—who, to Elle's relief, is *not* the one from before—takes down Elle's information. Their address, Tom's name and appearance. She can't remember what he was wearing the last time she saw him. "Probably a suit," she says. And she states her reason for concern: that it's her husband, but they've been fighting because he cheated, so she left the house, and when she came back, he was gone, and he's probably fine, but she can't figure out where he is, and so her imagination has been running rampant.

Their conversation is like a confession, and it feels good to tell someone, anyone, what she's been sitting with—the fact that it's a dispatcher, a complete stranger, makes her feel silly, but she's also more willing to open up. The woman on the other end of the phone has probably heard much worse. And who knows what might be pertinent?

"All right, Mrs. Hutton. Stay calm, and I'll have an officer stop by. Do you want me to stay on the line with you?"

"No, that's all right. Thank you."

The call ends.

An officer. Coming to her house. Elle isn't sure whether she should feel embarrassed or nervous or if she should call back and cancel the whole thing. Police make it daunting, all those scary images she imagined. She stands up, clears the coffee table, and runs upstairs to get dressed.

Once she's presentable, she goes back downstairs to wait on the couch. Fifteen minutes go by. Elle reaches up to pull her hair into a ponytail, her fingers weak. She wonders if she'll hear sirens, or if the cop will just show up, and should she wait outside, and how long will she have to wait? Rising, she paces. Then she stares through the blinds, over the branches of the rhododendron outside the window, to the empty street. Velcro rubs up against her leg, purring. She reaches down to scratch his head, and when she looks up again, an old blue Honda Civic is pulling into her driveway. She expected a real cop car.

She opens the front door and steps out onto the porch, wrapping her sweater tighter around her body, folding her arms. She can't see the man's face behind the glare off the windshield, but she sees him wave. The gesture is peculiar. When the man gets out, she realizes he's not a cop at all. He's Owen.

Her stomach seizes, hands clasping one another, her fingers instinctively reaching for her wedding ring to fiddle with, but she hasn't worn it in weeks. Her tongue prods at the spot where she bit her cheek last night, swollen and raw. As he approaches, Elle notices Velcro on the windowsill inside, staring out at her.

Owen stops at the bottom of her porch stairs, and she feels her eyebrows crease. "What are you doing here?"

"I tried the bakery first. The cashier gave me your address."

"No, I meant . . ." Elle spreads her hands, tongue tied, distracted by the thought of an officer on the way.

"You left some earrings at my place." He steps onto the bottom step, reaching, and hands them over, a pair of zirconium studs. She hasn't noticed their absence.

"Well, thanks," she says, pushing them into her jean pocket.

"You haven't returned my texts."

"Owen," Elle says, but before she can say more, she sees a cop car rounding the corner, heading for her driveway. Thank God the lights aren't flashing.

Owen turns to watch as the cop pulls in, blocking his Civic. His face contorts into an expression of confusion and panic. "You called the police?"

The knots in her stomach tighten. "Not on you."

She's not sure if she should go to the cop or stay on the porch, and then it hits her how *real* this is and how awful and embarrassing it is too. What if the neighbors see? All of a sudden she's even angrier at Tom for putting her through this, all of this. Still, she wants to know that he's all right. And she's mad at herself, too, for caring about him even after the despicable things he's done.

As the officer approaches, Elle starts down the stairs, pausing on the last step. Owen steps aside, the heels of his shoes meeting the edge of the flower bed. Again, Elle adjusts her sweater over her chest, staring at the cop sauntering over. Elle rarely ever sees cops in person—aside from in their cars—and she realizes how bulky his uniform is, one finger looped through his belt. Her eyes fall on the gun at his waist, then the radio hooked on his chest, his crisp white undershirt peeking out near his collar.

"Mrs. Hutton," the officer says, taking up a wide stance in the walkway. "I'm Officer Eduardo Grant. I'm here about your missing person report."

"Thanks for coming," Elle says, swallowing hard. She can feel Owen's gaze on her, burning through her. Fighting her urge to scream or run into the house and lock the door, Elle bites at the sore in her mouth.

After a considerable pause, Officer Grant looks at Owen. "You're not her husband, are you?"

He shakes his head. "No, just a friend."

Elle stares at the name patch sewn onto the officer's pocket: *E. Grant*. There's a loose thread hanging out from the *E*.

"Well, Mrs. Hutton, let's take a look around, all right?" His hand gestures toward the door, and she sees his wedding band, the smoothness of his hands. He probably has a wife at home, or a husband, maybe kids. Gets haircuts every other week, loves his mom's cooking, has a Seahawks jersey he wears every Sunday. Elle can feel her face flush, emotion rising to the surface. A home, a family. What is wrong with her that she can't have that? In that moment, the flour dust and stainless steel refrigerators of her bakery seem so cold in comparison to a family and a life.

"Call me Elle, please," she says to Officer Grant, leading him up the porch.

Owen clears his throat, and she remembers that he's blocked in.

Turning around, Elle says, "Oh, can you—" but stops herself short at the sight of a black Accord coming down the road.

The Accord slows, then parks on the street because the driveway is full. As Tom steps out of the car and walks up, a suitcase in hand, she can't help but start shaking—with anger, with humiliation, with relief. Her toes curl inside her socks. Her arms feel heavy and foreign. Again, she impulsively reaches for her wedding ring to spin on her finger, but it's not there. She is overwhelmed, swept up in the image of her husband coming toward her, their walkway suddenly crowded with men, all of whom she brought here one way or another, and she wishes she could sink into the ground and be done with all this chaos in her life.

"Is *this* your husband, Mrs. Hutton?" Officer Grant asks.

"I am," Tom says.

Elle can't help but stare at him, unshaven, his breath swirling around his face in the chilly morning air. He sets his suitcase on the ground, then stands tall, his six-foot frame squaring toward Officer Grant.

"What's going on here, Officer?" he asks.

"I should go . . ." Owen says, fingering his car keys.

Tom faces him, a strange look on his face. His voice is tense, level. "What did you do to my wife?"

"I didn't—"

Before Owen can finish, Tom pulls his arm back with the clear intention of a punch. Elle shrieks. Officer Grant grabs Tom's shoulders and hauls him backward before any contact can be made. Owen stumbles into their rhododendron, hand landing in the mulch to break his awkward fall.

"What did you do to my wife?" Tom shouts this time, his chest heaving against the barricade of the officer's palms.

"Nothing!" Elle says, but it's all she can get out, her esophagus clenching even tighter than before. She sucks in a desperate breath.

"All right, buddy, calm down," Officer Grant says, tugging at Tom's right arm.

Finding her voice again, Elle asks, "Tom, what the hell is wrong with you?"

He ignores her, staring at Owen. "What did you do to her?" His body is quivering, feet still.

"Nothing. I didn't do anything," Owen says, straightening his T-shirt. He brushes some dirt off his pants. "Christ, Elle, your husband is crazy."

Officer Grant says something into his radio, then, "Let's cool off in the cruiser, Mr. Hutton."

"Oh, please, Officer, that can't be necessary—" Elle protests.

"Ma'am, this is a verbal warning of no contact for all of you. I'm escorting him off the property," Grant says.

A small, alarmed yelp erupts from Elle's throat.

Tom's fists are still balled, but he nods, defeated. "It's okay, sweetheart. We'll do as he says."

"But—"

"There's a Days Inn on Aurora, the one we drive past; I can stay there for the night."

"Good plan." The officer regards Elle. "If I have to come back here tonight, he's going to jail." Then, to Owen, "I ask that you please leave the premises as well, sir."

"Officer Grant, this isn't . . ." Elle trails off—it's no use. She watches Grant lead her husband toward the cop car; over his shoulder,

Tom glares at Owen, but when the car door closes, his shoulders slump.

Elle is shaken, dumbfounded. She has never seen Tom so filled with rage. As Officer Grant starts the engine, she makes eye contact with her husband through the tinted back seat window. The look touches her deep in her core, an emotion she can't name, a sensation she can't place. His expression of concern and humiliation tears her apart.

Realizing her heart is pounding, she sits down on the porch step. "Are you okay?" she asks Owen.

"Christ," he says, straightening. His eyes are red. "Does he know?"

Elle shakes her head, trying to process the scene. "I think he does now."

Owen touches her shoulder, an unwelcome gesture, but she understands his sentiment. Resting for another few moments, she swallows hard and stands. "Thanks for returning my earrings. I'm sorry my husband tried to punch you."

Owen chuckles nervously. "He's not the first person to try to punch me."

~

Later that evening, despite the officer's orders, Elle picks Tom up from the motel. With Owen gone, there's no risk. Pulling out of the parking lot, turn signal clicking in the otherwise silent car, she can't help but sigh. Now what? She wants to look at him, touch his hand, even, but she can't bring herself to do either. She focuses on the road ahead, the sky dimming into dusk, pine trees falling away in an evergreen blur, houses congealing into neighborhoods, lights flicking on.

Running a hand over his face, Tom breaks the silence. "What *was* that?"

Elle feels her grip tighten on the steering wheel. "What was what?"

"*That*," Tom says. "At the house."

"That's what I want to know," she retorts.

"Why was the cop there, Elle?"

"You're lucky Owen didn't press charges," she says. "A verbal warning. You're lucky."

"Did he hurt you?"

"No, he didn't hurt me." She presses the brakes, coming to a stop at a red light.

"Who is he?" His tone pierces her chest.

"No one."

"Someone."

"No one."

Tom nods. "I see."

Shame fills her mouth, and she swallows it down. She wants to ask why he didn't answer her texts, why he didn't call back, but she's not sure she can handle his answer. "Where were you?"

"Atlanta," Tom says. "We might have a new investor."

"Oh." Buried somewhere in the shock of what just happened, she feels a semblance of relief. The light turns green, and she eases on the gas.

~

When they get home, Elle offers to put on some tea, but Tom refuses, wanting to take a shower and get to bed. "Long day." Elle makes some for herself and takes it up to the guest bedroom. For a while she just sits, listening to Tom rustling around in the next room, unzipping and zipping his suitcase, the clatter of toiletry bottles being unpacked, his footsteps down the hall. She is raw, ashamed. What does he think of her? She sips her tea. The memory of him lunging at Owen keeps flashing through her mind. She hates it, hates that image of him, his rage. She hates the mess he's made. Yet a small part of her wonders at the implication of his actions. Protective, even now. He called her sweetheart, didn't he? What did that mean?

Hearing the shower turn on, water sputtering through the pipes, Elle decides to lie down, and she falls asleep to the sounds of her husband home again.

April 18, 2015

About four months before Elle found out

It's their six-year anniversary. Elle is in her pajamas, sitting on the lid of the toilet. She's holding a pregnancy test, the purple cap already fitted back over the wet strip, a little foggy on the inside. Between Elle's fingers, the determining window of the test faces the floor. Tom waits in the doorway, his hand gripping the molding. He has a strange look on his face, his forehead creased, his lips tight, his eyes glimmering and fixated on his watch, hopeful. One minute remains.

Elle is sick to her stomach, but not in the pregnant way. Sick with anticipation, or dread. A volcanic burning at the back of her throat, the base of her chest. She thought that she would grow to want them, that perhaps one day she'd wake up with a maternal yearning in her belly. But that day has still not come.

Once, while making meringue, Elle broke an organic egg and found it filled with blood. Startled, she dropped the shell into her yolk bowl, and when she built up the courage to look again, she saw the chick fetus there, encased in a globby membrane, its eyeball clouded over, too big for its underdeveloped skull. Its body no more than a twisted sack, bleeding among the perfect yolks.

She felt sick then, too, that same curious burn.

With the memory clinging to her, Elle curls her numb toes on the tile. A few more seconds tick by, and then Tom looks up. Elle flips the test over to find a single line. All the muscles in her neck release. Tom has come all the way into the bathroom now, kneeling beside her. She tilts the result window toward him, watching as his face tightens, then droops. Each time they buy a test, he seems a little more drained. For Elle, it is always relief. How can she ever tell him that? Not after this many months.

"I'm sorry, sweetheart," she offers, dropping the pregnancy test in the trash.

He gathers her into an awkward embrace, her on the toilet, him on his knees on the floor. With his mouth pressed into her shoulder, she can feel the heat coming from his face, smell his aftershave mixed with the faint scent of the negroni he had with dinner. Her hand comes up to rest on his back, rubbing his cotton undershirt. They stay that way for a while, Elle coming to realize how hard this has been on him, the relentless disappointment. And how that single line calms the heat at the top of her ribs like a glass of chilled milk every time. So maybe it isn't working because she doesn't *want* it to work.

He tips back on his heels and looks into her eyes. "It might be time for us to go to a doctor."

Elle nods. "I can make an appointment tomorrow."

Tom kisses her cheek and stands, feet scuffing into the other room. Alone in the brightness of the bathroom, Elle cradles her head in her hands.

~

The next afternoon, Elle is just getting home from her shift at the bakery. Drowsy from the late night the previous evening, she sits down at the kitchen table and picks up a baking-supply catalog. She was talking with Bonnie, going over the bakery numbers, the profits, and thinking about another kind of child all day: a second bakery. It's not a new idea—customers have been asking about a second branch for years—but now the timing seems better. The more she considers it, the more she loves the idea.

Eyes fixated on the lists upon lists of new, state-of-the-art equipment, she's distracted when Tom comes into the kitchen from some yard work and kisses her cheek.

"Good day?" he asks.

Elle looks up from a spread of nonstick cookware. "Fine. Just tired from staying up late."

He runs the tap, filling a glass of water. "Did you make an appointment with the doctor?"

Swallowing hard, Elle says, "No."

"Why not?"

Elle closes the catalog. "Well, I was talking to Bonnie today . . ." She trails off, unable to say what she's thinking, afraid he won't understand.

"And?"

"We ran some numbers at the bakery—it's doing well. Really well, actually. And I saw this segment on TV about restaurant owners in Seattle." Elle brushes the hair out of her eyes, trying not to look too carefully at Tom. "And, well, I was thinking that I might want to open another bakery."

Sinking into a chair, Tom says, "Oh."

"A few regulars have brought it up too."

"So after months of trying to have a baby, you want to give up and open another bakery?" There's an edge in Tom's voice.

"Tom—"

"You just want to give up?"

"I want to build my career. There's nothing wrong with that."

"I thought we were on the same page about this."

"You know you always wanted a child more than I did."

He slaps his palm on the counter, startling her. "Since when?"

"Tom," Elle says, her eyes searching his face—for flexibility, for understanding.

"I can't believe this."

Heat growing in her cheeks, Elle says, "I stood by you when you got tired of grading papers, when you built your business."

"And I stood by you when you struggled with the bakery. And now that it's doing well, you want to drag us back into the stress of a new business? Right when we're getting comfortable?" He stands up, jaw clenched.

"Tom, please," Elle says, her voice soft.

"No, Elle. I'm upset."

Clasping her hands, she watches him pace. "Can we talk about this calmly?"

He stops and turns toward her. "A family . . ." He trails off. "I thought family was the next step, Elle. Don't you want a family with me?"

Elle scrapes her bottom lip with her teeth, not speaking. Her answer isn't a definitive no, but right now, it's not yes either. She refuses to acknowledge that her clock is ticking. She thought she'd be ready by now. Why isn't she ready?

"So that's how it is," he says. She hears him exhale, big and forceful.

"Can you think about it?" she asks.

Leaving the kitchen, he says over his shoulder, "I'm going to take a shower."

Alone at the table, Elle rests her head in her hands once again, and again she feels a burning in her gut.

September 29, 2015

Over six weeks after Elle found out

A hand touches her shoulder, shakes her awake. It's late, the guest room filled with shadows. She can barely see Tom in the darkness, kneeling at her bedside—just the silvery outline of his features.

"Elle," he says.

Panic fills her body, and she sits up. "What's wrong?"

"Shhh," he says. "Nothing's wrong." There's beer on his breath; his hair is mussed.

"Then what is it?"

"I got your message."

She doesn't understand. She looks at the clock, turns on the bedside lamp. "Tom, it's past midnight."

"You were worried about me?"

She realizes he's talking about her drunken voice mail on his phone. "Oh, God."

Again, "You were worried about me?"

"You *just* got that?"

"My flight was delayed, and my phone charger was in my checked bag, so my phone was dead the whole time I was at the airport."

"And you didn't just buy a new charger?"

She predicts his response before he says it: "I didn't want to waste money on a new one when I had a perfectly good one in my bag." He pauses. "But you were worried?"

"I was drunk," she says, trying to dismiss it.

"You were miserable?" Another pause. "So the cop was about me."

Elle sits up more, pulling her pillow upright, resting her back against the headboard. "Why did you wake me up?"

"You used the word *miserable*."

Her cheeks become hot, and she looks away, out toward the window. "You could've left a note."

"I didn't think you would care."

"That's beside the point."

"Is it?" He touches her arm, and their eyes meet. She can hear the clock on the nightstand ticking.

"Yes. And you left the cat to starve. What do you want from me?"

"Nothing," Tom says, standing.

He turns out the light, and she watches his figure move toward the door. Elle lies back down, taking a labored breath through her tight chest. She turns her back to the doorway but hears him exhale, long, a faint shudder at the end.

"I stopped seeing her," he says, his low voice piercing the darkness. "I think maybe I wanted to get caught. Maybe I wanted to break the stagnancy. But I wanted warmth too." He clears his throat. "I know there's no good excuse. I'm sorry, Elle. I just want you to know that as soon as you said something . . . I couldn't go on with it."

"You had no problem carrying on with it before I found out," Elle says. "For four months, you came home and acted like you weren't destroying our marriage." She turns around to see him, but he's not there. His shadow hovers in the hallway, the door cracked. Then the door clicks shut.

~

The next day, when Elle goes downstairs, Tom's in the kitchen. He's dressed in a suit, standing, eating eggs off a plate. For a split second, she considers going back upstairs, not wanting to face him, but he spots her and says, "I made extra." He points toward the covered skillet on the stove. It's the first time he's made breakfast for her in probably a year— yet she's angry about yesterday, humiliated, even. What is he doing to her? Reckless with her feelings, her attachment to him. Loving and then awful toward her. She feels like his emotional rag doll.

"Heading to work?" she asks.

"Is that all you have to say?"

"What do you want me to say?"

"After last night? Something, for Christ's sake."

Her chest flares. "Oh, yes, thanks for *not* cheating on me after I found out. You're a real class act."

"Jesus, Elle, are you kidding me? Who *was* that guy on our front porch yesterday?"

Elle's fists tense, and she glares at him from across the kitchen island, but words refuse to come out. Finally, she's able to say, "Just go."

Tom drops his plate in the sink, the loud clatter making Elle startle. Then he paces, hands on his head. She watches him in silence.

"I came in last night wanting to—the whole time I was gone I—I made you—" Finally, he lowers his hands and stops in front of her. "Do you even *want* to make this work?"

Elle stands stiff, the house silent except for their tense breathing. She slips her hands into her pockets to hide their shaking.

"Do you?" he asks again. "Elle?"

"Thanks for the eggs."

His lip quivers—only for a moment—and then he nods, his mouth pulling tight and straight. He picks up his workbag and leaves, the front door slamming behind him. Biting her cheek, she checks the sink to see if the plate broke. Seeing it still intact, she turns toward the stove and lifts the lid off the skillet.

April 18, 2009

Over six years before Elle found out

Elle is wearing a white gown with a neckline in a low but elegant *V* and a full, long skirt. The inner tulle itches around her ankles, but the breeze from the water is pleasant. Their wedding is not on a beach but near one. She decided to leave her hair down and free flowing, and now the wind brushes it gently. Her makeup is minimal. Tom's slate-colored suit brings out the blue in his gray-blue eyes—the second thing Elle loved about him, after his voice. He has a smile on his face, warm and soft and dreamy. In her heart, Elle feels a fluttering joy so exuberant she's faint.

Elle's mother and Tom's parents sit up front. Bonnie, her maid of honor, holds the bouquet Elle brought down the aisle. Chris is Tom's best man, and he has the rings. The rest of the family—cousins, uncles, aunts, grandparents—sit in white folding chairs on the low bluff, coarse beach grass swaying among the rows, yellow rose petals scattered across the ground, swept down the beach.

Her eyes refocus on Tom's smile, and it grounds her. She recalls their conversation that morning, Tom saying, "Even if your dress gets ruined and the gulls eat the food and everyone leaves because it starts pouring rain, it'll be a perfect day, because we will be married." His words linger in her mind as they are sworn together, as the ocean sighs behind them and clouds as white as her dress float above the vast horizon.

They made their vows identical and simple: "I vow to hold you and love you, always."

September 29, 2015

Over six weeks after Elle found out

In the late afternoon, Elle receives a call from Bonnie. At first, she worries it's the bakery—it's after closing time, and that's always when issues come up. But when she answers the phone, it becomes clear that the problem has nothing to do with the finicky industrial dishwasher or their flour supply.

As if reading Elle's unspoken concern, Bonnie says, "The bakery is fine. Good day, actually. But listen"—her voice becomes muffled, throaty—"I need you to do pastry prep. Something came up with my mom, and I need to go over there right now."

"Is she okay?"

"She's fine, but I need to drop in."

"I'll come to the bakery now."

"Whatever you want." There's some rustling on the other end. "Locking things up."

"Is there anything else you need?" Elle was folding laundry in the guest room when she got the call, and now she sits on the bed, right on top of the yet-to-be-folded T-shirts and tank tops and socks.

"Bake me something?" Bonnie says. "I'll need a heart-stopping sugar high once I get this shit sorted out."

Elle laughs faintly. "Done."

"You're the best," Bonnie says. "Wish me luck."

"Good lu—"

Click.

Elle lowers the phone from her ear. Her heart clenches for Bonnie; the struggle she's been going through is like a hangnail that gets worse with tugging. Coming to her feet, Elle leaves the guest room and descends to the kitchen to find her car keys, sorting through recipes in her head. By the time she reaches the bakery, she knows what she'll make.

Heart-Stopping Cheesecake

Break out your trusty springform pan. You'll need a pound of cream cheese (yes, a whole pound); set it on the counter to soften. Next, start the crust: 2 cups of finely ground graham crackers, ½ teaspoon of cinnamon, and 1 stick of melted butter. Coat your springform with butter; then combine the crust ingredients and press the crumbly mixture into the bottom and sides of the pan. Chill for at least 5 minutes.

There's something about cheesecake that pacifies emotional wounds. The bigger the tragedy, the bigger the slice. If you've never used cheesecake to soothe sadness, you've missed an opportunity.

Next, fire up the mixer. Beat the cream cheese on low until it's fluffy, add 3 eggs one at a time, and—with the mixer still thrumming—gradually pour in a cup of sugar. By now your mouth will be watering, the waft of cream cheese overpowering your senses as you hover over the mixing bowl. The filling will still be thick at this point; this is when you add a pint of sour cream. You'll need to scrape down the sides of the bowl to get it to incorporate—like a mother guides her daughter, this mixture takes tending.

Once the liquid is silky, add a few drops of vanilla. For tang, add the zest of a lemon (optional but highly recommended). Don't overbeat. Pour the filling into the prepared springform, using a spatula to smooth the top. Bake at 350° for about 50 minutes. The whole room will smell like comfort, and comfort is the first step toward mending a sore heart.

The cheesecake is done when the top turns gold and jiggles when you nudge the pan. You can serve it plain, with fruit, or even with a thin layer of jam on top. But after baking, it'll need to set in the fridge for a few hours. Just like aches and pains, a cheesecake needs heat and cold to come out right.

Elle quickly preps the pastries and finishes tidying up the bakery, and then—because she still has some house chores to do—she takes the uncooked cheesecake home to bake. Tom is still at work when she returns, and while the oven preheats, she finishes the laundry, starts the dishwasher, and refills Velcro's water bowl. When the oven reaches 350°, she carefully slides the cheesecake onto the rack. Some daylight remains, so she heads outside to check yet another chore off her list.

~

The cheesecake is still baking and Elle is in the backyard pulling weeds when Tom gets home from work. Having been listening for the kitchen timer, she hears the engine out front, the slam of a car door. She's on her hands and knees, picking tufts of grass from the cracks in the stone path that leads to their potting shed. Two-thirds done. Her back aches. Her father preferred dirt, but to Elle, it's just not the same as bleached flour.

Either Tom doesn't know she's in the yard, or he doesn't care. She spots him through the window, in the kitchen. His face is drawn; she's never seen him look so old, and she wonders if she looks that way to him. Wrinkled, frowning, eyebrows creased. For some reason the observation unsettles her. He's always been handsome in her eyes, but through the window, with the reflection of tree branches on his face, all she sees in him is betrayal—and it's ugly.

When she finishes weeding along the path, she stands up for the first time in nearly an hour. Stretching tall, her spine pops. There's still light in the sky, but the shadows are long, and the air is crisp and biting. She goes inside to check the cake; the kitchen is cozy, warm, and her cheeks feel numb. The timer has ten minutes left, but before she can peer into the oven, Tom comes downstairs. He's in workout clothes, unwinding a tangle of headphones.

For thirty seconds, the only sound is a slight gust of wind, the backyard salal bush rasping against the side of the house.

To ease the harsh silence, she says, "Going for a run?"

He nods, not looking up.

"About this morning—"

"Save it," Tom says. "Just . . . don't bother."

Elle looks at her hands, black with dirt, the creases in her palms like pink threads through the grit. Her nails are grimy; Tom stands between her and the kitchen sink. She wants so badly to scrub her knuckles until her whole life is shiny again, but it doesn't work that way.

She says, "I thought you wanted to talk."

"I changed my mind," Tom says. "I'm going for a run." He moves to step past her, but she stands in his way.

"I think we should talk."

Squaring up to her, he says, "What about?"

She holds his stare, searching for the softness she saw in his eyes last night, but it's no longer there. "Never mind." She steps aside, letting him pass.

"I'll be back in an hour."

She doesn't watch him go. Instead, she walks to the sink and lifts the tap. Her fingers tingle under the hot water, dirt swirling down the drain. All that worry, all that heartache over Tom going missing, only to go back to what? Bickering? Inaction? She exhales a long, quivering breath. Was he even in Atlanta, or was that a lie too?

Drying her hands, she recalls the flower receipt, the one that spurred her to leave the house. Roses. He said he had quit seeing the other woman, but the flowers tell a different story. Was he with the other woman all that time he was away? Or for even part of it? While she was agonizing, emailing her lawyer, staying home from the bakery, calling the police—was he with the other woman?

Like the ticking of a timer before it chimes, a thought comes to Elle, faint but ominous. *If you're that curious,* she thinks, *why don't you look on his iPad?*

She hesitates.

The cheesecake. Elle resets the timer before it goes off, as it had only a minute remaining. Donning oven mitts, she slides the cake from the oven and sets it on a daisy-shaped trivet.

You know you want to.

Before she can stop herself, she's climbing the stairs. She enters their bedroom. Now that Tom is home again, the place is like a relic of their marriage. It smells the same as always—a mix of lemon soap and tea tree shampoo, laundry detergent and dust. Yet she feels unwelcome, an outsider. Beyond the window, the sky is a blue-yellow bruise, clouds moving in. A breeze causes unseen timbers in the house to creak.

Tom hasn't finished unpacking. His suitcase lies unzipped, the cover flung back, a few shirts rumpled inside. Velcro is asleep atop the pile, a smear of orange-white hair clinging to the edges of the black suitcase. Bending down, she nudges Velcro aside; Tom's shirts are warm from the cat's body heat. Elle digs through the starched fabric and looks under his dress shoes, but she's quick to determine the iPad isn't there. She checks the front pockets of the suitcase but finds only Mentos wrappers and a book.

Sitting back on her heels, she feels dirty but unsatisfied. If she gives up now, it'll prod her all night long. She can't have gone through his suitcase for nothing. Growing desperate, she stands up, checks his nightstand—not there—before hurrying back downstairs. His briefcase is on the couch; it opens with a click. Laptop, a *Men's Health*, a notebook, some pens, but no iPad.

Elle sighs.

There's one more place she can look. Out the door, into their driveway; his Accord is unlocked. The interior is cavelike in the surging twilight. Clicking the overhead light, she checks the center console, glove box, and finds nothing beyond napkins and the owner's manual. Her bare arms succumb to goose bumps as she closes the front passenger door and opens the back. She climbs across the back seat on her knees, peering into the seat pockets.

That's where she finds it.

Without hesitation, she slides it out. The first time she read his iPad messages was an accident; this time, clear as a shrieking kitchen timer, it's simply an invasion of privacy. The bright screen illuminates the inside of the car with blue-white light. She taps on the messages icon.

"Elle?"

She startles, banging her head on the back seat ceiling. For a moment, her cranium pulsing, she doesn't feel guilty at all. Desperate, heartbroken, but not regretful. Tom's to blame. This is all his fault.

But of course, *that* feeling fades.

She drops the iPad on the seat and backs out of the car, slippers finding pavement.

"What the fuck, Elle?" Tom's standing there with his headphones slung over his neck, his cheeks colored but not yet red. "What the *fuck*?"

Like a tsunami gathering offshore, shame hovers over her like a hundred-foot wall of ocean. Yet she digs herself deeper into the sand: "I thought you said an hour."

"That—" Tom's hands come up to cradle his head before they fall back to his sides as fists. "I had the wrong headphones. Please, by all means, let me go back inside so you can continue invading my privacy."

The wave crashes. As if through a mouthful of salt water, she mumbles, "*Ughh.*"

Tom's voice could melt glass. "What are you doing out here, Elle?"

"You bought her flowers."

His face screws up in question. "What?"

"I found the receipt. You lied. You didn't break up with her; you bought her flowers."

"How else was I supposed to break up with her?" Tom asks.

Elle can think of a million ways. "Oh, I don't know, Tom. You didn't bring me flowers when you broke up our marriage. Were you really in Atlanta?"

"I have no reason to lie about that."

"What kind of investor business trip lasts over a week?"

"I don't know . . . a real one?"

"You weren't with her?"

He raises his voice, enunciating each word. "I. Broke. Up. With. Her." Then, "Is that what you were looking for? Evidence?"

Two houses down from their driveway, on the corner, a streetlight emits a loud pop, the bulb going out. Elle lifts her gaze to the fading yellow light. The bugs—directionless, all fluttering wings—disappear into the night. The neighborhood is hushed.

In the off-balance dusk, Elle hates who she has become. Selfish, jealous, vengeful. How good things were. She wants, desperately, for her life to go back to how it was, but it can't. She longs for a reality that has already slipped like sugar through her fingers.

"Who is she?"

"A woman from my building."

"An employee?"

"Of course not."

"Well, how should I know?" Her next words are poison in her mouth. "Did you love her?"

He looks down the street, toward the dark streetlight. "I ended it, didn't I?"

She shifts on her feet, crossing her arms.

"That's what you were hoping to find in my car, in my messages." He sighs. "You've never done anything so low, Elle. You know that, right?"

"Oh, I'm the one in the wrong?" she says, but her anger is already fading into a dull and bitter thickness in her lungs. "Why did you do this to us?"

"Sweetheart, it takes two people to ruin a marriage."

He steps past her, back toward the house, but she calls after him. "Yeah, you and the other woman."

He slams the front door before she can catch it with her hand. She turns the knob, following him into the kitchen. "We aren't done," she says, surprised by the firmness of her voice.

"Aren't we?"

Like a dough hook, she pries into him. "No, we're talking about this."

"Why?" Tom says. "Why bother?" His hand has come to rest beside the cheesecake, which is still cooling on the counter; she has yet to make room in the fridge.

"Why bother?" she repeats, nearly shouting at him now. "Do you want all of this to be a waste? Our time, our home, our marriage? Just—*gone*? That's it?"

"I tried. Last night, I—" He groans. "You act like this is all on me."

"It is," she yells. "This is *all* your fault."

He rolls his eyes, which steams her even more. "Like you're perfect."

"I've had my fair share of fuckups, Tom, but I would *never* cheat on you."

"No?" he says, lifting his palm up in question. "If I was never home, never loving, never asked about your day—you wouldn't have cheated?"

"What are you accusing me of?" Her throat is swelling with tears, and she forces them down.

"I've always come second to your career."

"Oh, fuck you."

"Yeah, sure, fuck me, right? Fuck you, Elle. Fuck all this." His voice is loud, now, filling the walls, making her claustrophobic. "You're so consumed by your own selfishness that you can't even hear what I'm telling you. What I've *been* telling you."

"You can't possibly be pinning this on me," she says.

"What if I am?" he shouts. His hands grip the counter before he slaps his palms down. Her eyes flicker to the cheesecake, worried he'll bump it. He follows her gaze, staring down at the golden top. "Even now, this is all that matters," he says, gesturing to the cake. "How sad is that?"

His eyes pierce her then, and he touches the edge of the trivet.

"Tom, come on," she says.

He leans toward the cake, elbow bending.

"You're being childish." There's desperation in her voice.

In one fluid motion, he springs his arm forward, shoving the cake right off the table with a force that sends it crashing against the wall, warm white filling splattering the baseboards, the dishwasher, the bottom rungs of the barstools.

Elle shouts, incoherent anger erupting from deep in her chest. It's as if he struck her, blood rushing to her cheeks.

"Now can you look at me?" he yells, spreading his arms.

She closes her eyes. "What is wrong with you?"

He laughs a harsh breath. "Why don't you tell me?"

"Did that make you feel better?"

"Honestly? A little."

She's infuriated, terrified. She's never seen him this angry, never thought he was capable of cruelty. "You're an asshole."

"Yeah, well, at least I know what I've done wrong."

"That was for Bonnie."

"You can make another." He steps over the mess, past her, upstairs.

Elle doesn't follow. Her throat is raw, and her teeth are chattering. She looks around at the splatter, the cake pan turned on its side like a wheel near the base of the oven. She shouldn't let him make her feel like all this is her fault, but in that moment she does. She takes on the whole burden of it, like a sack of sugar, bearing down on her shoulders until her neck stiffens and her back begins to buckle. Elle hangs her head. *I didn't do a thing*, she tells herself, but deep down she senses that she's missing something. That somehow, maybe, Tom's not the only one to blame.

September 30, 2015

The next day, when Tom gets home from work, Elle is reading on the couch. Her hair is still wet from a late shower, her eyes probably puffy and red. She stands as he comes through the door. She's been thinking all afternoon about him, not sure what they should do but knowing that they should talk. But before she can speak, he clears his throat.

"I went to a divorce lawyer." His voice is cool.

Elle sets her book down on the coffee table. "All right."

"I filed."

Elle nods, looks at the floor. "Don't you want to—"

"Here's his card," Tom says, handing it to her.

She stares at it, reminded of Miranda. She doesn't bother telling him that they met while he was gone—it seems moot, now. When she looks into his eyes, there's no warmth there. Nothing left. The man standing before her is no longer the man she married. And maybe it's for the best.

"You'll want to get your own lawyer."

"I already have one."

He disappears down the hall, and Elle is left in their living room, sinking into the couch. Upstairs, a door slams.

~

Hours later, Elle leaves a message: "Gina, this is Elle Hutton. It turns out I won't be able to lease anything right now; I'm sorry. Thanks for all your help." Next, she calls Bonnie. Then she calls her lawyer.

Not long after the calls, Elle googles Kelli's sister, the literary agent. She types in *Lily Zhang agent* and hits go. It's about time she did something for herself that wasn't tied to anyone else's money. Something all her own.

October 15, 2015

Bonnie is rifling through their chest freezer, her body half-inside its icy walls, one foot kicked up. Behind her, on the table, are all manner of frostbitten foods. Cellophane-wrapped pound cakes, crushed boxes of phyllo, and bags upon bags of frozen fruit. Elle can't remember the last time they cleaned out the old freezer, but it has been too long. The project was weighing on her like an unhad conversation.

Elle is standing by, wondering what she'll make with whatever they can salvage from the freezer. Upon spotting some newer bags of frozen peaches, she thinks of pie—perfect for the afternoon.

When Bonnie rights herself, Elle is smiling.

"You were checking out my butt, weren't you?" Bonnie asks.

Elle laughs. "I want to make pie." She grabs a few bags off the table, carrying them to her own work space. "Ginger peach?"

"God, yes," Bonnie says, grinning. She's been in a good mood since moving her mother to a new facility, and her attitude lifts Elle's waning spirits.

Elle nods, turning away to gather some dough, ginger, butter, and other supplies from the walk-in. When she comes back out, her arms full, Bonnie has the Jackson 5 playing: "I Want You Back." Having talked about her divorce terms all morning, Elle can't help but shake her head. "You trying to change my mind?"

"I'm trying to have some *fun*," Bonnie says.

Elle unwraps the prepped vodka dough, spreads some flour on her work space, and gets to work rolling it out. The dough is hard and unwieldy from being in the fridge, but as she works, it softens, moving smoothly under her pin as she rolls, turns, rolls, turns, sprinkling a tad more flour as she works.

"You wanna get the fruit ready?" Elle prompts Bonnie, who's standing over the freezer chest with a frown on her face.

"Yes, please," she says.

Ginger Peach Pie with a Friend

Pie is as easy to make as it is to eat, especially when you have a friend to help. Start with your favorite vodka-dough recipe—yes, vodka (you may have a sip). As the alcohol burns off in the oven, it'll yield a light, flaky crust. Just don't overwork the dough when mixing and kneading. 2 ½ cups of flour, 1 teaspoon of salt, 2 tablespoons of sugar, 12 tablespoons of cold butter, ½ cup of shortening, ¼ cup of cold water, and ¼ cup of vodka. Perfect.

Have your friend prepare the fruit by spreading it on a rimmed cookie sheet. Since peaches are already so sweet, sprinkle only very lightly with white sugar. For the perfect complement, use freshly grated ginger. If it's not freshly grated, don't bother. A tablespoon mixed in with the peaches is all you need. Slide the sheet into the oven and bake at 350° until the peaches are warm and bubbling but still firm, about 20 minutes.

By now, whoever is working the dough should have it in a greased piedish. You can do whatever you like with the crust, but fluting the edges is a tried-and-true decoration that is effortless upon practice—and if you have a good friend, you will be well practiced by now. Pie making is an underrated pastime.

For the top, do whatever you like: make crumble, do a simple dough covering, or get creative. Perhaps today you break out the cookie cutters. The music and the mood are lifting, and you want this pie to be more than ordinary. Your friend might find the heart-shaped cookie cutters, a whole set of different sizes. You roll out the remaining dough, and the two of you start cutting out hearts of all shapes and widths. Once the semicooled peaches are nestled in the center of the piedish, cover them in a flurry of dough hearts. And with a quick egg wash over the top, your pie is ready for the oven.

Bonnie sets the timer for thirty minutes, though Elle knows one of them will have to check on the pie and possibly leave it in longer. It's a matter of browning the edges and bottom now, since the peaches are primed. The spice of ginger pierces the air, and Elle, mouth watering, tries the caramelized peach juice left over on the cookie sheet. It's sweet, with a gingery kick. She smiles, looking at Bonnie. She thinks about everything they've been through, the years at the bakery. Starting out as employer and employee and moving swiftly into fast friends and partners, talking about everything from pastries to men.

Tom, Charlie. Elle glances at the floor.

How many years has Bonnie been happily married? And *still* Elle hasn't told her friend how she actually met her husband. Pickup lines and mild flirting have never seemed so shameful. Let alone their other encounters, always so uncomfortable. But as Elle recalls Charlie walking in on her in the bath, his horror, his apologies, his reassurance that he's always been faithful—maybe their meeting and subsequent awkwardness weren't so bad? Maybe Bonnie and Charlie are better for it.

"Where are *you*?" Bonnie asks, wringing out a rag.

Elle's eyes refocus on the bakery's back room. The worktable all messy with flour, dough, and sticky globs of peach juice. The oven timer counting silently down. The chest freezer, with its contents spread on another table, thawing in the warmth. And Bonnie, already starting to clean up.

"Just thinking," Elle says.

"About?"

Charlie, she thinks. "Life," she says.

"Only a few more days," Bonnie says. "Then you'll be a free woman."

"Not that. Bonnie, there's something—" Elle swallows. "There's something I haven't told you. Something I should. It's been bothering me, and, well . . ." It's time she let it out, time she cleaned up her life, bit by bit. And being honest with Bonnie is one way to begin to make her life right.

The freckles on Bonnie's forehead pinch together above her nose. "Sounds ominous."

"It's about Charlie." Her heart hiccups.

"He walked in on you in the bath again?"

Elle presses forward. "You remember that night you introduced us?"

"In the bar? Yeah."

"Well . . ." Elle glances down at her clasped hands, the crusty front of her apron. She should tell her, right? It's time she told her. Bonnie is her best friend. "When you went to the bathroom, he came over to me. I didn't know who he was—just some guy. He hit on me." The last words feel like molasses in her mouth.

Bonnie's face is blank. Elle fears the worst: a complete falling-out with her only friend and a blow to Bonnie's marriage too. This was a mistake. Maybe best friends shouldn't tell each other everything. Elle should've buried that secret forever.

"And?" Bonnie asks finally.

"And?" Elle scrapes her fingernails over the tips of her fingers. "I didn't stop him. And then you came over, and I realized, and—"

Bonnie chuckles. "That's it, then?"

"What? Yes."

"I knew," Bonnie says.

"You—?" Elle shifts on her feet, confused by Bonnie's expression, her words.

"I knew," Bonnie says again, stepping closer. "Elle, I saw him do it. Coming back from the bathroom, I saw everything. He hit on you—and I think you kinda liked it."

Now Elle is the one with the blank face, shame and horror swirling in her chest. Confusion and relief, too, given Bonnie's response. Elle's whole body is wound like a spring, tense and waiting.

The timer beeps, and Elle jumps.

Bonnie is unfazed; she turns on the oven light and peers inside, shaking her head. "Another ten minutes."

"You're not mad?" Elle manages.

Bonnie steps closer, her face kind. "I stayed friends with you, didn't I?"

"But—"

"After that night, I had a conversation with Charlie," Bonnie says. "The relationship conversation everybody has: Where is this going? Are we exclusive? We hadn't defined anything before then—hell, I flirted with men all the time. Seeing him with you—" Bonnie spreads her hands. "That's what made me realize how much I truly wanted him, how much I cared for him. Deeper than any man before. I didn't mind what he did. If anything, it prompted me to ask for something serious. So we moved forward, and he's been true to me; there's not a doubt in my mind about that." Bonnie smiles, stepping closer and placing a hand on Elle's shoulder. "So no, I'm not mad. I actually had forgotten about it."

Elle stands there, feeling dumb. "There were other instances. Things he said—"

"Awkward small talk?"

"Maybe . . ."

"He's the king of saying weird things during parties and dinners, trust me. Like everything else, you read too much into it." Bonnie smiles, genuine.

"I—I should have told you much sooner."

"Hardly anything to tell," Bonnie says. "But I appreciate you saying something now—clearly it has been weighing on you."

In that moment, Elle wants to laugh or cry or both. She thinks of Bonnie and Charlie and how happy they seem, how easily they love each other. No jealousy, no self-consciousness, no insecurity—just love. She wishes she were more like Bonnie.

"I'm embarrassed," Elle says.

Bonnie laughs, turning back toward the oven to check on the pie. "I would be too."

"I did like it, sort of," Elle admits. "I was flattered."

"I don't blame you. He's a good-looking guy." Bonnie winks playfully and then opens the oven door with a click, hot air whooshing out. "I think this is done."

Elle walks over, her flats brushing along the tile floor. Peering at the pie, she nods. "Yeah, it's done."

Bonnie slides it out, placing it on a hot pad on the cleanest corner of the worktable. Idly, she pokes the top, the crust perfectly browned and flaky underneath her inquiring finger.

"How does it not bother you?" Elle asks. "How do you see him next to me at your house or when we're having dinner and not think of how we met?"

She stands a little taller. "Sure, he flirted with you. But he chose me. He married me. He's my husband, and I trust him, Elle. Simple as that."

Elle wonders if she ever truly trusted Tom—she wants to believe she did. But did she ever fully trust herself? Did she ever let go of her own insecurity? *That* answer is a definite no. Elle presumes that Bonnie's confidence has something to do with her happiness too.

"You're my best friend, Bonnie," Elle says, staring at her from across the table. "I feel really lucky to have you around."

Bonnie purses her lips together. She spreads her arms and walks toward Elle, folding her into a tight embrace. "Good, because you're stuck with me."

October 24, 2015

Over ten weeks after Elle found out

As the moving truck pulls away, Elle sinks to the couch. Alone. The heater ticks, a ruffle of air stirring the dust on the opposite end of their—*her*—living room. Elle finds her thoughts going back to the night she found out about the affair. Scrolling through weeks of conversation. Again, what did the other woman have that she did not? Perhaps Elle didn't give Tom enough of her time: she was always busy. Or enough affection: always tired. Or enough . . . something: always distracted. She recalls a string of texts from the summer, not long before Elle found out. *V* said, *I miss you.* Tom said, *Really?* Her response: *Of course I do.*

Did Elle *ever* tell Tom she missed him? Did she ever truly show him that she craved his affection? Did she ever slow down, get over her shyness and jealousy, look into his eyes, and say, *I miss you when you're gone*?

That is one thing Elle can't recall.

December 19, 2015

Over four months after Elle found out

Tom and his lawyer are already there when Elle and her lawyer walk into the office. It has been over two months since she last saw them in this room, the place where they first negotiated, Elle staring out the window at the Bainbridge ferry gliding away; that evening, Tom left with his suitcase to sleep at a friend's house while the paperwork was sorted. And Elle stayed at the bakery, blind-baking piecrusts late into the evening, until she could barely lift her arms.

Now it's like déjà vu, only they've already parsed things out. She gets the house; he gets the Accord. She gets the KitchenAid; he gets the books. They don't allow pets at Tom's new apartment complex, so she gets the cat. She gets most of it all, actually, yet she feels as though she's losing everything.

She dressed in slacks, a plain button-down. Tom sits across from her in his work suit. It's his lunch break. After this, he'll go back to the office as if nothing has happened. He'll be free to call the other woman, or stay out all night drinking, or never see Elle again, and she'll have no right or reason to stop him or worry. He can't ask about Owen, and she doesn't have to tell him that she hasn't seen Owen since that day in September on their doorstep. Tom has already packed his things and moved out. Elle, alone in their big house, a place once filled with love, is now living in the tomb of their marriage. She wonders if, eventually, she'll move too. Sell their house and let it all be forgotten.

Her purse is wedged between her hip and the arm of the chair; she rests her left hand on top of it, fingers tracing the tan stitches along the opening. Last time they were here, she was unfeeling; the days between then and now, days without Tom at all, have softened her. Inside her purse is a piece of coffee cake, safe inside a shallow Tupperware. Blueberry. She was going to give it to him, but now she's thinking she won't. She wants to believe that she made it because she couldn't sleep last night, and it's all she had ingredients for. But who is she kidding? She knows she made it for more than just passing time. Embarrassed she brought the coffee cake at all, Elle closes her purse tighter while the lawyer finishes his explanation of the paperwork.

When it comes time to sign, Elle is numb. Pen in hand, forearm resting on the glossy wooden conference table, Tom seems to be a mile away. The ballpoint falls to rest on the page, and she drags it across, ink soaking into paper.

The page is tucked into a file, and the lawyers both stand. Tom rises from his seat too. When Elle stands, her purse slips off her chair, and the Tupperware skids across the floor, spilling its contents in a crumbly mess. Her face hot, Elle sinks to her knees, scooping up the coffee cake and picking fuzzy crumbs out of the carpet.

"It's fine," Tom's lawyer says. "We'll have someone clean it up."

Elle stands, her chest molten and anguished. She steals a glance at Tom. His expression is neutral, save for the small twitch of a frown. Is it pain that she sees? Or is he ashamed of her?

"I'm sorry," she mutters.

The lawyer gestures toward the door. "No worries. Take care."

She doesn't look at Tom again. Instead, Elle clutches her purse even tighter and rushes out the door. Her fingers are sticky with blueberry juice. *It's done*, she tells herself. *It's over.*

January 2, 2016

Four and a half months after Elle found out

Elle is arranging cheese, crackers, and fruit on a plate—an easy lunch for her day off—when she hears three knocks on her front door. Wiping her hands on a dish towel, she walks barefoot to the front of the house. The day started out hazy with frost, but now the sun is breaking, and the curtains are aglow. At first she guesses it's UPS, a Jehovah's Witness, or even a neighbor, but when she opens the door, it's the last person she would have expected: her mother.

Speechless, Elle swings the dish towel over her shoulder.

"Aren't you going to let me inside?" her mother asks, stepping past Elle into the living room.

Elle clears her throat, closes the door. "Mom, what are you doing here?"

Her mom drops her bags by the couch, turning around as if to survey the room. She's wearing a thick purple shawl, her hair done up in a stylish bun. "I'm here for you, dear." She opens her arms, and Elle, still raw from her divorce, falls easily into her mother's embrace. She smells of chamomile; she's thinner than when Elle last saw her.

Parting, her mother says, "How are you?"

Elle shrugs. "All right, I guess."

"Did you have a good holiday season?"

"Spent it with Bonnie," Elle says. "Do you want to sit down? I was just making lunch. I can brew tea."

"Lovely," her mother says, following her into the kitchen.

When her mother sits down at the island bar, she lifts a piece of Brie and a cracker off Elle's plate.

"So is it official?" she asks as if it's something to be excited about.

"It's official," Elle says, placing the dish towel by the sink. She begins filling the teapot, wanting to keep busy. Her mother has not been here since Elle and Tom bought the house, Elle always visiting her mother in California, if at all. "Why did you come here, Mom?"

Her mother eats the cheese and cracker, finishing completely before answering. "Is a visit not enough of a reason?"

"You hate Seattle."

"I don't hate *Seattle*. I hate the gray skies. I mean, seriously, does the sun ever make an appearance? How you don't slit your wrists during the winter is beyond me."

"It's sunny today," Elle exclaims.

"And bone cold. I stand by my opinion."

"*Anyway.*"

"Oh, fine, we'll cut right to the chase, then. I'm here because I have a proposition."

Setting the kettle on the stove, Elle sits down across from her mother. A strand of hair falls across her face, and her mother leans forward to brush it aside.

"You have the prettiest hair—why don't you wear it down more often?"

"Because I'm a baker, Mom."

"Not on your day off."

"Even on my day off." Elle would feel impatient with her mother's small criticisms, but her trepidation toward the unexpected appearance has her distracted. "Can you get to the point?"

Her mother arranges another piece of cheese on a cracker. "I'm here about your second bakery."

A spear of heat shoots through Elle's chest. "I don't have a second bakery," she says, her voice coming out pitchy. She distracts herself with her lunch—of which her mother has already eaten half—and picks up a few raw strips of bell pepper.

"Do you want one?"

Elle lowers the food from her mouth, not yet having taken a bite. "You're offering me a bakery?"

"I'm offering you a loan."

"A loan." Elle can't comprehend the words. When her father helped with her first bakery, her mother was furious, growing into cool indifference. Then, upon the news of a potential new bakery, her mother was less than thrilled. She claimed to be proud of Elle's overall success, but she never approved of Elle getting financial help from her father or, later, her husband. Her mother was of the belief that paying for Elle's college was enough, and she voiced that on numerous occasions.

For her mother to offer a loan . . . it can't be real.

"You think I'm joking," her mother says.

"Oh, Mom, I know you don't joke." The kettle begins to whistle, and Elle turns around, busying herself with the hot water, two mugs, and a tin full of tea bags. "Irish breakfast?"

"If you have milk."

Elle is already opening the fridge. Her mother takes her tea with milk and a pinch of sugar—the same way Elle has learned to enjoy it. She slides the steaming mug toward her mother. "You were saying?"

"Last time we spoke, you mentioned you're selling the house."

Elle nods. "I have another showing tomorrow afternoon."

"Will it leave you in a good financial position?"

"Enough to get back on track."

"If I helped you open a second bakery now, could you pay me back once the house is sold?"

With her tea to her lips, Elle's sharp exhale sends a spray rippling over the edges of her mug. She sets it down, wiping the mess with a paper towel.

"I would charge interest, but not as much as a bank."

"I'm not sure I'd have enough extra at the end of the sale—I still need to find another home for myself."

"And Bonnie?"

"I'm not sure what she has to spare, but I can ask."

Her mother smiles a rare smile, the wrinkles around her lips deepening. She sips her tea. "You prepared it perfectly—not too much sugar."

"Why are you helping me now?" Elle wants to know. "After all the resistance with the first bakery?"

"This is different."

"How?"

"Because you're on your own this time." Her mother reaches across the kitchen island to grasp Elle's hand; her fingers are cold but soothing, like sorbet. "No safety nets, no help from the men in your life. It's just you. And it's a loan. I'm not giving you a handout; I'm making an investment."

"A bakery isn't a sound investment."

She squeezes Elle's hand. "I'm making an investment in my daughter."

November 3, 2016

A year and three months after Elle found out

Elle is piping a birthday cake. Chocolate middle, pink frosting. Holding the piping bag, her fingers stained red, Elle rocks back and forth with each ripple along the base of the cake. Her hair falls in stray strands across her face. She and Bonnie managed to find a good location after all, and the new Eastside bakery is filled with the sounds of a busy day: Bonnie and their new hire up front taking orders, dishes clanging, ovens beeping, a child shrieking with delight. In the back room, however, those sounds are dulled by the whir of the fridges. It is a place of solitude amid the chaos, and Elle already feels at home here. Open only a week, and they're already on track to being a success.

Turning the cake on its swivel stand, Elle cleans up a splotch of frosting and repipes it. Now the top of the cake. Lifting the star tip up and down, up and down, she creates a simple ribbon along the outer edge. Then she takes up another piping bag, one with a petal tip, filled with red, and creates a few large flowers. Piping cakes is cathartic. She imagines the birthday girl—Laura—eating frosting off her fingertip, demanding a big piece with a flower. Her mother licking the bottoms of the purple-swirled candles. Everyone crowded around. Elle writes *Happy Birthday, Laura!* across the top of the cake, idly thinking about who will get the *Happ*, the *day*, the *ra!* when Laura's mom passes out the pieces.

Swiveling the cake once more, looking for imperfections to fix, Elle is startled when Bonnie pops her head in.

"You have a special request," she says, but her expression is off. It is not her usual easygoing half smile—instead, her forehead is creased, and her mouth is straight.

"Who is it?" Elle asks.

"You should come up to the front." Bonnie disappears back into the chaos.

Setting down her piping bag, Elle brushes her sticky hands on her apron and walks out of the back room. Despite the gloomy day, the bakery is filled with customers chattering and pointing at the cases. Sal, Henrietta, and their granddaughter, Rebecca, are among the many, conversing at a window table. Elle's new employee, Emily, is taking the next order while Bonnie grabs a pastry and slips it into a white pastry bag. Stepping fully into the front room, Elle tries to determine which customer has the special request. Her eyes scan the crowd, searching for someone off to the side who looks as though they're waiting. Then her eyes fall on a man in the back, tall, dark hair, a wool coat over charcoal slacks. A pang shoots through her chest, down into her stomach, and she feels suddenly overheated and disheveled in her apron.

Tom.

She walks over to him, not looking directly at his face but instead at the watch on his wrist. When she stops in front of him, she feels small in his presence. Trying to assume her high, airy customer voice, she says, "You have a request?"

"Elle." He shifts on his feet, as if he might lean in to kiss her cheek, but he doesn't.

She hasn't seen him since he moved out. She's barely spoken to him. It's just been too painful. What is he doing in Bellevue, in the bakery he didn't want her to have? "How are you?"

Tom nods, hands spreading. "Fine. You look good."

"Bonnie talked me into spin class."

A small smile tugs at the corners of his mouth. She had forgotten how much she missed that smile. Even his smell is distracting, a mix of Old Spice and tea tree shampoo that is as familiar and lovely to her as the scent of butter. She has gone out on five dates with five different men now, none of them going anywhere. She has spent more time with Bonnie. And Charlie, when he can come, things no longer so awkward between them. She thought she was making progress, but just the sight of Tom brings it all rushing back. What they had and lost. An acute sadness rocks her on her feet, as though she is being visited by a ghost: the source of her grief come back to haunt her.

"I meant you look . . . happy."

"You have a special request?" she says, trying to hide her fluster.

"We have a client coming in tomorrow for a breakfast meeting, and we want to impress. I'm sorry it's last minute."

She looks down at her apron, embarrassed by the mess of sugar all down her front, wondering why he came all the way to the Eastside to ask for her baking. "Did you have something in mind?" Tom hesitates, his hands clasping one another. Elle finds herself looking at them, recalling how they feel on her cheek, at the small of her back, or in her hair—and it makes her realize that she has made no progress getting over him at all.

"Yes, actually," he finally says. "Coffee cake."

Her eyes lift to his face, and for a moment the two of them are caught in a strange but knowing pause. She tries to speak, but nothing comes out, while her mind is firing at a million miles an hour, arriving, repeatedly, at the same question of *what does that mean?*

Just then, a family walks in with a young daughter, maybe five years old. When the little girl spots the cookies in the case, she rushes over, hands splaying on the glass, eyes widening until Elle can practically see the pink frosting reflected in the girl's pupils. Elle watches Tom watching the girl; there's a smile of longing on his face as her parents point to different cookies, the girl responding in varying levels of delight. When Tom catches Elle looking at him, his smile widens, only to fall away. For the first time, Elle does not feign interest in the child for Tom's sake. She loves the joy that baked goods bring anyone—young or old—but that's as far as her warm-fuzzy feeling goes. He seems to understand her expression in an instant. For Elle, her bakeries are her children. It's too late for her to have made this fact clear to Tom, but while they hold each other's stares, she finally feels resolved in who she is and where her life is heading.

The girl and her parents make it to the front of the line, and Emily helps them decide on a treat. Elle remembers why Tom's here in the first place: coffee cake.

"I—wouldn't you want something a little more"—Elle spreads her hands—"complicated?"

Tom seems to snap out of a reverie. His gaze is intense, knowing, and—hopeful?

Finally, he says, "I want to convey comfort, not complication."

Elle nods, regaining her composure. "So you've thought this through."

"I have."

She spots the bare ring finger on his left hand and touches her own. "Is this a new client?"

"It's . . . redemptive."

She feels his eyes lingering on her even as she looks away. "What flavor, then?"

His voice sinks to a low register, intimate, reaching a familiar place inside her that Elle has pushed down for a long while. A place she has tried to forget. "Surprise me."

$\sim$

After the bakery is closed and the lights are off and Bonnie has gone to their Greenwood location to help Mindy close down, Elle stands before her table, dark and silvery in the dimness. She remembers the recipe by heart. She remembers the many Sundays making it for Tom, in her *napron*, the grin on his face as he licked the spoon or following his first forkful of cake. She remembers the way it tasted on his lips, sharing bites between kisses.

The ingredients are spread before her. She takes it slow, savoring each step, letting the butter and sugar clump up, leaving lumps in the batter. Even the most perfect recipes have their flaws.

At last, when the dough has been poured into the cake pan, Elle turns her attention to the final addition. Resting in a plain bowl are two emptied bags of frozen fruit: blueberries and peaches. Elle rolls up her sleeves and sprinkles them with sugar. Then she lowers her hands into the bowl, tossing them together, the ice biting her skin. Only when they are thoroughly mixed does she pour them over the coffee cake batter. Sliding it into the oven, she sets the timer for forty five.

In the quiet of her new bakery, Elle methodically cleans up her mess to pass the time. Then she slides a box off a shelf; it's her cookbook, all done, the pages laid out flawlessly in their cardboard container. Lily Zhang, the agent, is already working on selling it to a publisher, but Elle couldn't help but print it out just so she can look at it on occasion, feel its presence in her new bakery like a guide, like pure luck.

Elle sits down on a stool at her silver table. In the darkness, she flips through the first pages, landing on the dedication page. She doesn't have to read the black letters to know what they say.

For my father, who convinced me to write this book.

And for Tom, one of few people whom I have ever loved more than baking.

From the other room, the timer goes off.

~

The following morning, Elle arrives early to help Bonnie bake and dress the pastries and cinnamon rolls. It's five thirty when she hears a knock on the front door—still a half hour until opening—and, with a sigh of mild frustration toward the eager early bird, rushes out of the back to encourage the customer to return in a half hour.

Only the early bird is Tom.

She pauses a yard from the door, staring at him through the glass. He's not wearing a suit but a sweater and jeans reminiscent of his teaching days. When she unlocks the latch and swings the door open, the CLOSED sign taps against the window. She didn't anticipate that he'd need to pick up the coffee cake this early.

"Come on in; I'll get the cake," she says, stepping aside.

He hovers just inside, his hands clasped behind him, eyes soft on her. "Take your time."

Elle is glad to turn away; it gives her a chance to allow the redness to drain from her cheeks. Bonnie is in the back, still working, and looks up when Elle rushes through.

"Impatient customers?" Bonnie asks.

"Tom," Elle says, ducking into the walk-in. She eases the coffee cake box off its shelf and carries it out. "Can you give this a dust?"

Bonnie comes over with a metal sugar duster and taps it over the top of the cake, the little blueberry globes and peach crescents turning frosty white with powdered sugar.

"Looks good." Elle closes the lid, sealing it up.

Bonnie touches her shoulder. "Deep breath."

Elle inhales sharply and darts away, the cake box clutched in her hands. Tom is standing by a far table staring out the window when she returns. He straightens as she approaches, reaching out to take the box; his fingers brush her fingers. Shifting the box in his arms, he opens the lid. Elle flushes with heat when he sees that she made blueberry peach.

"Does it look all right?" she asks.

He looks up, mouth pursed in neither a smile nor a frown. Under pinched brows, his eyes glisten. Barely audible, he asks, "Do you have time to share this with me?"

She tips her head. "What?"

He gestures to the table behind him; a single peony has been laid across the top.

"I thought you—" She breaks off, sinking into the chair.

Tom retrieves two forks from the self-serve station near the register. "This new space is beautiful," he comments, sitting down across from her.

He hands her a fork and pushes the coffee cake box toward her. He meets her eyes, and she's swept up in his gaze. Something different lies in his stare; it feels as if he's seeing her for the first time, and she sees him too.

"I don't understand—your meeting?" she manages.

Tom says, "This is it."

Acknowledgments

A million thank-yous to Michelle and Alicia for seeing the potential in this book and for believing in my abilities as a writer. I'm so grateful to have an agent and editor who get it. Thanks, also, to my incredible team at Lake Union.

This book would not be what it is without the encouragement of the Woodshed Writers' Workshop—you know who you are. Thanks also to Wayne for helping me realize I am a writer.

April and Marcia, though we have lost touch, your kindness and wisdom during my baking days were the spark that set this story alight.

None of this would have been possible without the patience and support of my husband, Joe. Thank you for the many nights of staying up late in solidarity while I edited, edited, edited. And of course, for buying me celebratory margaritas and ice cream after every milestone.

Finally, to my parents, Terry and Cathy: What can I even say? You instilled in me a thirst for knowledge and a zest for life that continue to drive me forward. Thank you for always believing in me—and for teaching me how to believe in myself.

Questions and Topics for Discussion

1. Elle's initial response to Tom's affair is insecurity rather than anger. If you were in Elle's position, would you have had a different gut response?
2. Do you think Elle treated Owen fairly? Why or why not?
3. Many of Elle's mistakes stemmed from her self-consciousness. How do you think the story would've been different had Elle been more forthright with her feelings?
4. How does Bonnie and Charlie's relationship compare to Elle and Tom's relationship? What do you think Bonnie and Charlie got right that Elle and Tom got wrong?
5. Do you think Elle's mother had a positive or negative influence on Elle's life? What about her father? Why?
6. Was it selfish of Elle to refuse to have children with Tom? Do you think a couple can end up together despite a major disagreement over something like the decision to have children?
7. Toward the end of the book, Tom suggests that Elle is in part to blame for the ruin of their marriage. Do you agree or disagree? Why?

8. The story is left somewhat open ended. Do you think Elle and Tom get back together? Do you think it's possible for them to work through their differences? Would you forgive Tom?

9. Do you have recipes that remind you of certain times in your life? Which recipe in the book had you drooling?

About the Author

Jennifer Gold believes love is sweet and life is messy, which is probably why she has a passion for writing about the relationships of career-focused women. When she's not writing books, Gold spends time with her witty husband, sassy horse, and two snuggly cats. Gold holds a master's degree in writing and lives in Washington State. You can find out more at http://jennifergoldauthor.com.